CINDERELLA IS DEAD

CINDERELLA IS DEAD

Kalynn Bayron

BLOOMSBURY

NEW YORK LONDON OXFORD NEW DELHI SYDNEY

BLOOMSBURY YA
Bloomsbury Publishing Inc., part of Bloomsbury Publishing Plc
1385 Broadway, New York, NY 10018

BLOOMSBURY and the Diana logo are trademarks of Bloomsbury Publishing Plc

First published in the United States of America in July 2020 by Bloomsbury YA

Bloomsbury books may be purchased for business or promotional use. For information on
bulk purchases please contact Macmillan Corporate and Premium Sales Department at
specialmarkets@macmillan.com

Library of Congress Cataloging-in-Publication Data
Names: Bayron, Kalynn, author.
Title: Cinderella is dead / by Kalynn Bayron.
Description: New York : Bloomsbury Children's Books, 2020.
Summary: Queer black girls team up to overthrow the patriarchy in the former
kingdom of Cinderella.
Identifiers: LCCN 2019048162 (print) | LCCN 2019048163 (e-book)
ISBN 978-1-5476-0387-9 (hardcover) • ISBN 978-1-5476-0388-6 (e-book)
Subjects: CYAC: Fantasy. | Lesbians—Fiction. | Feminism—Fiction. | Sexism—Fiction. |
Blacks—Fiction. | Characters in literature—Fiction.
Classification: LCC PZ7.1.B386 Cin 2020 (print) | LCC PZ7.1.B386 (e-book) |
DDC [Fic]—dc23
LC record available at https://lccn.loc.gov/2019048162

Book design by John Candell
Typeset by Westchester Publishing Services
Printed and bound in the U.S.A. by Berryville Graphics Inc., Berryville, Virginia
2 4 6 8 10 9 7 5 3 1

All papers used by Bloomsbury Publishing Plc are natural, recyclable products made from wood
grown in well-managed forests. The manufacturing processes conform to the environmental
regulations of the country of origin.

To find out more about our authors and books visit www.bloomsbury.com
and sign up for our newsletters.

For Amya, Nylah, Elijah, and Lyla

CINDERELLA
IS DEAD

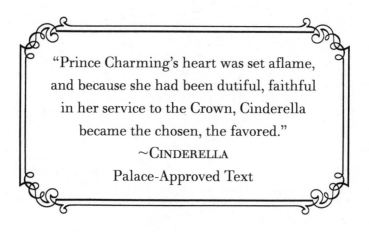

"Prince Charming's heart was set aflame,
and because she had been dutiful, faithful
in her service to the Crown, Cinderella
became the chosen, the favored."

~CINDERELLA

Palace-Approved Text

1

Cinderella has been dead for two hundred years.

I've been in love with Erin for the better part of three years.

And I am about two minutes away from certain death.

When the palace guards find me, and they will, I am going to die in the forest on Lille's eastern border. But I don't care. The only thing I'm focused on is Erin, who is pressed up against a tree directly across from me. The palace guards don't see her yet, but they are headed her way. They stop a few feet from where she's hiding. Her eyes grow wide in the shadowy confines of the forest. I meet her gaze across the wide swath of carriage pathway that separates us.

Don't move, Erin. Don't make a sound.

"I fell asleep in the tower last night," one of them says. "Someone woke me, but still. I was lucky. If the king found out, it'd be my head on a pike."

"You going to the ball?" one man asks.

"No," says another. "All work and no fun for me, I'm afraid."

"That's a shame. I'm hearing the girls in this year's group are the prettiest lot in a generation."

"In that case, is your wife going to have an *accident?* It'd be a shame if that first step down to your cellar suddenly came loose."

They laugh from the gut, hissing and sputtering, and from the sound of it, they are falling all over themselves. Their voices move away from us until I can't hear them anymore. I pull myself up and run to Erin, who is still cowering behind the tree.

"They're gone," I say. I take hold of her hand and try to calm her.

She peers around the tree, her face tight with anger, and jerks away from me. "Of all the impossible things you've ever convinced me to do, coming out here has to be the worst one. The guards almost spotted us."

"But they didn't," I remind her.

"You asked me to meet you here," she says, her eyes narrow and suspicious. "Why? What is so important?"

I've rehearsed what I'm going to say to her, practiced it over and over in my head, but as I stand in front of her I'm lost. She's angry with me. That's not what I want. "I care about you more than anything. I want you to be happy. I want *us* to be happy."

She stays quiet as I stumble over my words, her hands clenched at her sides.

"Things feel hopeless so much of the time, but when I'm with you—"

"Stop," she says, her expression a mask of anger. "Is this what you brought me out here for? To tell me the same thing you've been telling me since forever?"

"It's not the same thing. The ball is so close now. This may be our last chance to leave."

Erin's brow shoots up in surprise. "Leave?" She comes closer, looking me dead in the eye. "There is no leaving, Sophia. Not for you, not for me, not for anyone. We are going to the ball because it is the law. It is our only hope for making some kind of life."

"Without each other," I say. The thought makes my chest ache.

Erin straightens up but casts her gaze to the ground. "It can be no other way."

I shake my head. "You don't mean that. If we run, if we try—"

Laughter in the distance cuts my plea short. The guards are circling back. Erin ducks behind the tree, and I dive into the brush.

"You don't get to work in the palace if you don't know

how to say yes and shut your mouth," says one of the guards as he comes to a stop directly in front of my hiding spot. "If you don't have the stomach to do some of the things he's asking for, you're better off here with us."

"You're probably right," says another man.

Through the branches, I see the tree Erin is hiding behind. The hem of her dress has caught on a rough patch of bark and is poking out. The guard looks in her direction.

"What's that?" he asks. He takes a step toward her, his hand on the hilt of his weapon.

I kick against the bush. The entire thing shakes, causing a cascade of rust-colored leaves to rain down on me.

"What was that?" one of the men asks.

They turn their attention back to me. I shut my eyes tight. *I'm dead.*

I think of Erin. I hope she'll run. I hope she'll make it back. This is all my fault. I only wanted to see her, to try to convince her one last time that we should leave Lille once and for all. Now I'll never see her face again.

I glance toward the tree line. I can make a run for it, draw the attention of the guards away from her. I might be able to lose them in the woods, but even if I can't, Erin can get away. My body tenses, and I pull my skirt between my legs, tucking it into my waistband and slipping off my shoes.

"There's something in there," a guard says, now only an arm's length from me.

The guards move closer, so close I can hear them breathing. I glance past them. There's a flash of baby blue between the trees. Erin's made a run for it. A clanking sound cuts through the air, metal on metal—a sword drawn from its scabbard. Over the rush of blood in my ears and the pounding of my own heart, a horn blasts three blaring notes.

"We've got a runner," a gruff voice says.

I freeze. If I'm caught this far into the woods, the guards will make an example of me. I picture myself being paraded through the streets in shackles, maybe even stuffed into a cage in the center of town where Lille's people are so often made to endure public humiliation as penance for stepping off the beaten path.

The men's voices and footsteps move away from me.

I'm not the runner they are talking about. I haven't even started running yet. My heart crashes in my chest. I hope they can't gain on Erin quickly enough.

The guards' voices trail off, and when they're far away from me, I tuck my shoes under my arm and run into the shadowy cover of the forest. Ducking behind a tree, I peer around the trunk as several more guards gather. They've got an older woman with them, already bound at the wrists. I breathe a sigh of relief and immediately feel a searing stab of guilt. This woman is now at the mercy of the king's men.

I turn and make a break for it. With my legs pumping

and lungs burning, I think I hear the snap and snarl of hounds, though I can't be sure. I don't dare look back. I trip and smash my knee on a rock, tearing the flesh. The pain is blinding, but I pull myself up and keep going until the trees start to thin.

At the path that leads back to the heart of town, I pause to catch my breath. Erin is nowhere to be found. She's safe.

But this is Lille.

No one is ever really safe.

2

As I trek home all I can think of is Erin. The forest is deep and dangerous and, most important, off-limits. I know she won't stay hidden. She'll make her way home, but I need to know she's safe.

The bell tower in the town square rings out the hour. Five loud clangs. I'm supposed to meet my mother at the seamstress's shop for a fitting, and she specifically told me to come there bathed, with my hair washed and a fresh face. I look down at myself. My dress is smudged with dirt and blood, and my bare feet are caked with mud. I escaped the king's men, but when my mother sees me, she'll probably end me herself. Guards patrol the streets. Many more than usual now that the ball is so close. I keep my head down as I pass by. They aren't too concerned with me.

They're on high alert because of what people in Lille are calling *the incident.*

It happened two weeks ago in the northern city of Chione. There were rumors that an explosion damaged the Colossus, a twenty-foot likeness of Mersailles's savior, Prince Charming, and that the people responsible were ferried into Lille under cover of night and taken into the palace to be questioned by the king himself. Whatever happened, the details he was able to pry from them sent him into a state of panic. For the first week after the incident, he ordered the mail stopped, our curfew was moved up two hours, and pamphlets were distributed that assured us the incident was nothing more than an attempt by a rogue band of marauders to vandalize the famous statue. It also stated that the perpetrators were put to death.

When I get home, the house is empty and silent. My father is still at work, and my mother is waiting for me at the seamstress's shop. For a moment, I stand in the center of the floor, looking up at the wall hangings over the door.

One is a portrait of King Stephan, haggard and gray; it shows him as he was before his death only a few years ago. Another is of King Manford, the current king of Mersailles, who wasted no time in pushing out his official royal portrait and requiring that it be hung in every house and public space in town. Our new king is young, only a few years older than I am, but his capacity for cruelty and his lust for absolute control rivals his predecessor, and it is on full display in the third frame hanging over our door. The Lille Decrees.

1. A minimum of one pristine copy of *Cinderella* will be kept in every household.
2. The annual ball is a mandatory event. Three trips are permitted, after which attendees are considered forfeit.
3. Participants in unlawful, unsanctioned unions will be considered forfeit.
4. All members of households in Mersailles are required to designate one male, of legal age, to be head of household, and his name will be registered with the palace. All activities undertaken by any member of the household must be sanctioned by head of household.
5. For their protection, women and children must be in their permanent place of residence by the stroke of eight each night.
6. A copy of all applicable laws and decrees along with an approved portrait of His Majesty will be displayed in every household, at all times.

These are the hard and steadfast rules set forth by our king, and I know them by heart.

I go to my room and light a fire in the small hearth in the corner. I consider staying until my mother comes looking for me, but I'm worried that she already thinks something terrible has happened. I'm not where I should be. I bandage my knee with a clean strip of cloth and wash my face in the basin.

My copy of Cinderella's tale, a beautifully illustrated version my grandmother gave me, sits on a small wooden pedestal in the corner. My mother has opened it to the page where Cinderella is preparing for the ball, the fairy godmother providing her with everything her heart desired. The beautiful gown, the horse and carriage, and the fabled glass slippers. Those attending the ball will reread this passage to remind themselves what is expected of them.

When I was small, I used to read it over and over again, hoping that a fairy godmother would bring me everything I needed when it was my turn to go to the ball. But as I got older, as the rumors of people being visited by a fairy godmother became fewer and farther between, I began to think the tale was nothing more than that. A story. I told my mother this exact thing once and she became distraught, telling me that now I certainly wouldn't be visited if I voiced so much doubt. I never said anything about it again. I haven't looked at the book in years, haven't read it aloud like my parents want me to.

But I still know every line.

An ivory-colored envelope sits on the mantel, my name scrawled across the front in billowing black script. I take it down and pull out the folded letter from inside. The paper is thick, dyed the deepest onyx. I read the letter inside as I have done a million times since it arrived the morning of my sixteenth birthday.

Sophia Grimmins

King Manford requests the honor of
your presence at the annual ball.

• • •

This year marks the bicentennial of the first ball,
where our beloved Cinderella was chosen by
Prince Charming. The festivities will be grand,
and made all the more special by your attendance.

• • •

The ball begins promptly at eight o'clock
on the third of October.

• • •

The choosing ceremony will begin
at the stroke of midnight.

• • •

Please arrive on time.
We eagerly await your arrival.

Sincerely,
His Royal Highness King Manford

On its face, the invitation is beautiful. I know girls who dream of the day their invitation arrives, who think of little else. But as I turn it over in my hand, I read the part of the letter that so many of those eager young women miss. Along its outer edge, in a pattern that reminds me of ivy snaking its way up latticework, are words in white script that give a dire warning.

You are required to attend the annual ball. Failure to comply will result in imprisonment and seizure of all assets belonging to your immediate family.

It is the first of October. In two days, my fate will be decided for me. As terrible as the consequences will be if I'm not chosen, the danger in being selected might be worse. I push those thoughts away and shove the letter back in the envelope.

I leave the house and make my way to the dressmaker's shop, taking the long route and hoping I'll run into Erin. I'm worried to death about her, but I know my mother is worried about me too.

The shops along Market Street are lit up and bustling with people making last-minute preparations for the ball. A line winds out of the wigmaker's. I peer into his shop window. He's really outdone himself this year. Elaborately styled wigs crowd his shelves. They remind me of wedding cakes, tiers upon tiers of hair in every shade, the ones on the top shelf featuring things like birds' nests with replicas of eggs tucked inside.

A young girl sits in the wigmaker's chair as he places a four-tiered piece atop her head. It's layered in fresh pink peonies, topped with a small model of Cinderella's enchanted carriage. It teeters precariously as her mother beams.

I hurry past, cutting through the throngs of people and ducking down a side street. The shops here aren't ones that my family and I have ever set foot in. They're for people with enough money to buy the most outrageous and unnecessary baubles. I'm not really in the mood to feel bad about what I can and can't afford, but this is the quickest way to the town square, where I can cut across and find Erin before I meet my mother.

In the window of one shoe store, Cinderella's glass slippers sit on a red velvet cushion, illuminated by candlelight. The little placard next to it reads, Palace-Approved Replica. I know if my father had the money, he'd snatch them up immediately, hoping they'd set me apart. But if they're not enchanted by the fairy godmother herself, I don't see the point. Shoes made of glass are an accident waiting to happen.

Farther down there is another line snaking out of a small shop with shuttered windows. The sign above the door reads Helen's Wonderments. Another sign lists the names of tinctures and potions Helen can brew up: Find a Suitor, Banish an Enemy, Love Everlasting. My grandmother told me Helen was just some wannabe fairy godmother and that her potions were probably watered-down barley wine. But that didn't stop people from putting their trust in her.

As I pass by, a woman and her daughter—who looks about my age—hurry out of the shop. The woman has a heart-shaped glass vial in her hand. She pops the cork and pushes it to the girl's lips. She drinks the whole thing in one long gulp, tilting her head back and looking up at the evening sky. I hope the things my grandmother said weren't true, for that poor girl's sake.

3

I make a quick turn and hurry toward the town square. The Bicentennial Celebration has been going on for a week and will culminate with the annual ball. Until then, the festivities continue every night. Before curfew, people crowd the square to make music and drink, and tonight is no exception. As I push through, trying to cut directly across the square, vendors are hawking their goods in the shadow of the bell tower, a gleaming white structure with four tiers topped by a golden dome. There are jewelry and dresses from the city of Chione in the north, and satin gloves, makeup, and perfume from the city of Kilspire in the south.

As I zigzag through the booths, searching the crowd for Erin's face, I notice a young woman standing on a raised platform. She is reciting passages from *Cinderella*. The palace-issued volume sits on a book stand in front of her.

"The ugly stepsisters had always been jealous of Cinderella, but seeing how lovely she looked that night, they realized that they could never be as beautiful as she and, in a fit of rage, tore her dress to shreds."

People who've gathered around jeer and boo. I keep walking. I still don't see Erin, and an all-consuming terror creeps in. I tell myself she's at home, but I have to get there to make sure.

A booth, much more crowded than the others, sits near the middle of the square, and a crowd of people blocks my path. As I try to maneuver around them, I see that all the fuss is over a game being played in the booth. There are shoes piled up, and little girls pay a silver coin to be blindfolded as they pick one set of slippers and try them on. If they fit, they win a small prize—a beaded bracelet or necklace, along with a little slip of parchment that reads "I Was Chosen at the Bicentennial Celebration." A little girl with a crown of bouncy brown ringlets beams as her tiny foot slides into a violet-colored shoe with a tall heel. It's all good fun until another little girl picks the wrong size shoes and wins a slip of paper with a small portrait of Cinderella's fabled stepsisters, their faces twisted into hideous smiles.

She looks at her mother. "Mama, I don't want to be like them." Her bottom lip trembles as she chokes back a sob.

A palace guard laughs uproariously as her mother scoops her up and carries her away.

I slip through an opening and move from the booth toward the center of the square where a fountain, a life-size replica of Cinderella's carriage, stands. Made entirely of glass, it shimmers in the fading sun. Water spouts up around it, and in the bottom of the pool are hundreds of coins. It's tradition to make a wish, much like Cinderella did so many years ago, and toss a coin, preferably silver, into the fountain. I remember tossing coins in when I was younger, but I haven't done that in years.

"Sophia!"

Liv bounds toward me; her long brown hair is pulled up into a bun on top of her head, and her rosy cheeks look like candied apples on her tawny skin. She looks me over.

"What happened to you?"

I look down at my dress, which I hadn't bothered to change. "You don't want to know."

"Where are you off to?" she asks.

"I'm looking for—" I hesitate. It's too dangerous to talk in public about what happened out there in the woods. "I'm going to my fitting."

Liv's face twists up in a look of disbelief. "You were supposed to do that weeks ago. The ball is two days away."

"I know," I say. "I've been avoiding it." There's an opening and I move to leave, but Liv loops her arm under mine.

She shakes her head. "You are so stubborn. Your mother must be pulling her hair out." She laughs and holds up something wrapped in a shiny silver cloth. "You'll never believe what I won at one of the booths." She unwraps the object.

It's a stick.

I look at Liv and then back to the stick. She is beaming, and I am thoroughly confused.

"Are you feeling okay?" I put my hand on her head to see if she's running a fever.

She laughs and playfully bats my hand away. "I'm fine. But look. It's a wand. A replica of the very same one the fairy godmother used."

I glance at the stick again. "I feel like you got taken advantage of."

She frowns. "It's a real replica. The man said it came from a tree in the White Wood."

"No one goes into the White Wood." Erin steps out from behind Liv, and my heart almost stops. It takes everything in me not to grab her and pull her close to me.

"Close your mouth before a bug flies in," says Liv, looking around nervously.

"You're safe," I say, relieved.

Erin nods. "And you're a mess."

I wish I'd taken the time to clean up a little better before I left my house.

"Still lovely, of course," she says quickly. "I don't think you can help that."

I glance at her. "Maybe Liv can use her wand to help me clean up."

Liv points the stick at me and gives it a flick. She frowns. "I always hoped that one day I'd develop some magical powers. I guess today is not that day."

I pat her arm. "No one has seen that kind of magic since Cinderella's time. I doubt it even exists anymore."

A hush falls over them, and they exchange worried glances.

"Of course it exists," Erin says in a whisper. "You know the story as well as anyone. If we are diligent, if we know the passages, if we honor our fathers, we might be granted the things Cinderella was."

"And if we do all those things and nothing happens— no fairy godmother appears, no dress, no shoes, no carriage—then what? Do we still believe it?"

"Don't question the story, Sophia." Liv steps closer to me. "Not in public. Not anywhere."

"Why?" I ask.

"You know why," Erin says in a low tone. "You must put your faith in the story. You must take it for what it is."

"And what is it?" I ask.

"The truth," Erin says curtly.

I don't want to argue with her.

"She's right," Liv says. "The gourds in the royal garden are grown at the very spot where the remnants of her carriage were gathered up. And I've heard that when her tomb was still open to the public that the slippers were actually inside."

"Another rumor," I say. I remember hushed conversations between my grandmother and her friends about the tomb. No one has seen it in person in generations. Just more stories to trick young girls into obedience. Liv and Erin both look like they've had about enough of me.

"Well I'm still hoping to earn the favor of a fairy godmother," says Liv.

Liv's plan seems risky. My mother hopes for the same thing but has arranged for my dress on the off chance I don't find a magical old lady in my garden the night of the ball. If anyone shows up with anything less than a gown fit for Cinderella herself, they'll risk their safety, and I don't think the king cares if it comes from a fairy, a dress shop, or someplace else. What matters is that we *look* like a fairy godmother blessed us with her magic.

"Do your parents have a plan in case that doesn't work?" I ask. I don't want Liv to be in danger because they waited too long to get her what she needed. This will be Liv's second trip to the ball. A third is permitted, but it would break Liv's spirit and send her family to ruin.

"Do you ever get tired of trying to get yourself arrested?" Erin asks. "Talking like that is going to get you locked up."

"Okay," says Liv, stepping between us and shaking her head. "Here." She reaches into her satchel and pulls out a handful of coins. "They're not silver, but they'll have to do. Let's make wishes in the fountain like we used to." She takes my arm and leads me to the fountain.

Erin comes up beside me, her shoulder brushing against mine. I think I hear her sigh, and she gives a little shake of her head. Behind us, music continues to play, and people laugh and chatter away. Palace guards roam the square, their royal blue uniforms neatly pressed, their swords glinting in the lamplight. Liv hands Erin and me a coin each.

"Make a wish," says Liv. She closes her eyes and tosses in her coin.

I look at Erin. "I wish you'd leave Lille with me. Right now. Leave Mersailles, leave all this behind, and run away with me." I toss my coin into the water.

Liv gasps. Erin's eyes flutter open, her brow furrowed, her mouth turned down. "And I wish you'd just accept the way things are." She tosses her coin into the fountain. "I wish I could decide that nothing else matters, but I'm not like you, Sophia."

"I'm not asking you to be like me," I say.

Erin's eyes mist over, and her bottom lip trembles. "Yes, you are. Not everyone can be so brave."

My chest feels like it's going to cave in. I step away, and Erin rushes off, disappearing into the crowd. I don't feel brave. I feel angry, worried, and doubtful that anything will ever change. I prepare to run after her, but Liv catches me by the arm and pulls me back.

"You have to let it go, Sophia," Liv says. "It cannot be."

She leads me away from the fountain, and I push away the urge to cry, to scream out. We move around a large circle of blackened grass. Liv looks down at it.

"What is this?" I ask.

"Something happened here a few nights ago. Rumor is that someone created an explosion, tried to destroy the fountain. They failed." Liv turns to me, worry plastered on her face. "Don't you see? There is no resisting. We can't go against the book or the king."

I shake my head. I don't want to accept that this is all there is for me.

Liv glances around and then leans close. "A group of children found a body in the woods by Gray Lake."

"Another one?" I ask. "How many is that?"

"Six since the leaves have started to turn. A girl, just like the others."

I try to tally up how many young women have turned up dead in Lille in the years since I've been old enough to understand such things. The dead number in the dozens, but the missing are more than I can count.

"Go to your fitting, Sophia," Liv says, squeezing my hand. "Maybe someone at the ball will take you away from all this."

There is a ring in her voice. Maybe Liv wants to be taken away. I can't blame her, but that's not for me. I don't want to be saved by some knight in shining armor. I'd like to be the one in the armor, and I'd like to be the one doing the saving.

⟋

I make my way to the seamstress's shop in a daze and arrive a full two hours late. Peering through the window, I see my mother chatting away with the other women in the shop. They laugh and smile, but her mouth is drawn tight as she rests her chin on tented fingers. I hate that I've made her worry. I take a deep breath and open the door.

My mother stands and exhales, letting the air hiss out between her teeth, a look of relief on her face. "Where have you been?" Her gaze wanders over me. "And what have you been doing?"

"I was—"

She puts her hand up. "It doesn't matter. You're here now." She glances past me, out to the street. "Did you walk here alone?"

"No," I lie. "Liv and Erin walked with me to the end of the street."

"Oh, good. I'm sure you've heard about the incident at Gray Lake."

I nod. She shakes her head and then forces a quick

smile and instructs the seamstress and her helpers to get to work.

The pieces of my dress are sewn into place to ensure a perfect fit. My mother fusses over the color of the piping along the hem of the gown. Apparently, it's supposed to be rose gold, not regular gold, so it has to be taken off and reattached. I think the entire ensemble would look very nice at the bottom of a wastebasket, maybe doused with lamp oil and set on fire. No one asked me what color I'd like it to be or how I'd like it to fit.

My mother wrings her hands together and paces the floor in front of me. She is worried sick about every little detail, as if my life depends on these things. I try to silence the voice inside me that tells me it very well might.

"It's gorgeous, Sophia," my mother says as she looks me over.

I nod. I can't think of anything to say. I still can't believe this day has actually arrived. I'd hoped to be far from Lille at this point, maybe far from Mersailles altogether, with Erin by my side, leaving the king and his rules behind us. Instead I am here, preparing to give in to this terrible inevitability.

The seamstress helps me out of the dress so she can pack it up and send it home with us. A plum-purple bruise colors the side of her neck; it has started to turn green around the edges.

"What happened to your neck?" I whisper, though I know the likely source of her pain. So many women in Lille carry around similar burdens.

The seamstress looks at me quizzically and quickly adjusts her collar. "Don't you worry about that. It'll be gone in a week. Like it never even happened."

"Sophia," my mother interrupts. "Why don't you go out and get some air? But stay on the path where I can see you." I stare down at the seamstress, whose smile does little to mask her pain.

I gather up my skirts and walk out to the footpath leading up to the shop. The sun fades as the lamplighters begin their nightly rounds. Even in the encroaching darkness, the watchtowers loom in the shadows. Stone sentries, their lookout windows facing inward.

A mural of the king mars the side of a building across the street. He's pictured on a horse at the head of an army of soldiers, his arm outstretched, holding a sword. I bet he's never led an army anywhere except across the squares of a chessboard.

Hard as I try, I cannot set aside thoughts of what it will be like to be chosen. In two days' time, I could be given to a man I know nothing about, who knows nothing about me. My own wants and needs will be silenced in favor of what he thinks is best. What if he thinks nothing of putting a bruise on my neck? And if I'm not chosen, what then? And Erin. My dear Erin. What will become of us? I shiver as a knot grows in my throat. My mother comes out into the street and throws a shawl around my bare shoulders.

"You don't want to catch a chill so close to the ball, Sophia." She looks around cautiously, lowering her voice. "I wish it didn't have to be this way, but—"

"Yes, I know. This is just how it is." I grit my teeth, stifling the urge to scream for the thousandth time. I look at her, and for a split second she lets the mask slip, and I see the pain in her face. She seems older in the pale light of the evening sky. Her gaze moves over my face and down to my dress for an instant before she looks away.

"Does it suddenly seem real to you?" I ask.

She presses her mouth into a hard line. "Yes."

"I've wished that this day would never come," I say.

"So have I," she says quietly. "But here we are, and we must make the best of it."

My mother returns to the shop, but I linger for a moment before joining her as the seamstress and her helpers finish packing my dress. I look up at the starry sky. Things will be different now and forever. There will be no going back once the ball has taken place. I feel a sadness, almost grief-like in its depth, threatening to consume me. I pull my shawl tighter and hurry inside.

4

Mr. Langley, a friend of my father's, has a son who's agreed to drive our carriage for us while my father is working. He meets us at the road and helps us load up the dress. He locks eyes with me and smiles as I climb into the carriage. I look away from him. I'm not in the mood to pretend to be flattered.

My mother climbs in behind me, and the carriage moves jerkily down the road. Heavy curtains cover the windows, but the chilly night air still makes its way inside. I tighten my cloak around my shoulders and pull the hood down, covering most of my face, but this isn't a clear enough signal to my mother that I don't want to talk.

"He's quite a handsome young man, isn't he?" she asks.

I watch my mother as she eyes me carefully. "Who?"

"Mr. Langley's son. Of course, if he were to find you agreeable, he would have to make an official petition for you at the ball. I'm sure he won't be the only one interested."

I shake my head. "Is there ever a time when you're not thinking up ways to marry me off to the first half-decent man you can find?"

"Half-decent might be the best we can hope for." She looks down into her lap, pressing her lips together.

I pull open the curtain and look out the window, more to keep my eyes from rolling back into my skull than to take in the view. I'm not angry at her specifically. Her way is the way of most people in Lille. Always looking for an opportunity to make the dark seem brighter. She's good at it, but I'm not. I can't help but see the ball for what it really is.

A trap.

We ride through Lille's twisting streets. In the distance, the palace's massive turrets stick up over the sloping landscape. It is extravagant, gaudy, a reminder to the rest of us that no matter how hard we try, we will never be completely worthy of that kind of wealth, that privilege.

Just outside the palace grounds is the gated section of Eastern Lille, where the highest-ranking members of the aristocracy live. Close enough to the king to make themselves feel special but far enough away so they didn't get the impression they were equal to him. The people there hoarded their wealth, improving their own lives while the rest of the city fell into decay.

As our carriage pulls into the western part of the city, the identical houses along the cobbled alleys lean on one another as if they might collapse in on themselves without the added support. The evening hours bring with them a particularly confusing mixture of smells. Scents of freshly baked bread and boiled meat waft through, but they are tinged with the distinct smell of excrement, human and animal alike.

No lamps light my street other than the ones people keep in their windows. We roll to a stop, and my mother climbs out. I stand on the carriage step for a moment, hoping to put some distance between us. She isn't going to let me go to bed without having a talk. She reaches the front step and looks back at me, a sorrowful expression drawn across her face. Mr. Langley's son places the dress box on the doorstep, then clears his throat. I glance over at him, and he flashes another wide smile. I'm about to tell him that he looks ridiculous and is clearly making a fool of himself when my mother calls to me.

"Sophia, come inside."

She knows me too well.

She pushes the door open as the bells toll, signaling curfew for Lille's women and children. Her foot keeps time with the thunderous gongs. At the final stroke of eight, we are meant to be inside, behind our locked doors. Sometimes I stand on the front stoop as the last bell tolls, just to see what might happen. On those occasions, my mother darts around the house in a fit, wishing I would sit down and stop trying to get myself arrested like some damned fool. When I was little my mother told me that if I wasn't inside at the toll of the final bell that the ghosts of Cinderella's evil stepsisters would swoop in and take me away. Now that I'm older, I understand that it's not vengeful spirits I need to be afraid of. The king and his men pose the biggest threat.

I step out and make my way to the door, avoiding my mother's stare and squeezing past her as she closes and locks it behind me. I head for the stairs.

"Sit," she says as she pulls a chair out from our dining room table. She walks to the other side and sits down.

I want to go upstairs and fall into bed, but we'll have to have this little talk first. I join her at the table and stare across at her.

Most people think my mother and I are sisters, so alike are our features. Our dark, curly hair is identical except that her strands are lightly flecked with gray. We share the same deep-brown complexion, but she has lines set in at the corners of her mouth. People call them laugh lines, but I'm certain hers are from frowning.

"I was chosen by your father my first year at the ball, and it was a good match," she begins. "He was the son of a land baron, and he is a decent man, a good man."

"I know." She's told me this before, but an urgency tints her voice now, like she's trying to convince me that there's some glimmer of hope.

"But some are not so lucky," she says, her tone deadly serious. "Do you understand what that must be like? To not be chosen? What the repercussions of that would be?"

"Of course I understand." That possibility scares her almost more than anything else. Girls who aren't chosen by their third ball are considered forfeit, ending up in workhouses or in servitude. But in recent years, several girls have disappeared into the castle and were never heard from again.

My mother runs her hands over the pleats in her dress and sighs. "Tell me something, Sophia. Do Erin and Liv know how difficult you can be? How stubborn?"

"Yes," I say. It is a half-truth. Erin and Liv are my closest friends, and I can be myself around them for the most part. But even in their presence, I feel like I have to hold back because Lille has left its mark on them, too. They hear me speak of leaving, of resisting what is expected of us, and they tell me to lower my voice. Those things are simply not done. No one leaves. No one resists who isn't courting death.

"I do hope Liv finds a match this year," my mother says, staring off. "Her parents are very worried, and if she's not chosen this time, she'll only get one more chance."

That a girl is considered a spinster if not married by

eighteen is wrong, and that the boys don't even have to attend the ball until they want to is a sickening double standard. "It's not her fault she wasn't chosen."

Liv hadn't been selected at last year's ball. Erin and I had discussed it, and neither of us could understand why. Liv almost never brought it up, but I'd gleaned that someone had made a claim on her and at the very last minute had chosen another girl.

Now Liv was brandishing a replica wand, hoping to conjure some magical assistance. After everything they'd seen and gone through the previous year, Liv and her parents still hoped she'd receive a visit from a fairy godmother. They had convinced themselves that one didn't show up the year before because they hadn't been pious enough in following Cinderella's example.

"I'm not going to be visited by some magical old crone," I say, frustration bubbling up inside me.

"Maybe not," my mother says in a whisper. "But you'll look like you were, and that is what the suitors and the king care about most."

"You'd think they would care about me, about what I feel." Even as I say the words, I know they fly in the face of everything I know to be true, and my mother agrees.

"Why, in the name of King Manford, would they ever think that?" she asks. She squeezes her hands together like she's praying, but the skin over her knuckles is stretched tight. "You've—we've—got one chance at this. You must find a match. Going back to the ball a second time is an embarrassment."

Her words cut me like a knife. "Is Liv an embarrassment? How can you say that about her? It's not her fault some disgusting old man changed his mind."

She looks away. "She knows what's at stake. Foolish wishes and magic aren't going to save her. She must conform, know her place, and do whatever must be done to find a match, and so do you." She leans toward me. "I know you're different, and that this will be hard for you, but you have no choice."

Different.

That's how she sees me, and every time she uses that word, a distinct air of disapproval accompanies it. Lille has left its stain on her, too.

"I want to be with Erin."

"I know," she says, glancing around as if someone might hear. "But you will keep that to yourself." Her tone is flat, emotionless. It's how she protects herself from the reality of what I'm facing.

I was twelve when I told my parents that I would much rather find a princess than a prince. They had gone into a state of panic, from which they emerged with a renewed sense of determination. They told me that in order to survive I would have to hide how I felt. I was never very good at it, and the weight of that mask grows heavier with each passing year. I want nothing more than to cast it aside.

"You don't have to resist every little thing. It will do you no good, and I will not lose you," says my mother as she grips the edge of the table. "I can't. You must attend. You must play the part." She sits back as if she is exhausted, letting her shoulders roll forward and exhaling slowly. "Your father is working on brokering another sale as we speak to bring in the extra money we need for—" She stops. Her voice catches in her throat. Her eyes become glassy as she puts her hand on top of mine. "I love you very much. I would do anything to ensure you are the most beautiful girl in the room when you make your entrance."

"My whole life has been a buildup to this. This isn't some *little thing*. Everything I do, everything I say, it's all about the ball. My path has been chosen for me since birth. My future is already written, and I don't have a say in any of it."

"Yes. And?" She stares at me blankly as if she can't understand.

"Don't you want me to be happy? Isn't that what matters most?" In the brief moment before her answer, I imagine she'll say yes and tell me I don't have to go. I think of what it would feel like to have her on my side.

"No." My mother lets go of my hand. Bitter disappointment envelops me. "What matters is that you are safe. That we follow the laws. They are clear as day. Right there." She motions to the front door. "Happiness is a bonus, Sophia. You're not entitled to it, and the sooner you accept that, the easier your life will be."

"And if I don't want an easy life?"

My mother stares at me. She parts her lips to speak and then presses them together, dropping her gaze to the table-top. "Be very careful what you ask for. Because you just might get it."

"May I be excused?" I ask.

She nods, and I push my chair back from the table and go upstairs. As I reach the top step, I hear my mother cry-ing. A part of me wants to go to her, but a part of me doesn't. I love her, and I know she loves me, but that's not enough. She will not break the rules even if they require me to deny everything about myself. I go into my room and close the door.

5

The next morning, I awake just before sunrise. My father is already gone for the day, and my mother has begun her work preparing breakfast. Dough sits rising under a cloth by the wood stove, which she stokes and sets a kettle on. I join her in the kitchen and tie an apron around my waist. My mother places a small plate with two biscuits and a sliced apple on the table. She speaks to me over her shoulder as she turns out a ball of dough onto the floured surface of the countertop.

"The floors will need to be swept and scrubbed, like always, and it's washday for the linens upstairs. Take the rugs out and give them a good beating. Your father said he might be home early, so we must get to it. When he arrives, be sure to recite the story as soon as you can because I know he'll be tired and will want to rest."

"You want me to recite it out loud?" I ask. I know that's what we're supposed to do. It's more of a tradition than a rule, but I hadn't done that in a long time.

"Yes," my mother says curtly. "Maybe you're a little rusty, and with the ball coming up you'll want to know it backward and forward in case a suitor wants to test your knowledge."

I don't even respond. It's the dumbest thing I've ever heard. The suitors will test me? I have a strong urge to tell my mother that I'm pretty sure the men gathering at the castle haven't even read the story all the way through because none of it is actually meant for them. It's meant for the rest of us. I just nod. I put on a cloak and start lugging the rugs outside.

Would there really be suitors wanting to test me? And does my father really want to hear it, or is my mother just thinking of every single way someone might try to trip me up once I'm at the ball?

"*The wife of a wealthy man grew ill and knew that her end was near,*" I say aloud. It's still there in my head. Every word.

I'm beating the rugs out when my mother opens the front door, a concerned look on her face. "Sophia, I need you to go see Mrs. Bassett. I'm afraid I forgot the ribbons that match your dress at her shop, the ones for your hair."

"You don't want to go?" I ask. I get a clear look at her for the first time that morning. She has dark circles under her eyes like she hasn't slept.

"No, I'm not feeling well. I've sent Henry to tell Mr. Langley's son to be here within the hour to take you."

I glance around to see if Henry, our neighbor's young son, has already left.

"I can walk," I say. "Or I could take the carriage myself?"

She shakes her head. "Alone? Sophia, please. My nerves are already shattered. Don't add to it with your penchant for trying to break the law."

"It's not a law."

She plants her foot on the stoop with a loud thud. "You'll be taken up to the palace in chains if you're caught driving a carriage, and if you go walking alone you might end up in a far worse situation."

Something in her tone strikes me. Her emotions, usually tightly coiled, seem to be fraying more and more with each passing day. I won't tell her I'd walked through the woods and into the city on my own yesterday. She might not survive the shock.

"Mr. Langley's son will be here soon," she says. "He'll take you."

She goes inside, and I wait in the yard. As scheduled, he comes strolling up through the dissipating mist. He leans on the gate and gives me a little nod.

"Morning," he says. He shows me that mischievous smile again.

I'm fairly good at reading people, but this boy is a puzzle. The curl of his lip and his smug smile make me think I'm missing something.

"Ready?" he asks.

I nod as he pulls out the wooden cart that we take to the market instead of the covered carriage we use to travel. It's made to haul sacks of grain and has only one wide seat in the front. He hitches it to our horse and climbs up.

"It's cold," I say. "We should take the carriage."

"But I've already got this one ready to go. Don't you want to sit next to me?"

"Absolutely not. And if you'd asked me beforehand, I would have told you to hook up the carriage. But you didn't, so here we are."

He raises an eyebrow. "So you run the show around here? That's . . . different."

"Different," I say quietly. Different never means anything good.

The front door creaks open behind me.

"Is she giving you trouble?" my mother calls from the doorway. I don't turn around, but I can feel her eyes boring into the back of my head.

"No problems, Mrs. Grimmins." Mr. Langley's son shoots me a quick wink. If he expects a thank-you for not telling my mother what I said, he is going to be sorely disappointed.

I climb up, sitting as far away from him as the seat allows. He yanks the reins, and the cart lurches forward.

The temperature stays cool, even as the sun rises. I pull my cloak in tight around me, but the air still seeps through. Mr. Langley's son sets the reins in his lap and removes his coat.

"Here. It's not much, but it should help." He places the coat over my shoulders, and I lean away from him, watching his hands and his eyes. I don't know him enough to trust him, and most times when a man does a woman a favor it is because he wants something in return. "Am I that off-putting?" He raises his arm and gives a whiff. "Do I smell? I just bathed last week."

He's trying to be funny. I don't respond.

"My name's Luke. In case you were wondering."

"I know," I say flatly. We've never been formally introduced but I've heard my parents speak of him a little too often.

"You're always with your mother. She doesn't let you get a word in edgewise."

I watch him out of the corner of my eye. "Or maybe I don't have much to say."

"Okay." He grimaces a little. "I was surprised at your outburst back there with the cart. I've never seen a girl refuse a man's request so openly. That's a dangerous thing to do."

"Are you joking or threatening me?" I angle my body so I can raise my leg and kick him over the side of the cart if he gets any ideas. Girls are harassed and manhandled on a regular basis in Lille, and because of that I actually have a plan for what to do if someone ever tries to hurt me. If Luke makes one false move, I'll smash his nose back into his skull, maybe kick him where he'd feel it most, and then run. I can also grab the reins, pull the horse off the road, and flip the cart over. I don't care if I get hurt in the process. I'm not going quietly.

"I wasn't joking, but I wasn't threatening you, either. I'm sorry." He looks at me and smiles again. His demeanor is abrasive but not malicious. He can't be more than twenty, tall and lanky, brown skin, black hair, with only the slightest air of self-importance. I still have a hard time reading him.

I keep my body in a position to upend him but pose a question as a distraction. "Are you preparing for the ball as well?"

He tosses his head back and laughs. It catches me so off guard that all I can do is stare at him. He composes himself and shakes his head. "Not if I can help it. Things are different for me."

"Why?" I ask. He's lost some of that bravado he had when he strode up to my front gate. We stop in front of the seamstress's shop.

"You're friends with Erin, aren't you?" He doesn't meet my eyes.

The question seems out of place, and I bristle. "Yes. She's one of my best friends."

"Hmm," he says, nodding. "Then you'll understand what I mean when I say things are different."

The knowing look in his eyes terrifies me. I've seen it before. It's the same look my mother gives me every time I speak Erin's name. I immediately hop out of the cart and toss his coat back to him. "Just wait here, please."

"Sure," he says.

I worry that his friendly manner is just a way to get me to feel comfortable enough to drop my guard.

I hurry to the door of the shop and go in. None of the lamps are lit yet, and the dappled light from the barely risen sun casts shadows through the room, which feels oddly at rest without the seamstress and her bevy of helpers bustling around. A measuring tape hangs over the edge of the table, and dozens of glass beads litter the floor as if they've been knocked over without anyone bothering to clean them up.

I see the ribbons my mother left behind sitting on a table in a canvas bag, and I pick them up. Just then, a whimper comes from under the table. I step back and look down to see someone sitting there. A young boy. His knees pulled to his chest, as he rocks back and forth.

"Hello?" I say gently. The boy's head pokes up from behind his knees, his eyes rimmed with tears. He sucks in a gulp of air and wipes his nose with the back of his hand. He's dressed in a tattered pair of slacks and a faded shirt a size too small. The sleeves expose his delicate, thin wrists. He seems so fragile. I want to put my arms around him and tell him everything is going to be okay even though I have no idea what's wrong. He sobs again.

"Oh no. Please don't cry. Are you all right?" I put my hand out, but he scurries back, knocking into the leg of the table and sending more beads scattering to the floor. "I won't hurt you, I swear." The eerie silence of the shop sets me on edge.

"I don't know you," he says.

"No, I don't think we've met. My name is Sophia. The seamstress is helping me with my dress, and I just came to pick these up." I crouch down and hold out the bag of ribbons. "See?" His expression softens. "Why are you crying?"

He opens his mouth to speak but hesitates. Then he scoots closer so he is almost out from under the table.

"He's too loud," he says, cupping his hands over his ears and shutting his eyes.

"Who's too loud?" I ask, confused.

A man's voice, shrill and grating, echoes from somewhere over my head. Heavy footsteps pound across an upstairs room. I look up as the entire structure of the house quakes. Dust, shaken free from the wooden beams criss-crossing the ceiling, falls down through the shadowy confines of the shop and settles like a fine powder on the tables and chairs. I fight the urge to pick up the boy and bolt out the door.

The boy lowers his hands, his eyes wide. "My father. He's yelling at my mother. He's always yelling at her."

The light streaming through the shop windows illuminates the boy's face. He is nearly identical to the seamstress. They share the same brown skin, dark eyes, and dimples at the outer corners of their mouths.

A loud crash followed by a woman's scream pierces the momentary silence. I stand up, and the boy scurries back. I look out the front window and see Luke still perched on the cart.

What a man does in his home is his business. That is the rule. I should leave, but I can't do that.

"You just stay here, all right?" I say.

"Okay," he answers from under the table.

I creep to the rear of the shop, where a staircase leads up to the second floor. I put my hand on the rail and listen. The silence is almost as unbearable as the woman's screams. At the top of the stairway is a door, and a soft light streams from underneath it. The stairwell is dark and shadowy, with thin shafts of light from under the door illuminating bits of dust floating in the air. I take one step up.

I don't know what I will do when I get to the top. Knock? Call out? Can I even stop what is happening? The man's voice sounds again, and this time I hear the words clearly.

"You've kept the money from me, haven't you?" he bellows.

Then comes a woman's voice. "No! I would never!"

"Every cent you make belongs to me." There is a loud thump like someone ran into the door at the top of the stairs, and the door creaks open a few inches. I step up onto the landing and peek inside.

"I know that—I swear, I work hard." The seamstress cowers against the wall of the small upstairs room. Tears stain her face. Her husband stands over her, his fists clenched.

"Then what is it? There's so little money in this pouch I wonder why you even bother. Either you're a terrible seamstress, or you're keeping the money for yourself." He flings the pouch at her, and it breaks open, sending a shower of coins tinkling to the floor.

"Everyone is having a hard time," the woman says. "The king has taxed us so steeply that we can scarcely afford grain. Others are suffering, too, but they need to make their girls ready for the ball. I take what they can afford to give. That's every red cent, I swear it."

"You take what they can afford to give? What are we—a charity?"

He raises his fist, and the woman winces as if he's already struck her. I put my hand on the door, and the floorboard groans under my weight. I cringe as the man's head whips around. He is short and stocky but his hands are massive.

"I-I'm looking for the seamstress," I say, trying to keep my voice from cracking.

"Who the hell are you?" He sticks out his neck and glares at me.

"My mother purchased some ribbons, but she left them here. Can you help me find them?" I look directly at the seamstress as I tuck the ribbons out of sight. "If you could, I would appreciate it." The man steps in front of the woman, blocking my view. I scowl at him.

"Watch yourself before I send you up to the palace to be forfeited," the man snaps.

He can do it. Any head of household could. The only person who can disagree is another head of household. Money, power, class, all those things come into play, but the founding tenet of our laws is that women, no matter their standing, are at the mercy of the fickle whims of men. That's how little control I have over my own life. I continue to glare at him as he shuffles off to an adjoining room. The seamstress scrambles to her feet and comes rushing out the door, swiping at her eyes.

"Your son—" She grabs me by the elbow and leads

me to the main room of the workshop before I have a chance to finish my sentence.

She bends down, pulls the boy out from under the table, and wraps her arms around him, all the while glancing nervously toward the back staircase. Her son melts into her, grasping her tightly and sobbing. Tears well up in my eyes, and I have a hard time figuring out if it is my anger or my absolute heartbreak for the seamstress and her son that is getting the better of me. The seamstress gently nuzzles her nose into his hair. She spots the bag of ribbons in my hand.

"I see you've found your missing ribbons. I'm glad you remembered to come pick them up. You'll look lovely." If I hadn't seen what just happened or the welt on her cheek, her tone would have convinced me that nothing was amiss.

"I didn't mean to intrude—or maybe I did—but I saw your son and heard your husband upstairs." The woman's body tenses as if she's bracing for what I might say next.

She stands, pulling her son up with her, and straightens out his clothes. He looks to be no more than seven or eight years old, but the bags under his eyes are those of a child who's seen too much. She kisses him and points toward the room directly across from the main work area.

"You go get something to eat. Breakfast is on the table." She smiles at him, and he looks to the stairs and nods. He embraces her again. She looks down at the boy. "Papa knows best, my love. You will grow up to be a good man, just like him." The boy doesn't smile as he disappears into the other room. The seamstress straightens out her dress, avoiding my gaze.

A sigh escapes me, and the seamstress glances over, her mouth turned down. "Don't pity us. Please. That isn't what we need."

"What do you need?" I ask. I step toward her. "You don't have to— I mean— I could—"

"What could you do?" The woman laughs lightly. "Oh, you poor thing. You're one of those girls who thinks there's a way out, aren't you? That something will come along and make everything better." She sighs and shakes her head like she's angry. "I wish there were. I swear I do. I wish I could tell you to run, to hide, but it would never work." Her voice is so low I have to lean in close to understand. "Nothing can be done. Not a damn thing."

I want to believe there might be a way out, but with every passing day, that feeling fades. I wonder when this woman gave up hoping.

"You've got your ribbons, and I've got work to do. You'd best be off."

I hesitate. "You deserve more than this." We all do.

The woman pauses. I can see a small cut over her eye. Her lips part, on the verge of saying something, but she holds back.

"Please go."

6

I slowly walk out of the shop to find Luke standing next to the cart. "Everything all right?"

"No," I say, climbing up and taking a seat. "Let's go."

Luke glances back at the shop and joins me in the cart. I'm sick to my stomach as the cart starts to move.

"How many people do you think are poorly matched at the choosing ceremony?" I ask, numb. I try to wrap my head around what I just witnessed.

"Like a clash of personalities?" Luke asks.

"No. I mean like a man takes a wife and then mistreats her. Hits her."

Luke looks at me out of the corner of his eye. "You didn't know that sometimes happens?"

"It happens all the time," I say. "That's my point. I can't

think of how terrible it is to have to deal with the king's rules and then go home to have your husband beat you."

"I understand," Luke says.

"How could you? You aren't being beaten in front of your own child. You're not being forced to go to the palace for the ball. You're what—twenty? And you say you've never been to a ball. We don't have that luxury."

Luke stares at me in silence. He pulls the horse into a slow trot, and we meander in the general direction of my house.

"Is there a reason you're going so slow?" I ask.

He smiles warmly. "Just hoping to get to know you a little more before, well—"

"Before the ball?" I ask. "Before some man decides I'd make a pretty prize and everything in my life is changed forever?"

Luke looks a little taken aback. His big brown eyes dart around like he's rehearsing what he is about to say. "You're a rare person, Sophia."

"I don't even know what that's supposed to mean," I say, still skeptical of his intentions.

He continues to guide the cart along the road as others pass us. We come to a rise in the road, and Luke brings the cart to a full stop.

My heart ticks up. "What are you doing? Why are we stopping?"

Luke looks out over the wide swath of land to the east. The sun is high above the horizon now, casting an orange glow through the wispy clouds and across the apple orchards. The trees there are every shade of russet and gold as the land prepares to sleep for the winter.

He glances at me with his brow furrowed, his mouth drawn into a tight line. "I wonder if I might share something with you." He is calm, soft-spoken. He seems very serious, and my curiosity is piqued. But I keep my guard up. Just in case.

"All right. What is it?"

He doesn't speak right away. He gazes off, biting his bottom lip.

"I've been mentally calculating how I'm going to get away from you if you try anything," I say. "I'm pretty sure you're not going to hurt me, so I want to hear what you have to say."

"Hurt you?" He looks puzzled. "Why would I want to do that?"

I give an exaggerated look around. "Because this is Lille. That's what happens here."

"I can't blame you for feeling that way, but not everyone is like that."

I pinch the bridge of my nose and shut my eyes for a second. I know that. My father is a good man, Liv's father is a good man, and even Luke's father seems like a good man. But these good men aren't making the rules. These decent men are turning a blind eye to indecent acts. "If you're not one of the men who would jump at the first chance to put a woman in her place, then I'm not talking about you."

He hesitates for a moment before sighing. "That's fair."

A high-pitched whistle sounds from behind me, and I turn to see two young men strutting up to us, their chests pushed out, smirking.

"Shit," Luke says under his breath. He moves closer to me.

"What's wrong?"

"Nothing. Just some people from school."

"Luke!" one of the young men shouts. He is smiling wide, but Luke isn't. "What are you up to on this beautiful fall morning?"

"Just out for a ride." Luke's tone is biting, angry.

"Out for a ride? With a girl?" the taller man asks. The ring in his voice makes me pause, and he looks me over. His beady brown eyes remind me of the glass marbles the children on my street play with.

"Do I know you?" I ask.

The man's head snaps up. "Not yet, but maybe we can do something about that."

"Shut up, Morris," says Luke.

"Morris?" I ask, glancing up at Luke. "What a lovely

name. Sounds a lot like moron." This time Luke smiles wide.

"You've got a smart mouth," Morris says, glaring at me.

"Don't you have somewhere to be?" Luke inches closer to me. His body has gone rigid, and his fists are clenched.

Morris smiles, but it makes me uncomfortable. There's nothing kind about it.

"Are you claiming this wretch at the ball?" Morris asks.

Luke bristles. "Why does it matter to you?"

I cross my arms. I hate this kind of talk, especially when I'm sitting right here.

"She doesn't seem like your type," Morris says, grinning as if he's said something hilarious.

I've missed something. Fear clouds Luke's eyes.

Morris looks back and forth between us. "Oh. Oh!" He claps his hand on the other man's back, and they laugh. "She doesn't know, does she?"

Luke looks down at the reins gathered in his lap. Morris steps forward and takes my hand. I try to pull away, but he has me by the wrist and holds it tight. "Luke here has all kinds of secrets. You should ask him about them sometime." He looks at Luke. "What was that young fellow's name? Was it Lou—"

Before he can finish, Luke's fist connects with Morris's right cheek, sending spittle and at least two teeth flying from his mouth. He lets go of me and stumbles back, clutching his jaw. The other man stands still, stunned. Luke hops out of the cart as Morris clutches his face.

"If you ever so much as breathe a syllable of his name in my presence, I will make you regret it," Luke says. "Consider this your only warning."

Morris's face is ruddy, dripping with sweat, his mouth bloody. He tenses, like he's going to attack Luke again, though I can't understand how he thinks that will be a good idea.

"Don't do it," his friend says to him, reading his expression. "Let's get out of here." He takes Morris by the arm and pulls him away until they disappear down the road. Luke hops back into the cart.

Morris's broken teeth lie like pearls in the cracks of the cobbled street. "Should we pick those up and return them to him?" I ask. "Maybe put them on a string he can wear around his neck?"

Luke chuckles, massaging his hand and straightening out his shirt. "I'm sorry about that."

"You don't have to apologize," I say. I would pay money to see despicable men get socked in the jaw. "Morris was trying to get under your skin. Why does he dislike you so much?"

Luke looks at me and shakes his head. "It's . . . complicated."

"Morris said I'm not your type. It's okay. I'm not offended. You're not my type either." I'm trying to lighten the mood, but Luke frowns.

"Oh, I know."

My skin pricks up.

Luke sighs and leans back in his seat. He struggles with something, and with each passing moment, I grow more afraid of what it is.

Luke looks thoughtful as he stares off. "Everything we do is measured against Cinderella's story. But what happens if . . . well, let's say—" He shifts around, fumbling with the reins. "Why is that story the only way of doing things?"

"I'm not sure what you mean," I say. "But we should get going. My mother—"

Luke glances over at me. "When my sister read that story as a child, I—"

"Luke—" I start.

"I remember thinking Prince Charming would make a good husband—for me."

"What?" I'm breathing so fast that little orbs of light dance around the edge of my vision.

"Did you want to marry the prince? Or maybe the princess?" he asks.

"Why are you asking me this?" My voice is barely a whisper, and my heart pounds. "I have to go."

"I don't want to make you uncomfortable, and I swear

I'll never say a word about any of this to anyone." His face is tightly drawn, his eyes downcast. He struggles to find the words to continue. "It's just that I—I know about you and Erin."

A sinking feeling overtakes me. "What about me and Erin?"

"I overheard your mother talking to my mother." He watches me carefully, reading my expression.

"What did she say?" I can't imagine my mother telling anyone about my feelings. She doesn't even want to hear *me* talk about it.

"She said she was afraid you couldn't hide your feelings for Erin, that sometimes it was like you didn't even want to."

The world has suddenly become unnaturally quiet. Carriages pass by us, but I don't hear their wheels on the road. I don't see anything but Luke's face. It never occurred to me that my mother would confide in anyone other than my father.

"Why would she do that?" I ask. "Why would she talk to your mother about me?"

He angles his body toward me. "It's true then?" An almost hopeful look spreads across his face.

I don't say anything, but my silence is confirmation enough for him.

"I know what it's like to feel as if everyone wants you to

be something you're not." His eyes soften, and he sighs. "When I was seventeen, I fell in love with a boy named Louis. That's who Morris was referring to. He was a light in a world that was so dark. So dark, Sophia. You can't imagine—"

"Yes I can," I say without thinking. Being face-to-face with someone who might understand how I feel overwhelms me. I wait for him to continue.

"He allowed me to envision what life could be like for me. When I was with him, nothing else mattered. We planned to flee, but when Morris and his brother, Édouard, found out about us, they told our classmates and of course the news reached Louis's parents. They asked him if it was true, and he would not deny it. They took him to the palace as a forfeit. I never saw him again." His eyes fill with tears.

"They gave him up? Just like that?" It's horrifyingly simple for some people to forfeit their own children. I've seen it happen dozens of times, but it never gets any easier to imagine. I reach out and put my hand over his. "I'm so sorry."

He blinks back tears. "My parents would have done the same to me if my sister hadn't convinced them that our relationship was a phase that I'd grow out of. She knew it was a lie, and I think my parents did as well, but they chose to believe it rather than surrender me to the palace."

My heart shatters into a thousand pieces for what he has lost. What we've all lost.

"People who don't fit nicely into the boxes the kings of Mersailles have defined are simply erased, as if our lives don't matter." Luke hangs his head. "Have you ever heard of a man marrying another man? A woman being in love with another woman? Of people who find their hearts lie somewhere in the middle or with neither?"

"Only as a cautionary tale that ends with people imprisoned or dead." I slump down against the seat, crushed by the hopeless feelings that always seem to find me.

Luke picks up the reins, and we begin to move. "I can avoid the ball for as long as I choose," he says. "And people wouldn't think twice if I'm old and gray before I go out to the palace." He shifts as if he is uncomfortable with what he said. "You don't have that privilege, and my heart breaks for you and Erin and for all the rest of us who have to hide."

"All the rest of us?" I ask.

Luke nods. "The kings that have ruled Mersailles would like you to believe that you're alone, but it's not true. People wear masks so they can fit in and stay safe. Can you blame them?"

"No, I guess not," I say. Isn't that what I am doing? Hiding. Pretending. Just trying to stay safe.

As we approach my house, the weight of our revelations

bears down on us, and the feeling of utter despair is palpable. I climb out, taking the bag of ribbons from the bed of the cart.

"What will you do?" Luke asks.

I shrug. "I don't feel like I have any choices."

"We should look for an out," says Luke. "And at the first opportunity, we should run. As far away as possible."

"Do you think things are different past the towers?" I think of what might lie beyond the capital, beyond the farthest borders of Mersailles.

"Maybe. For now, just try to stay safe. That's all either one of us can do." He reaches out and presses a few silver coins into the palm of my hand. "Your mother feels better when she pays me for driving the cart, but I've told her it's not necessary. Maybe you should keep it. Prepare for your great escape."

I take the coins, even though I don't think that there will be an escape. Not for Erin and me. Not for Luke or Liv or anyone else. We are all trapped here, our stories already written.

7

My mother is standing over me, nudging me out of bed.

"I've drawn you a bath," she whispers. Her hands are like ice as she pulls the blankets off me. I blink repeatedly. "Get up, Sophia. We have work to do."

I look out my bedroom window to see the sun cresting over the horizon. Against my sincerest wishes, the day of the ball has arrived, and my mother is already preparing. I slide out of bed and plant my feet on the cold wood floor. My mother shakes her head as she looks at me.

"What is it?" I ask.

"Nothing." Her voice cracks, and she quickly looks away. "Into the tub. We don't have much time."

"It's dawn," I say. "The ball doesn't begin for hours." I

want to crawl back into bed and pull the covers over my head.

She stops in my doorway, her hand resting on the jamb. She doesn't look at me. "We'll be at this all day. Best to get started right now." She disappears into the hallway.

I trudge into the washroom and bathe, stalling until the water turns cold and my fingertips wrinkle. I slip into a dressing gown my mother has left for me. Uncontrollable hopelessness sweeps over me, the feeling of hurtling off a cliff and not being able to do anything about it. I could be chosen, and my life would be only what my husband said it could be. Or I might not be chosen at all. I wonder if my parents could forfeit me so easily, the same way Louis's parents had.

A knock at the door startles me out of my thoughts. I open it to find four women waiting for me on the other side. I don't recognize any of them. I move to close the door, and one woman pushes it open again.

"Now, now, dearie," she croaks. "No need to be nervous."

They pounce on me instantly, and I push them away as they pull at my dressing gown.

"Mother!" I call out.

"For goodness' sake, Sophia, they are dressers," my mother says as she stands in the hall.

"Is this really necessary? I've been getting dressed on my own since I was seven. I'm sure I can manage."

"You hush now and let them do what I'm paying them for."

The women begin again. Two of them help me into a set of undergarments, while the other two rub scented oils into my skin. My mother oversees every detail, like the perfectionist she is.

"Make sure the garters are knotted tightly," she says. "We can't have her stockings rolling down."

"Oh no. We can't have that. What would people say if they knew about my droopy stockings?" I exaggerate every word, and one of the dressers cackles. My mother is stone-faced. I know I'm being silly, uncooperative, but I don't see how my stockings make a single bit of difference in all this. They tug at the corset, and I let out a yelp as someone yanks the laces together. "Does it have to be this tight?"

"Yes," says my mother. "We'll need to move downstairs to fit the farthingale. There's not enough room up here."

The women buzz around me as I go downstairs. I'm trying to figure out what a farthingale is, while focusing on not breathing too deeply. The walls and ceiling switch places right before my eyes, and I hear a high-pitched ringing in my ears. Someone lightly tugs at my back, and then suddenly I can take a deeper breath. I gulp in air and glance at the woman behind me. She winks. I'm not going to faint, but vomiting isn't completely ruled out.

The curtains in our front room are drawn, and a stool sits in the middle of the room. My mother brings in a petticoat and a camisole that I slip on. As soon as I stumble onto the stool, the women tug at my hair. Tears well up in my eyes as I tip my head back to keep them from pouring down my face.

"Aww, don't cry," says the woman who had loosened my corset. "You'll catch a husband like a fish on a hook with a face like that."

"No, it's not that." I try to slow my breathing and concentrate on not running out the front door. My mother watches me with concern in her eyes.

"We should straighten her hair with an iron," one of the women says. "It would be prettier that way. And I've heard that the king himself prefers it."

"Or we could leave it the way it is," I say through clenched teeth. They all laugh as if I'd made a joke. It isn't funny. It feels like another part of me is being changed to fit someone else's vision of what is pretty. I especially don't want to do anything the king prefers.

"Pull it straight and pin it up," my mother says. "And use the ribbons."

It takes hours for them to finish my hair. When they are done, they set to work on my makeup.

"Which one do you like?" asks one of the younger women. She holds up three small tins, each with varying shades of pink. "It's for the lips."

I reach out to touch the least ostentatious of the three when my mother steps in and chooses the color most akin to actual blood.

After the women finish my makeup, they bring in something that looks like a large hoop made from reeds with bits of fabric connected to the rim and gathered in the middle. They place it on the floor, then motion for me to step into the center. As I stand in the middle, they pull the hoop up, attaching the fabric strips around my waist like a belt. I can just barely touch the edges of the thing as it hangs around me.

"It looks wonderful," my mother says.

"How am I supposed to sit down?"

"You don't need to sit. You need to mingle. Dance, if you're asked. The shape of the farthingale is accentuated when you stand."

"Please don't say farthingale anymore," I say dryly. "It sounds like a torture device." Which is accurate.

My mother goes into the next room and returns with the main part of the gown. She and one of the other women pull the light-blue frock out of its cloth sack. They slip the upper part over my head and adjust it before attaching the skirt to the hoop. The weight of it all holds me in place, like an animal in a trap.

When my mother brings out my shoes, I almost faint and not because I can barely breathe. The heels of the glittering monstrosities are nearly five inches tall, and the toes are so pointed that a normal human foot could never fill its proportions.

"Am I supposed to wear those?" I ask.

"Obviously," my mother says.

I'm reminded that this isn't about what I want or what I like. It's about what everyone else thinks is best, and I'm not sure how much more of this I can take.

My shoulders sit exposed, and the woman beside me dusts my décolletage with a fine pearly powder that sparkles in the dancing candlelight. I try to tune out their chatter about the king, the ball, how they had all met their husbands at an event just like this one, and how Cinderella herself had once sat by her prince to preside over the gathering.

"She was a beauty, to be sure," says one woman. "And not just on the outside. She was a kind person. Heart of gold. Something about her shined. Everybody was drawn to her."

"It's a tragedy that she died so young," says another of the women. "I think she would have loved to see all the young women following in her footsteps."

"I picked the blue to honor her," says my mother.

I look down at the dress. Its pale-blue color matches the

descriptions of the dress in the story, but I think that is where our similarities end. Would Cinderella really have been delighted to see so many girls unhappy, dreading this moment?

"It's all we can do now, isn't it?" asks one of the helpers. "To honor her we have to do it in these small, sentimental ways. We used to be able to pay our respects in a more traditional way."

My mother's face grows tight, which always means someone is saying something they shouldn't be.

"What do you mean?" I ask.

The woman sighs, and my mother shoots her a pointed glance. She continues anyway. "My great-grandmother told me that her grandmother had actually seen Cinderella's tomb with her own eyes, that people used to leave flowers and trinkets for her."

"Why?" I ask. "Why leave anything for her?"

The women all stare at me like I have two heads, and I stop talking. My mother looks like she might faint. Cinderella's story is the reason I'm being forced to go to the ball, the reason my parents have gone into debt to provide me a dress and shoes and all the pretty things I could ever need. Her story is the reason why none of the things I want for myself matter.

"Are we finished?" my mother asks.

"Finished," the woman says.

The other women step back, admiring their handiwork. They drag a full-length mirror into the room, and I gasp at the sight of myself. My painted face, the dress squeezing me in at the waist—it isn't me. It can't be. The dress, though beautiful, is not something I would have chosen. My hair and makeup are done in a way that I wouldn't have picked. My eyes well up, and my mother rushes in to catch my tears on a handkerchief before they roll down my cheeks.

"Now, now. We'll have none of that," she says, her voice soft.

"Here." One of the women presses a small glass vial into my hand. "Drink."

I hold it up to the light. The liquid inside is yellow. "What is this?"

"A little something from Helen's Wonderments," says the dresser. "I was going to give it to my niece, but—" Her eyes glaze over, and she shakes her head. "Well, never mind that. Drink up."

"A potion?" I ask.

I see my mother bite the inside of her lip.

"For luck," says the woman. "You look lovely. You'll be the prettiest girl at the ball and I'm sure you won't need it, but—just in case."

I turn to my mother. I want to tell her again how much I don't want to go, but before I have a chance to speak, the front door creaks open behind me and my father steps in.

The women fall silent. I tuck the vial between my skin and the corset as my mother takes his coat and hat while he stands watching me. He doesn't look at my dress. He stares directly into my eyes.

"Would you all excuse us for a moment?" The helpers scatter, but my mother hovers nearby. "What do you think?" he asks.

I don't answer. What I think doesn't matter. Smoothing out his vest and rumpled sleeves, he comes to stand in front of me. He is tall. His frame next to mine makes me feel small, but not in the way I feel when I stand by men in the market or in town. He wants to protect me, but he, like my mother, has no real idea of how to do that.

He reaches into his breast pocket and produces a small package secured with brown twine. His eyes, deep and brown, mist over as the firelight casts shadows across his warm umber skin. He presses the package into my hand.

"You must be feeling quite conflicted," he says.

"That's one word for it."

"Angry. Resentful. Those are probably much better words."

"Probably."

"You are rebellious. Always have been. Where you get your fiery spirit, I'll never know." He gives me a knowing little wink and motions toward the package. "Are you going to open it?"

I pull the wrapping apart, and a beaded necklace with a sapphire cut into the shape of a heart falls into my hand.

"Just a trinket. It pales in comparison to you." He takes the necklace and clasps it around my neck. "It was your grandmother's. She asked me to give it to you when the day came for you to go off to the ball."

"Is that really what she said?" I ask.

He narrows his eyes at me. My grandmother was like a storm, wild and unpredictable and sometimes a little too harsh for my father's comfort. When she would speak about the ball, she never made it seem like it was something that was inevitable. She always used the word *if* when she spoke of it. *If* the day came for Sophia to go to the ball. *If* we were still doing this when young Sophia got older. It was her spitfire spirit, her hatred of the way Lille was run that got her killed. She had said too much to the wrong person, and the palace guards came to get her on a cold rainy afternoon. She kicked one of them on the way out the door.

A week later my father received a letter that informed him where he could pick up her body for burial.

My father sighs and casts his gaze to the floor. "She said *if*, not *when*. I miss her every single day, but I hate that she planted such nonsense in your head."

I press my lips together. I don't dare tell him that once while I sat in her lap she told me that *if* I ever went to the ball, I should set the palace on fire and dance on the ashes.

It was a fun but dangerous little secret the two of us kept. A knot grows in my throat.

"I hope you understand why you must stifle the urge to resist this," my father continues. "I know you want to. I can see it in your eyes. It feels wrong to ask you to deny who you are, but it's necessary."

I step forward and look right up into his face. "I don't want to go." I refuse to let the tears fall. "You love me, don't you?"

"Of course. More than anything." He lowers his eyes, his hands resting gently on my shoulders.

"Then stand with me. Behind me, beside me, something. Please." I hate how out of control I feel.

"Sophia, please." He is pleading, desperate. "I'm trying to save you. I know it's not right. You think I want you to be unhappy?"

"Then just stop. Don't make me go. Don't let this happen." I beg him to spare me from this, but it's like he doesn't hear me.

He throws his hands up. "I'm not the one in charge, Sophia." He slumps down into a chair. My mother puts her hands on his shoulders. "It's not fair, but I'd rather see you unhappy than imprisoned or killed."

"For being who I am?" I ask. "For not wanting a husband? How is that wrong?"

My mother keeps glancing at the front door like

palace guards might knock it down and drag me away at any moment. "Keep your voice down," she says in a whisper.

"I can't change how you feel," says my father. "But you cannot disobey the king. Your feelings, my feelings, none of that matters to him." His voice gets lower and lower as he speaks to me, his eyes downcast.

"He is not the only one who thinks solely of himself." The words slip out like a curse, and my father winces as if I've cut him. That's not what I want. "I'm sorry. I don't want to hurt you. I—I'm sorry I can't be who you want me to be."

A knock at the door startles us both. When my father composes himself enough to answer it, a man in a finely tailored navy-blue suit stands in the doorway.

"Good evening, sir." The man bows low. "The carriage is ready."

"It's time," my mother says.

She tries to take me by the elbow, but I pull free from her grasp and reluctantly walk out of the house and down the footpath. The carriage, decorated with lavender curtains and matching ribbons, sits there like a beautiful vision ready to ferry me into a nightmare. Two snow-white Clydesdales are hitched to the front, each wearing a lavender sash to match the carriage. Through the glass window, I see Erin seated inside.

"We split the cost of the carriage with Erin's parents," my mother says. "It will give you a chance to say your goodbyes, make peace with the situation."

She slips the invitation to the ball into my hand. As the reality sets in, an unfathomable sadness wells up inside me. There will be no more stolen moments, no more rendezvous at the park, no more secrets shared between us. I climb into the carriage.

"You look stunning, Sophia," Erin says. I watch her gaze move over me before she looks away.

"Thank you," I say. I lean toward her and reach out to touch her hand when my father's face appears in the window. I sit back immediately.

"Try to enjoy yourself, Sophia," he says through the glass.

He can't be serious. I begin to speak, but Erin beats me to it.

"We'll try, sir," she says. She gives me a pointed look, and I reluctantly nod back.

My father and mother watch from the door as the carriage pulls out of the drive and begins the short journey to the castle.

"I can't wait to see what the palace looks like on the inside," says Erin, staring out the carriage window. Her voice is low, her words measured. "I hear they have tables and tables of food and wine and peacocks just walk around the grounds. Can you imagine it? Real live peacocks."

Erin wears a maroon wig that has been elaborately styled and placed on her head in such a way that strands of her dark hair are still visible around the edges. I reach forward and tuck them away, letting my fingers linger near her cheek.

She is all I want.

Suddenly, she takes my hand in hers and presses my palm to her lips. She pulls my hands into her lap and leans forward, pressing her forehead against mine.

"We're out of time," she says, her eyes closed.

"We're not," I say, gripping her hands, breathing her in. "We can stop right now. We can run."

"Where can we go? If I thought we could make this work—"

My heart leaps as a glimmer of hope springs to life. "We can. You just have to say it's what you want. That's all. It's easy."

She smiles, and as I go to put my arms around her, she presses my hands down into her lap, holding them there. "It's not. And I know you don't want to hear this, but this isn't what I want."

That spark of hope is immediately extinguished, replaced by a numbing ache. "Please don't say that. You don't mean it."

Erin was my first friend, the first person I cared about as more than a friend, the first and only person I've ever kissed. In the beginning, I'd been so afraid to tell her how I felt about her that I lied and said another girl had feelings for her, just to see how she would react. Apparently my ability to lie convincingly wasn't as good as I thought it was, because she saw straight through me. She told me that she cared about me, too, but that we had to keep it a secret. I didn't want to keep it a secret. But I did. For her. And the moments we shared sustained me, gave me something to look forward to.

Over time, as the ball grew closer, something began to change. She didn't want to hold my hand or even hear me talk about us being together. It wounded me in a way I didn't even know was possible.

She sits back, her face a mask of pain and hurt. "My parents have made it clear that if I put one foot out of line, they'll take me to the palace as forfeit. There's no place the king couldn't find me if I tried to escape. Lille is his capital, but he holds just as much sway in every other city in Mersailles. You've seen the convoys when they come through town, bearing gifts, emissaries groveling at his feet. Every king who has ruled over Lille since Cinderella's time follows the same path. You think it's any different outside our borders? It's not."

"That's not true," I say, scrambling to find a way to make her change her mind.

"The ball may lead to something wonderful for us." It

sounds as if she's reading the words from a piece of paper, stiff and unfeeling.

"How can you say that to me?" I ask in disbelief. "How can you pretend like this isn't tearing you apart?" I refuse to believe that everything we've shared suddenly means nothing to her.

"*You're* tearing me apart," she snaps. "Why do you have to question everything? Why do you have to make this so hard?" Anger invades her voice, but it isn't loud enough to drown out the sadness. The same sadness that colors everything we do because we know these stolen moments are rushing us toward a catastrophic end. She crosses her arms hard over her chest. "I don't want to fight for us, Sophia. I don't want to fight for something that will only bring us pain. This is wrong. Everyone says so, and they're right."

"It's not wrong," I say. "I choose you, Erin. I want you, and I'm willing to risk everything for that."

Tears slide down her face, and she pats them dry with a handkerchief before they have a chance to leave streaks on her cheeks. "I can't do this. I can't be an outcast. Our families are depending on us to make them proud, to find suitors who will provide for us. Disobeying the king for an impossible situation won't do that."

"I don't care about what the king wants," I say.

"Because you're selfish," Erin says bluntly. "Because

you've never once stopped to think that maybe I don't want to be different. I don't want to stick out. Accept it."

I choke back tears. Then I give in and let them fall. Maybe letting them flow freely will give me a temporary relief from the crush of sadness that comes with knowing that Erin isn't saying she doesn't care about me; she is saying she's choosing not to. But relief never comes. The ache creeps into every part of me and lingers there, burning and painful. I can only look at her as she avoids my eyes and stares out the window.

I find the little vial the dresser had given me and open the top.

Erin glances at me. "What is that?"

"A potion. For luck."

Erin's eyes grow wide. "Really? Where'd you get it?"

"One of the dressers gave it to me. It's from Helen's Wonderments."

I drink half and offer Erin the remaining part. She hesitates for a moment but then takes the vial from me and gulps it down. I hope against hope that it works, but something tells me we'll need much more than luck to get through this night.

The carriage bounces along over a ridge. Erin shifts in her seat, and a gasp escapes her lips. The palace comes into view outside the window, and it looks like something out of a painting. On any given day, the palace is extravagant, a beacon of wealth, power, and privilege. The sprawling ivory façade can be seen from miles away, but when the ball is held, it looks like something out of a dream. I wonder how he manages to do that, to make something so terrible seem so inviting. This isn't a dream; it is a nightmare made real, and there is no waking up.

8

Lamps line the drive; their low, undulating light gives the entire area an ethereal glow. Every window is dressed with red-and-blue sashes. Lights hang along the covered parapet walks, and the ramparts are decorated with gonfalons displaying the royal crest: the body of a lion with the talons of an eagle and the head of a hawk. The golden mantling is set against a crimson background, with the royal motto emblazoned across the bottom: *A Deo Rex; A Rege Lex*, which my father told me means "From God, the king; from the king, law."

The palace guards, dressed in colors matching the crest, line the length of the footpath just outside the main entryway, their gleaming swords holstered at their sides, their faces stoic and unchanging. A wave of panic washes over me. I dread going inside.

The queue of carriages extends behind us almost all the way out to the main road. We inch along, waiting for our turn to exit.

"This is more than I could have ever imagined," Erin says, staring up at the castle.

"That something could look so beautiful and still be a nightmare is terrifying," I say as I look at her.

"You don't know that it will be a nightmare."

"I wasn't talking about the palace."

She shoots me a frustrated glance as she climbs out of the carriage. I follow her, my heart galloping in my chest, my nerves getting the better of me with each passing moment. There are sideways glances, hushed whispers, and more than one catty laugh. I've never felt so exposed. I look through the crowd, and for every judgmental face I see, another is drawn tight with fear and apprehension.

I struggle to keep my balance atop my heels as I approach the guard and hand him my invitation, my fingers trembling. He checks it and crosses my name off a list. Erin does the same, and we push through the crowd of young women that has flooded into the main entry hall of the palace.

Gilded cherubs line the walls on either side of the long hallway. A portrait of Cinderella hangs over a set of enormous double doors overlaid with gold lilies and the royal family crest. In the painting, she is seated with her hands delicately clasped in her lap. She looks serene, smiling gently. Her golden hair falls around her shoulders in tight ringlets. Wearing her iconic blue dress, she gazes at us, her shining hazel eyes reflecting the candlelight. She is watching us.

A pair of guards pull open the gold-framed double doors at the end of the long entryway. The rush of girls spills into the grand ballroom, but Erin stays by my side even though the tension between us remains.

The ballroom is as large as a field. Dozens of crystal chandeliers hang over the space, their light washing us in a warm glow. I can see my reflection in the ice-like surface of the polished marble floor. The smell of fresh-cut flowers permeates the room. An entire orchestra sits readying their instruments, and random notes float through the air as they prepare to play.

I can hear Erin sucking in quick gulps of air beside me. I want to comfort her even though she'd all but ripped my heart out. "Try to take a deep breath," I say, quickly glancing at her.

She nods, slows her breathing, and readjusts her wig. The girls break off into groups, and I scan the room for Liv but can't find her among the sea of ruffled dresses. I hope she's been able to get to the palace on time. More girls than I was anticipating crowd the room, and each of them seems to be stunned by our lavish surroundings.

Just then, I am struck hard on the shoulder by someone

walking past. I turn to see a girl glaring at me. I don't recognize her, and I think for a moment that she is looking past me at someone else.

"Who do you think you are, wearing a dress like that?" she hisses.

"Excuse me?" I ask, bewildered at the hatred dripping from her voice.

"Cinderella's dress? More like a cheap knockoff. You look ridiculous, but you probably couldn't afford anything better," she says, her breath shallow and eyes wide. Fear lingers just below the surface.

"Do I know you?" I'm growing angrier by the second.

She rolls her eyes. "No. But that's because I don't run in the same circles as peasants trying to steal the spotlight from the rest of us. Pathetic."

I figured there would be men who might have something rude to say and that I would be required to keep my retorts to myself. I didn't think that the harshest words would come from another girl.

"Sophia," says Erin as she takes hold of my arm. "She doesn't know what she's saying."

"Yes she does," I say, shrugging off Erin's hand and squaring up with the other girl. "Does it make you feel better about yourself to put me down?"

Her face flushes crimson. "Don't be ridiculous. You're no competition."

"Then why say anything at all?" I walk toward her and look her dead in the eye. "You're just as afraid as the rest of us, so don't take it out on me."

"I *know* I will be chosen," she says, her voice trembling.

"That's exactly my point. Do you even know what that will mean for you?"

"My parents aren't stupid. They've made sure I'll come out ahead."

She's implying her parents either paid money to have her picked by someone specific or that a suitor has already purchased a claim on her.

"Do you think your money makes a difference?"

She glares at me. "I would expect someone like you to say money doesn't matter."

Erin tugs at my arm again.

"Money won't keep your future husband from using you as he sees fit. And your privilege won't keep you safe. You and I are exactly the same in the eyes of the king and the suitors."

Her face pales a little. Regardless of her abrasive front, we share the same fears. A small crowd has gathered around us, a mixture of alarm, hope, and uncertainty in all their faces.

A trumpet blares. Everyone looks around, unsure of where to go or what to do as a throng of guards marches in, their boots pounding the floor, sending a shudder through the entire room. They push the girls into a line, positioning them so they all face the front of the room where a three-tiered platform stands, the king's empty throne at the very top. It's a massive seat made of gold, inlaid with rubies. A giant lion's head is carved into the backrest, its mane designed to give its occupant the appearance of having a golden halo.

A squat guard takes Erin by the shoulder and shoves her into line. I step between them and push the man's arm down.

"Don't touch her."

"Sophia," Erin says, her eyes pleading. "Don't."

"Listen to your friend, little girl," the guard says. A man nearly a foot shorter than me has the nerve to call me little.

He grabs me roughly by the elbow, shoving me into line next to Erin. I yank my arm out of his grip and scowl at him. He smells of sweat and cigar smoke.

"Feisty now, ain't we?" He smiles, exposing every one of his yellow and rotting teeth.

"Leave me alone," I say.

The man raises his eyebrows, and the corner of his mouth turns up. He grabs my arm again, this time digging the tips of his fingers into my skin. If I act quickly, I can break his nose and run away before he has a chance to catch me. I ball up my fist and draw my arm back. The trumpets sound again, and he hesitates for a moment before letting go of me and walking away in a huff. I push away the tears, refusing to let them fall.

The atmosphere changes as the guards direct a line of girls across the grand ballroom. A palpable sense of fear descends as those who were excited to arrive soon realize that this is no happy social gathering. It isn't even a well-disguised trap.

Erin stands silently, a big forced smile plastered across her face, her hands shaking. I purse my lips. I have to get us out of here. My arm throbs in time with my frantic heartbeats. Glancing around at the other girls, I finally spot Liv.

She wears a plain cotton frock, no makeup other than a bit of rouge on the apples of her cheeks. Her hair is draped over her shoulder, and a crown of baby's breath encircles her head. She stares at the floor, and I watch her chest rise and fall in the rhythm of someone who is quickly losing her ability to pretend that everything is fine. She looks lovely, but as she glances up, I see only sadness in her eyes. She shakes her head, and I know that something has gone wrong. She hadn't been visited by a fairy godmother, and her parents couldn't afford to make other arrangements. Her gaze moves down the length of my gown and back up again. She smiles and presses her hand against her chest.

I swallow hard. I know what Liv will be facing if she isn't selected, and my heart aches for her. The king might grant her a pass to work in Hanover or maybe even Chione, but that isn't a solution as much as a punishment. The people there run workhouses where forfeits labor day and night with a small amount of compensation sent directly to their heads of household. I desperately try to find what Luke had called "an out" but can't think of a single thing that doesn't end up with us in prison—or worse.

A guard stands at attention and clears his throat as a set of doors at the side of the room open and a procession of men files in. "His Majesty's honored guests," he announces.

The suitors.

"The Marquess of Eastern Lille," the guard says.

The marquess marches in. He always dresses audaciously and makes a point of showing off whenever he can, but he has outdone himself this night. His suit is the color of freshly bloomed marigolds and is so tight it looks like it's been painted on. The fabric creeps into all his creases, and I see outlines of things that make me wish I could poke my eyes out. In the brim of his three-pointed hat is a plume of brightly colored feathers. His shoes are made from some kind of animal skin but have been dyed yellow to match his suit. He climbs to the tier just below the throne and stands there like a very awkward bird. The Marquess of Eastern Lille is the highest-ranking man in Mersailles besides King Manford himself.

"The Earls of Hanover and Kilspire, and the Viscount of Chione," says the guard.

These men and their entourages are less officious than the marquess, but they still think themselves better than the rest of us. They are smiling, some of them laughing, and all of them dressed in their finest attire. They walk in and take their places on the second level of the three-tiered platform.

"The barons," the guard says, his enthusiasm waning. "And peasantry." He says that last part like a curse.

The last of the suitors file in. Some of them are old enough to be my grandfather, but that doesn't stop them from shamelessly ogling the young girls. I cross my arms as one man looks at me from his perch, and I stare at him unflinchingly. He only smiles wider. Most of them are well-to-do men—not quite commoners, not quite aristocracy—who stand on the bottom tier of the platform. Their attitudes are more reserved, but they are here, so they can't be that concerned with the well-being of the girls present. Some of them admire us, while others look around the grand hall as if they, too, are in awe of the lavish surroundings. It's hard to believe that the king found so many like-minded men within riding distance of Lille, and it doesn't surprise me that even the men considered peasants by the palace are positioned above all the girls here.

Surely there are good men among the ones gathered here, but if there are, they won't stand up to be counted. The men on the bottom tier seem restless, wringing their hands or tapping their shiny boots on the marble. One man stands quite still, gazing out into the crowd. I know him.

Luke.

9

I clear my throat loudly, and he looks in my direction. He catches sight of me and smiles. I smile back, but I'm immediately struck by a sickening sense of apprehension. He said he could avoid the ball for as long as he wanted. So why is he here? Had he lied to me? And if so, had he lied about other things? I'd been more open with him than I should have, and now I regret it. He continues to stare at me, and I clench my fists at my sides. I swallow hard and kick myself for being so trusting. Now I'm worried he'll tell, but I temper my fear. He'd told me things about himself, too. His gaze wanders to the upper part of the wall, and I follow it.

Portraits of the kings of Mersailles hang all around the ballroom. Some of them are as wide as a barn door.

Prince Charming's portrait hangs by the tiered platform. His hair is gray, and his skin is creased at the corners of his eyes and mouth. A fur is draped around his shoulders. He lived to be almost one hundred and was Mersailles's founder.

Paintings of his successors are hung up as well: King Eustice, King Stephan, and of course, King Manford.

Since the time of Cinderella, the throne has been passed to a successor of the king's choosing. All new kings are handpicked from a city beyond the Forbidden Lands that does nothing but work to produce a suitable heir. The city's name and exact location are a closely guarded secret because the rulers of Mersailles fear someone might interfere in their process of always putting the most detestable fools on the throne. Cinderella hadn't had any children, and her Prince Charming had ruled alone for nearly seventy-five years, dying a decrepit old man and passing the throne to his successor, King Eustice.

Three notes from the trumpeters blast through the room, and the guards scramble to form two parallel lines near the door. Everyone turns as the royal anthem blares, and King Manford appears in the doorway. He strides in, draped in a bloodred fur cape and all black underneath. He proceeds to the platform, ascending the steps as three servants follow him up. Each of the men already standing there bow low, and when he gets to the top,

Manford unclasps his collar and tosses the cape at the servants, who gather it up and scurry away.

There is an audible intake of breath from the crowd as the music fades. He stands in front of his throne, and I get a good look at him. The last time I saw him in the flesh was at his coronation. I'd only gotten a glance at him then from very far away, but I see him now, clearly. He has dark wavy hair that curls up just above his ears. His eyes are dark and his skin is a warm golden brown. He is tall and commanding and absolutely possessed of self-importance.

Some of the other girls in line seem completely smitten, even before he's had a chance to speak. They stare up at him, their mouths open, smiling, as if he and his predecessors aren't the sole reason most of their parents have gone bankrupt funding their trip to the palace.

"I am honored to have you here tonight," says the king in a booming, gravelly voice that echoes off the walls. The girl beside me sighs, trying her best to catch his attention by batting her eyes repeatedly and poking out her chest. She raises her hand slightly to wave at the king, but she inadvertently attracts the gaze of another on the lower platform. A stocky little man, who furiously dabs his forehead with a piece of cloth, blows a kiss to her. She quickly lowers her hand and looks down at the floor.

"The men you see before you are some of the most upstanding members of our community," says the king.

"I doubt that very much," I say under my breath.

"They have journeyed from near and far to see what the young ladies of Lille have to offer, and I must admit, gathered here tonight are some of the loveliest faces I've ever seen." He pauses and cocks his head to the side. "Except you." The king narrows his eyes and raises a long slender finger, pointing it directly at someone. Anger flashes across his face, and for a moment he appears gaunt, pained. I blink several times and look to the girls on either side of me. Surely they'd seen it too, but their expressions remain unchanged.

"You there. Step forward," the king commands.

A guard passes behind our line and pushes one of the girls forward. She stumbles into the open space at the bottom of the platform.

Liv.

"Your—Your Majesty," she sputters. She curtsies and then stands, wrapping her arms tightly around her waist.

Erin's breathing becomes frantic, and I take a half step forward.

"I see so many beautiful gowns, beautiful faces. And then I see you." The king glares at her. "Were you not aware that this is a formal event?"

The men on the platform laugh, and so do many of the other girls. Luke is silent, staring ahead. My heart races as

I take another step forward. The king's lips curl into a hideous smile.

"My—my parents, they couldn't afford—" Liv starts.

"Excuses are for the weak," the king says. "The ball was obviously not a priority." He takes stock of her again, his face twisting into a mask of disgust. "Do your parents care that now, looking as you do, you will not be picked by one of these fine gentlemen?"

Liv sobs. "I'm so sorry, Your Highness. I'd hoped a fairy godmother would see fit to visit me."

The king descends the steps to stand in front of her. Just behind my shoulder a hulking guard looms over me.

"Get back in your place," he says, just above a whisper. I hesitate. He doesn't look at me as he speaks and seems much more concerned with what the king is doing. I slowly step back into line.

"You are indeed sorry," says the king. "You didn't earn a visit from a fairy godmother. Didn't you consult the book? Didn't you do as Cinderella would have done?" His tone is taunting, sarcastic, cruel.

No one makes a sound. Even the men on the platform quiet themselves.

"I did, Your Highness," Liv says, her voice choked with what I can only imagine is some combination of fear and dread. "I study the book every day. I have worked my fingers to the bone in service to my father, to my king—"

"And here you are," says King Manford. "Disgracing us both." He walks around Liv like an animal circling its prey. My stomach turns over. He touches the fabric of her dress, running his hand over the seams of her sleeve. He stands in front of her again. "Did you make this dress yourself, or did you find it in the gutter somewhere?"

Nervous laughter erupts from the men on the platform. None of the girls laugh this time. It could easily have been any one of us standing up there.

"I made it," says Liv. "I—I didn't have a choice."

"There are always choices. They may not be ones you like, but there are always choices. You could have worked harder, couldn't you? Your parents could have sold something. You could have gone out to work in Hanover. They are always on the lookout for *talented* young women like yourself."

Girls who voluntarily go to Hanover instead of attending a second or third ball must get a pass from the king himself, and many of them never return.

"Alas," the king sighs. "You chose to wear this abomination to my ball. A terrible choice. But . . ." He leans in so his face is almost touching Liv's. "Now that I look a bit closer, I can see that you are quite lovely." He reaches out to pull her hair through his fingers, sighs, and gazes past her. "While your beauty surpasses some of the other faces here, I simply cannot allow you to come dressed like that. What will people say? They'll think I've lowered my standards, and that, my dear, simply will not do." The king nods to a nearby guard, who steps forward and loops his arm under Liv's.

"Wait!" she screams as the guard drags her toward the side door. "Please—I'm sorry!"

The king claps his hands twice as he ascends to his throne. A barrage of men in white coats and matching toques blanches come in, pushing carts with silver platters piled high with succulent hors d'oeuvres. The band starts to play a chipper melody.

"Let the festivities begin!" says the king.

The crowd disperses as the men descend from their platform to mingle with the girls. I'm frozen. I can't breathe. I pull at the corset, but it won't budge. Looking across the room, I gauge the distance to the door to see if I can make a run for it, but there are too many guards.

I watch the king surveying the room as he sits atop his golden chair. He runs his long, thin fingers over his chin. Suddenly he stands and his servants scramble behind him as he descends the platform and disappears through the door where the guards had taken Liv.

I grab Erin by the wrist and duck away, weaving through the crowd until we end up beside an elaborately decorated table with a gleaming glass bowl filled to the top with bloodred liquid.

"What will they do with her?" Erin asks.

"I don't know. I don't know where they took her." I look toward the door again.

"They probably put her out. Oh, Sophia, this is terrible. What will she do now? This is already her second ball. I don't know anyone who's actually gone to a third. She'll be a forfeit."

"Don't say that. Maybe we can find a way to get to her and then leave."

"We can't. They haven't even started the selection ceremony yet." Erin dabs at her eyes.

"No. I mean I want to leave Lille. I want to leave Mersailles. I want to get as far away from here as possible." We have to run. Fear envelops me as I take Erin by the arm.

"Shh!" Erin looks around to see if anyone heard me. "You can't say things like that. People are listening."

"I don't care." A few people glance in my direction. I lean in toward Erin. "We have to get out of here."

"I can't leave," she says through gritted teeth and a fake smile. "My parents have invested so much, and so have yours."

"They can't keep us safe. Look around you, Erin. Who are our parents to do anything? They won't defy the king. And I don't care what they've invested."

Without warning a hand grasps my shoulder, and I turn,

expecting to see some bumbling idiot ready to make a claim on me.

"Sorry," says Luke with his hands up. "I didn't mean to startle you."

I exhale slowly, relieved, but then I remember his words from the other day. "Were you lying to me? You said you didn't plan on coming here."

"No, I knew you'd be here, and I wanted to see you."

"Sophia?" Erin watches Luke with the eyes of a hawk.

"Miss Erin." Luke gives a little bow.

"Do we know each other?" Erin asks, an edge of anger in her voice.

"Yes. Well, no. What I mean to say is that you know my sister. Mila."

"Your sister? I wasn't aware the Langleys even had a son."

"Uh, surprise?" Luke spreads out his fingers and shakes his hands awkwardly. He turns to me. "I knew you'd be here, and I was worried."

"You're worried about me?" I ask, a little surprised. We'd only just met, and while our conversation had been intense, I didn't expect him to feel any obligation to me. "What did you plan to do once you found me?"

"I was going to choose you. If that's all right, I mean."

"What?" Erin asks, taking the word right out of my

mouth. Her entire demeanor changes. Her body goes rigid as she looks back and forth between Luke and me.

"You want us to be . . . together?" I ask, utterly confused.

"I thought if you and I could be matched, you'd be spared from having to be with one of these dolts. It would be a ruse, of course, but it could buy us some time."

He is willing to pretend in a way that might benefit us both, and a glimmer of hope springs to life inside me. "This could work."

"Nothing has changed. I meant every word I said to you in the other day." He lowers his voice. "We could get out of here, and then we could make a plan to leave Lille for good."

Erin makes a noise like she's choked on a bit of food. Her jaw is set, her eyes narrow. "You'll never make it past the towers."

"We can try," I say, echoing what I'd told her in the carriage. We have to try. We have to do something. "Come with us. She can come with us, right?" I look at Luke.

"I don't know how, but I'm sure we can think of something." I can see he isn't at all convinced of that.

"I don't want to go with you," Erin says angrily. "Go get yourself killed if that's what you want, but I'm staying here and doing what my parents and the king expect me to do."

"Erin, please, I—"

Out of the crowd appears a young man, about the same age as Luke, who wedges himself between us.

"You look absolutely ravishing," he says to me, taking my hand and kissing it roughly. He winks at Erin. "And you're quite pretty, too. I think this may be my lucky night."

10

The man moves his lips down onto the inside of my forearm. I snatch my arm away and move to Luke's side.

"Excuse you," I say sharply. "But I'm spoken for." Saying no isn't good enough, but he might respect another man's claim on me.

The young man looks at me and then at Luke. I peer around him and catch sight of the back of Erin's head as she disappears into the crowd.

"Luke Langley," the man says.

"Édouard." Luke says the man's name as if it leaves a foul taste in his mouth.

"I hear you've had a run-in with my brother," Édouard says. From behind him steps a bruised and gap-toothed Morris.

"Shit," Luke says.

Morris frowns.

"I bet he thinks his name is Shit," I say to Luke. "It's the first thing you say whenever you see him."

Luke bites back a smile.

"What did you say?" Morris asks. He seems dumbstruck that I can form actual words.

"Oh, don't worry," I say. "The name suits you. Just embrace it."

Morris is furious, but Édouard seems amused. "Settle down, Morris." He looks to Luke. "I must admit I'm surprised you're here. After all, none of the prospects are boys."

"And I'm not surprised to see you here," Luke says. "And seeking more than one girl? That seems about right." Luke squares his shoulders and leans toward Édouard.

"Seems like you've come into your own, Luke. Where is that scared, pathetic little outcast I used to know?" Édouard lurches at Luke, forcing him back a step. "Ah. There he is."

Édouard laughs and then reaches out, slipping his hand under my chin. I move to bat him away, but Luke beats me to it. He catches Édouard by the wrist, wrenching his arm down. I grab a small cup from the table to my left, dip it into the punch bowl, and toss the drink at Édouard.

The red liquid cascades down the side of his ivory jacket. Édouard's face twists into a mask of rage as he looks at his ruined clothing. Luke puts his arm under mine, and we rush off, leaving Édouard in a sputtering, hissing fit.

I frantically search for Erin as we cut through the heart of the crowd and end up on the opposite side near the powder room entrance. I catch a glimpse of her just as the band strikes up a waltz, and the young women pair off with different men. Everyone moves in a dizzying circle in time with the music, and I lose sight of her again.

My heartbeat pounds in my ears. I lean down and put my hands on my knees. "How did one family end up with two complete fools in the same generation?"

"They get it from their father," says Luke. "He gave up their mother as forfeit when we were in school so he could take a new wife. He was cruel to her, and still Morris and Édouard want nothing more than to be exactly like him. Their family has gained favor with the palace. They support everything the king does, without question."

"Why?" I ask.

"Morris and Édouard's family have ties to outside traders in cities beyond the Forbidden Lands in the west. They support the king, sharing their profits, and in return the king lets them do whatever they want. Sometimes they invite envoys to bring their goods to trade and then rob them on the way into Mersailles."

"How do you know all this?" I ask. "It seems like something you'd want to keep secret."

"It's Morris. He loves to talk about his special privileges and thinks that he'll never have to face any consequences. He's probably right."

Luke puts out his hand, and I take it. He pulls me into the swirling mass of couples, and we spin to the tune of the waltz. I glance toward the king's throne. It's still empty.

"We need to get as far away from here as possible," I say.

"Exactly." Luke lifts his arm as I duck under it, stepping back to take his hand again.

"And how do we get past the watchtowers? Even if we're married, the king would never allow us to just walk away."

"I think we could sneak out. We could find a way. I'm sure of it."

I remember how the guards had called for the executioner when a runner had tried to cross the border. "I've never heard of anyone leaving without the king's consent."

"Neither have I, but that doesn't mean it hasn't happened. We've also rarely heard about people like us and yet here we are. Just because they deny us doesn't mean we cease to exist."

It's entirely possible that someone has attempted an escape and the palace had hushed it up. But could someone actually escape? Has anyone ever actually done it? That would be a secret worth keeping. I think of the circle of blackened grass at the fountain. Maybe there is something to what Luke is saying.

"The border is guarded all the way around Lille," I say.

Luke lowers his mouth to my ear. "Less so on the western edge."

"No," I say. "The western edge of the city butts up to the White Wood, and we can't go through there. It's too dangerous. No one is stupid enough to actually try and escape that way."

"We *shouldn't* go through there," Luke says. "But we *can*. We have to decide if we're willing to take that risk."

The alternative is staying here, falling in line, being at the mercy of the king and his rules. It's not a way to live. I'm willing to risk leaving by any path necessary.

"I need a minute," I say. My head is spinning. We're going to do this. We're going to make our escape.

Luke gestures to the powder room door, and I nod.

"When you come back, I'll let the registrar know that I'm going to make a claim on you." He shakes his head. "I'm so sorry that I have to say it that way, and I'm sorry that you can't be with Erin."

I smile at him, and he kisses me gently on the cheek before I duck off.

The powder room is bigger than some of the houses in town. In the center sits a circular sofa covered in fabric decorated with pink roses. It smells of lavender and fresh flowers, and girls are lounging about, talking among themselves.

"No one has even looked at me," one girl says. "Is it my dress? My hair? I did everything my father told me to do."

"You look gorgeous," says her friend, glancing at her shyly. They clasp hands and go out arm in arm.

I go to the mirror and stare at my reflection. I will allow Luke to choose me, and together we'll find a way out of the kingdom. I'll convince Erin to come with me, and we'll have to find Liv first, but what about the others? All the girls left behind will be at the mercy of the king and his deplorable cohorts.

My painted face stares back at me like a stranger. I dip my hands into the basin and splash myself with water. The rouge runs down my cheeks in thin rivulets, and I pull my hair out of its coils, letting it fall around my face. Other girls come into the room and look at me as if I've lost my mind.

A loud bang, like someone dropped a stack of plates, comes from the ballroom. Shouts ring out as the other girls scurry from the room, and I follow behind them.

A crowd gathers in the grand ballroom, all pressed together, staring at some commotion. As I push through the crowd, I glance toward the door where they'd taken Liv. The door stands open. Through the forest of people, I see the king walking briskly from the room, and I catch a glimpse of an old woman with hair as white as snow being propped up by a palace guard. The door closes, and

I move to the front of the crowd to see what the commotion is about.

Two guards stand holding another man between them. He struggles against them, and the guard on the left delivers a swift punch to the man's ribs. He doubles over. I feel like I'm going to be sick.

Luke.

Édouard, in his stained jacket, his brother Morris at his side, stands in front of Luke. "This man thinks he can make a mockery of this time-honored tradition, and I will not stand for it!"

The king appears at the other side of the crowd, flanked by his guards. He smiles as he watches the scuffle, and I am taken aback by how happy he looks. His eyes seem lighter than they had when he was perched atop his throne, his face seems less stern, and his entire demeanor has changed.

"Luke knows full well my brother intended to claim—" He searches the crowd until his gaze lands on me. "Her."

I stifle the urge to vomit. Morris grins, and I think back to what could have made him assume I was remotely interested. He doesn't even know my name. But I realize that it has less to do with me and more to do with making a fool of Luke.

"The rules are clear," Édouard continues. "Morris comes

from a family of higher class, better breeding, and so Luke's claim is void. But I admire his efforts. Truly."

Luke slips the guard's grip and lands a clean jab on Édouard's chin, sending him stumbling back. Édouard rushes in, his fist raised. I scream out in terror, and the king's head snaps up. He looks directly at me.

"Enough," orders the king.

Édouard stops in his tracks, lowering his hand. The king signals his guards, and they scoop Luke up and drag him through the same door where they'd taken Liv. As the crowd disperses, some of the guards laugh with Édouard and Morris.

My heart sinks. Luke was my only chance to get out of here, but beyond that, now I'm worried something terrible is going to happen to him. Scanning the room for Erin, I don't see her, but the suitors are watching me. I hear some of them whispering. Stumbling over my own feet as the crowd presses in, I catch sight of Édouard whispering something to Morris, who then makes his way straight toward me.

"Hello again," he says. "I'm very sorry you had to see that." The air whistles in and out between his broken teeth as he lies to my face. "I think you and I should get to know each other a little better now that I've made my intentions clear." He runs the tips of his fingers over the exposed skin of my shoulders.

"Where have they taken Luke?" I ask.

"I'll ask you, because I'm a gentleman, not to mention his name," says Morris, pressing in on me. "But I'm sure he'll be dealt with in whatever manner the king feels is appropriate."

Tears well up. "You made no mention of a claim. You were lying."

Morris frowns. "Don't tell me you were actually happy about Luke's claim on you."

"I was."

He sighs heavily and takes my hand in his, squeezing it tight. "Do not embarrass me in front of all these people. I'll need you to smile, and even if you're not happy, you'll need to act the part." He leans in and presses his lips to mine. I try to pull away, but he holds me close. He smells like wine and sweat, and all I want to do is get away from him.

I step back and bring my knee up as hard as I can— right between his legs. His blunted yelp makes the people around us stop and stare. The look on Morris's face switches from anger to bewilderment, and finally agony. Before he has a chance to recover from the shock, I duck off and run to the empty powder room. I slam the door closed and frantically look for an exit.

The only door is the one I just came through, and there is only one narrow window. No closet, no wardrobe, nowhere

I can hide. My heart crashes inside my chest. I glance at the window again.

I reach under my skirts and rip off the farthingale, unhooking it and letting it fall down around my ankles. I strip off the underlayers of petticoats, leaving just the shell of the dress. Reaching behind me, I struggle to untie the knot at the back of the corset. I can't manage it. After kicking off my shoes, I push open the small window and hoist myself up. I'm halfway through when someone grabs ahold of my ankle.

11

W e've got a runner!" the guard yells.

Images of the woman they'd caught on the border flash in my head. I bring up my leg and kick the guard as hard as I can, breaking his grasp. I pull myself the rest of the way through, tumbling down onto the roof of another structure just under the window.

The air is chilly, and I can see out over the rear of the castle grounds. The wind catches the hem of my gown and whips it around my ankles. I struggle to keep myself upright as I inch along the roof. The guard yells, trying to come out the window after me, but he can't fit. I keep moving and glance over the edge. The ground isn't too far. I can make it if I jump.

I gather myself and prepare to leap when the roof I'm

balancing on gives way with a sickening crack. Grasping at air, I fall, landing on my back, the breath punched out of me.

I roll onto my side, heaving, pain spiraling down my leg. I scramble to my feet and look around. Cold and dank, the narrow passageway smells of dust and stale water. It's unlit except for the moonlight that shines through a row of small windows at the top of the outer wall and through the hole in the ceiling that I'd fallen through. Several doors line the interior wall, all of them bolted from the outside with big brass locks. The sound of water dripping echoes down the corridor, and music from the great hall wafts in like a whisper.

I walk along the cramped hall, looking back, half expecting palace guards to come barreling in at any moment. When I come to the end of the hall, a door juts out from the exterior wall.

This has to be a way out.

As I turn the handle, I hear a faint sound. So faint that I almost lose it in the distant melody of the band's waltz. I stop to listen. The sound comes again. It could only have been emanating from the door directly opposite me. I press my ear against the wooden slats. A faint, flickering light comes from the crack near the floor. Someone sobs quietly behind the locked and bolted door.

"Hello?" I call out.

The sobbing stops, and I hear a rustling noise. I press my ear harder against the door. "Hello?" I call again. There's a small shift at the door, as if someone is leaning against it from the inside.

"Hello?" a voice says just above a whisper. "Is someone there?"

I look down the corridor, afraid of losing my opportunity to escape. "Yes. I'm here."

"Why are you here?"

What an odd question coming from someone behind a locked door.

"There is a ball," I say. The crying resumes. "Who are you? Why are you locked up?"

"Run away. Don't ever come back. Save yourself."

"Where has she gone?" A man's voice cuts through the darkness and echoes down the corridor, and a shriek escapes my throat.

I bolt out the door in the exterior wall, across the manicured grounds, until I find cover in the wooded tree line. Crouching low, I peer out to see lamps moving around like fireflies in the distance. I want to find Luke, Liv, and Erin, but I can't go back. If the king's men apprehend me, they will execute me. I turn and run straight into the woods.

Stumbling over the thick underbrush and exposed tree roots, I'm sure I'm heading away from the palace because the trees become thicker and the darkness more complete. But I have no idea if I'm on a course to the main road or just walking in a circle. The canopy blots out what little moonlight is still visible in the night sky.

The voice from behind the door sticks in my mind. I'm ashamed for leaving whoever she was there, but I need to focus on escaping.

I push forward for what feels like hours. The cold is biting, and the sting of it on my arms and on my stocking feet leaves me numb. I haven't come across a road or trail or any of the fencing that runs along the outer edge of the palace grounds. The estate is vast, and I fear that I may be too lost to find my way out. What have I gotten myself into?

My teeth chatter together, and I shake uncontrollably. Struggling to see in the dark, I notice that the trees are beginning to thin. I hope it's the forest's edge, but it is only a clearing. On the other side are more trees and more darkness.

I step into the open space where a large rectangular structure stands. As tall as my own house and nearly as wide, the structure shimmers in the slivers of silver moonlight. Charcoal-gray veins run through the white marble walls. As my eyes adjust, I realize that it is a mausoleum, and the name carved in flowing script on its edifice is as familiar to me as my own.

Cinderella

12

Ivy creeps up the entire façade, covering the structure in a tangle of tendrils. The surrounding grass stands as tall as my knees, and all of it is dead and brown. The tomb looms in the dark, and as I stand before it, in the dead of night, breaking the king's rules for the umpteenth time, I feel like I'm seeing something not meant for anyone to see. This place isn't supposed to exist.

I wade through the brush and come to three wide marble steps leading up to the doors of the mausoleum. Bushels of faded, crumbling flowers clutter the stairs. Small toys and hundreds of folded pieces of paper in varying stages of decay litter the monument. Some of them are only yellowed a bit at the edges, while others are nothing more than little piles of dust. I pick one up that looks sturdy

enough to handle. Unfolding it, I read the words scribbled
inside.

*Please allow my daughter to be chosen. Please make her stand
out among the others.*

Picking up one note after the other, I read as many as I
can find that are still legible.

Please help us find a way to pay for her gown.

*Meet me at the place where the man took our sister on the
last day of the growing season. Bring only what you can
carry.*

They are all essentially the same. Pleas for help or good
fortune, for luck, or for protection. The last one sounds like
someone was trying to plan an escape. Clearly whoever it
was meant for never got it, because it is rotting here in the
shadow of Cinderella's tomb.

They were more than trinkets, as my mother's helpers
had said. They were petitions, prayers. Looking up at the
tomb, I wonder if Cinderella has heard their cries. Or if she
even cares at all. More likely, she is laughing at how miser-
ably we've failed to live up to her expectations.

I climb the stairs to the pair of double doors guarding

the entrance. Etched into the stained glass of the door panels is a depiction of Cinderella's carriage drawn by four white horses.

A flicker of light shines through the glass doors, and I freeze. A white-blue flash illuminates the inner sanctum of the mausoleum and lingers a moment before dying out again. I try to see through the colored glass, but only a faint glow toward the rear of the chamber remains.

I should be running home. I need to get away from here before the guards find me and drag me back to the palace.

A branch breaks in the distance. Someone is out there. Taking my chances with the flickering light, I push the doors open and go inside, closing them behind me. I don't hear anything, but I stay still, holding my breath.

Directly in front of me, Cinderella lies on a slab in the middle of the crypt.

I jump back, my heart thudding in my chest. Two hundred years in a crypt should have rendered her body dust and bones. I squint in the shadows and see that the figure on the slab is only a marble rendering of Cinderella. Sighing heavily, I lean against the inner wall of the tomb.

At the end of Cinderella's story, she and Prince Charming embrace, they kiss, and she goes off to live a life of luxury in the palace. It doesn't say anything about how she hid in the castle while her people suffered, the prolonged illness that took her life, or why she now lies in an abandoned tomb in the middle of the woods.

The walls of the tomb extend high above my head. Frigid, musty air fills the space, and I rub my arms, trying to warm my freezing limbs. I walk along the inside wall, studying the lifelike carving of Cinderella. The sculpture looks a lot like the portraits I've seen of her. She lies on her back, her hands clasped over her chest holding a bouquet of marble flowers. The rectangular box that extends down to the floor is also made of gleaming white marble.

That strange light flickers again in the rear of the crypt, lighting up the darkness in short bursts. In an alcove, a small, square glass housing sits atop a pedestal with metal trim wrapped around it like a cage. The panes of the glass box are foggy, and broken leaves clutter the space. I clear away the debris and clean a spot on the glass with my fingers so I can see inside. The white-blue glow lights up the box. A pair of shoes, small and almost completely translucent, rest inside. These are the fabled glass slippers.

"I guess the legends were true," I say aloud.

"Not entirely."

I spin around, knocking my knee against the pedestal's base. A figure appears in the crypt. The person wears a long cloak with a hood covering their face.

"I didn't mean any harm, I swear," I say, clutching my knee.

The figure is silent. Have they come to take me back to the palace? I scramble to think of what to do.

"Cinderella is dead," says the figure, the voice light, airy. "I doubt she'll mind you lurking around her tomb."

"I'm not lurking," I say, searching for something within arm's length that I can use as a weapon. "And if you lay a hand on me—"

"Lay a hand on you? I wouldn't dare." The person reaches up and pulls their hood back. A shock of lush reddish curls frames their face. It's a young woman. She tilts her head to the side, looking me over. "Not unless you wanted me to."

I am struck silent.

"You're—you're not working for the king, then?" I'm having trouble figuring out who she is and why she's here.

"I would choose death over serving him." Her tone is suddenly serious.

I keep Cinderella's sarcophagus between us as I move toward the door. "I was just leaving."

"And where are you off to?" she asks. In her hand, she holds a small lantern, lit just brightly enough so I can see her face. We are matched in height and build and are probably close in age as well. Her fawn skin, dewy and smooth, seems to glow from within.

A ripple of guilt runs through me. I should not be admiring some stranger's beauty at a time like this. "I'm trying to get home."

"On a night like this? A pretty girl like yourself should be at the palace looking for a suitor." She watches me carefully as she speaks.

"I've just come from there," I say. The way she said the word "pretty" gives me pause. It's a compliment, but there is something else in her voice. I avoid her eyes. "I'm not going back. I don't care how many guards the king sends after me."

"Don't you want to find a husband and settle into your proper role?" Subtlety isn't this girl's strong point. Sarcasm permeates every word.

"I don't want anything to do with a husband or any sort of proper role."

"And why is that?" she asks.

"Because that's not my choice. That's not what I want." It's probably a mistake to spill my secrets to her, but I feel like I have less and less to lose with each passing moment.

She smiles at me and my face flushes hot.

"So, did you come here to pay homage to Cinderella?" she asks. She places her lamp on the ground and pulls a small bundle of flowers from the folds of her cloak. I shiver as she walks up to place them on Cinderella's coffin, running her hand over the smooth marble.

"No," I say curtly. "But from the looks of it, lots of other people have. I didn't think this place still existed." My teeth clang together as I try to bite back the cold.

She walks toward me, takes her cloak off, and places it around my shoulders. "Better?"

"Yes. Thank you." I almost swoon in the warmth of the cloak. I breathe in her scent, a mix of wildflowers and lavender. I have to remind myself to focus.

She's wearing a pair of close-fitting trousers and a tunic. A thick belt encircles her waist and from it hangs a gleaming dagger. She goes to the doors and peers out through a little chip in the glass. Her face relaxes as she turns to me.

"Why are you dressed like that?" I ask. She looks lovely, but I've never seen a woman wear pants and a tunic before.

"The pockets," she says. She puts her hands in them and gives a little twirl. "I love pockets."

I smile, despite the cold, despite the terrible circumstance. "You said before that I was wrong about the legends being true. What did you mean?"

Her gaze drifts to the glass slippers. "All fairy tales have some grain of truth. Picking apart that truth from the lies can be tricky, though."

"Questioning the story is against the law."

She stiffens.

"I'm sorry. I'm not threatening you," I say quickly. "It's just that I've rarely heard anyone say that even parts of the story are fiction. Most people believe every word."

"And you don't?"

"I don't know what I believe anymore." The weight of everything that has happened falls on me all at once. "I have to go. If the guards find me . . ."

"They won't if you stay here," she says.

"How do you know that?" I ask frantically. A wave of panic rushes over me. "I don't know what I'm supposed to do now, but I have to do something."

The girl stares at me for a moment. "West of the city center, about five miles, the road branches out into two forks. The far right one meanders for a few more miles and leads to a gate. Meet me there tomorrow."

"I probably won't be alive tomorrow," I say. "I'll be rotting in some dungeon on the king's orders by then."

Her brows knit together as if this troubles her. She ducks behind the coffin and picks up a small bag. After fishing around inside, she takes out a set of clothes—a pair of pants and another tunic, a pair of boots—and tosses them to me. "Put these on."

I set her cloak aside and pull on the trousers, casting aside the shell of my dress. I slip the tunic over my head as the girl steps toward me, a small dagger glinting in the lantern light. My heart skips. I realize what a fool I've been to so blindly trust a stranger. I turn to run, but in one quick motion she slices the strings of my corset, and for the first time all day I can breathe. My heart pounds in fear, but also something else. Exhilaration? Panic? It feels like

I'm free from something much more than fabric and strings.

"Stay here," she says as I face her. "Stay hidden. And tomorrow, come to meet me if you can, because I think you're probably right about the king's men. They won't stop searching for you." She straightens up. "What's your name?"

"Sophia," I say.

"I'm Constance," she says. "I'll lead the guards away from you. When you leave at first light, stay off the main road."

"I don't even know which way to go," I say, feeling more hopeless with each passing moment.

"City center is in the direction of the rising sun," she says. "Remember, leave at first light."

She moves to the door, and I hold out her cloak.

"Keep it," she says. "You can give it back when you come see me."

13

I don't sleep, and as soon as daylight touches the sky, I leave Cinderella's tomb. Following the rising sun, I cut through the woods, stumbling along in boots that are two sizes too big. The main road is visible through the trees after a while, but I don't take it. I stay in the shadowy confines of the tree line until the road is clear at the junction that leads into the heart of Lille.

I hesitate as I think of the girl. Constance. If I go now to meet her, my parents will be left wondering what happened. The king will send his men to the house, I'm sure of it, but what will they say? Will they admit that I slipped through their fingers? I can't leave my parents wondering if I'm dead or alive. I keep the hood of the cloak up as I cut across the main road and make my way home.

When I arrive on my street, a trio of palace guards are storming out of my house. They mount their horses as I sink low, pressing my back into a garden wall. They ride past, raining bits of earth and pebbles down on me. As the sounds of the horses fade, I scramble to my feet and dart around to our rear entrance. The door is locked. I rap gently on the glass until my mother's tear-soaked face appears. She flings it open and pulls me inside, cupping her hand over my mouth. My father appears in the doorway, and his eyes grow wide. He glances back over his shoulder.

"Hurry up with that tea, woman," a gruff voice calls from the front room.

My mother goes to the stove where a kettle sits steaming. My father motions for me to move away from the doorway. He walks to the front room.

"I'm going out to the front garden to pull down the lines," my father says.

"That's woman's work," the other man says.

"It is," my father replies. "But my wife is getting your tea."

The man huffs. The front door opens, and a moment later my father cries out.

"Sophia!"

The man in the front room clambers to his feet and out the door. "Where is she?" he barks.

"I saw her! There!"

The man's boots pound the ground as he runs in whatever direction my father has pointed to.

My mother wraps her arms around me as my father sweeps over in a silent rage.

"They came looking for you," he says through gritted teeth. "They have guards posted at the end of our street."

My mother steps aside. I've never seen him so angry.

"Is it true you assaulted one of the suitors and fled on foot?" my mother asks.

"I didn't have a choice," I say.

"How could you put us in this position?" my father asks.

"What about the position you've put me in?" I can't believe that they are making it seem like this is my fault.

"We put you in a position to succeed in finding a good match. You could have wooed the king himself. You would have been chosen by someone." My father rubs his forehead, squeezing his eyes closed.

"You don't even know what happened up there! It was worse than anything I could have imagined. Some of those men were older than Grandpa, and some of them were looking for two girls at a time."

My mother looks as if she's going to be sick. "It's disgusting, Morgan," my mother says to my father. I'm struck silent. She so rarely expresses any doubt about the king's laws or the ball itself.

"You have broken the law," my father says. "Do you care for nothing except your own selfish desires?"

The words strike me like an open hand. I stagger backward into a chair at the kitchen table; a dizzying torrent of utter despair washes over me. My father hasn't even bothered to ask me if I am okay.

"You put us in a terrible position, Sophia. We can't defend you. The palace may think we're complicit." He glances at my mother and then back to me. "You can't be here when the guards return."

"Where am I supposed to go?" I ask, bewildered. I look at my mother, who hangs her head.

"You've given me no choice." My father's eyes are wild and searching. He slumps down, and my mother puts her arm around his waist. "Your friends probably found suitors. You come home dirty, disheveled, and wanted by the palace guards."

"The king humiliated Liv in front of everyone, tossed her aside like a piece of garbage, and you're worried about my dirty clothes?"

"Her family is not one of means, Sophia," says my father. "They tried their hardest to make sure she was prepared, but they failed her. I did not want that for you. I have worked hard to make sure you were ready and now . . . now you'll be a forfeit."

My mother shakes uncontrollably. She rushes to me

and holds me close. "No! I will not allow it!" She clings to me, digging her fingers into my back.

"There are no other options, Eve."

"I'm not going back to the palace," I say. "I'll leave if that's what you want, but I will not be a prisoner to the king."

My father stands firm, and I watch him. This man who I adore so very much has turned into someone I don't want to know. His words crush me. I walk to the back door in a haze.

"Wait," my mother says, rushing to block the door. "Please, we can hide her. We can make her apologize to the king. We can—"

"She has to go, Eve."

The pain of this is too much. I begin to weep as my mother screams at my father. "Morgan, stop this! Stop it this instant! This is our child. She needs us to—"

"To what?" my father snaps. "To continue to break the law? To continue to defy the king? Her best chance is escape." He flings the back door open wide. A gust of cold air stings my face. "Go. Get as far away from here as you can."

I look into his eyes. The tears stream down my face, but I keep the urge to scream and sob bottled up.

"I can't protect you here," he says. "Neither can your mother. You have to go, or we will all be dead."

"And if I leave it will just be me who ends up dead?" He doesn't answer, and I am again taken aback. He knows this. He's willing to let this happen. "You can't keep me safe because you're too afraid to stand up to the king."

My words hurt him. His eyes brim with tears. He blinks them away. "Please, go while you still can, before the guards return. This is the best chance for all of us. Your mother and I can avoid suspicion if I tell the guards that you never made it home."

I want to scream, to shake them and tell them to open their eyes, to see how wrong this is. I step out onto the stoop. The door closes and locks behind me. My mother's cries ring out inside the house, and my father's muffled voice tries to calm her as she screams my name.

I walk to the street, tears streaming down my face and an anger growing in the pit of my stomach, so hot it courses through me like a raging fire.

I stay close to the buildings to avoid the patrols and lamplighters. Behind closed doors, I imagine some girls are feeling the keen sting of rejection, while others celebrate their matches, none of them knowing what the future will bring.

Even as my head swims with my father's words, I can only think of my friends. Liv and I will be outcasts, and while I don't know what has become of Luke, whatever happened is my fault. He wouldn't have been there if it wasn't for me.

I pull the cloak in around me, and the lavender scent envelops me, reminding me of the girl from the crypt. Five miles west. That's where I need to go. It is the only place I can think of.

There is only one road leading west that extends right up to the city's border. As I make my way there, the rumble of carriages and horses puts me on edge. The king's men are searching for me, but how many of them could pick me out of a crowd?

The farther away from town I get, the fewer people there are. After a while I am alone, and all I can think of are my parents, of Erin, of what has happened.

On the road behind me, there is the chatter of men's voices, and I quickly take cover in a small grove of trees just off the road, pressing myself against a tree and trying not to breathe. Their voices carry as they stop at the edge of a steep embankment across from me.

"Are we sure she was at the ball?" one of them asks.

"Her parents said she was, but she's too old," says another. "Look at her hair. It's white as a sheet."

I peer around the tree. Guards. They are all looking down at the embankment.

"She's seventeen. That's what her mother said. Described her clothing and everything. It's a shame, sending her to the ball dressed like that."

One of them nods. "Well, we'll need a cart. And one of

us should go back to the house to make sure her father doesn't come down here."

They all turn and ride back up the road. I stand still until they are out of sight, and I can no longer hear their witless banter. My heart crashes wildly in my chest as I walk toward the embankment. Something deep inside compels me to look.

The steep slope leads down into a ditch where a few inches of water have gathered. Lying there is a person. My breath catches. I recognize her dress. Eyes that once sparkled with laughter and a mouth that once whispered silly jokes are open wide, caught in a scream. I cup my hand over my mouth to stifle the nausea. My dear Liv.

I have never seen a dead body. I don't know what it should look like, but what I see seems foreign. Liv's hair, once brown, is now white as snow. Her skin is shriveled and ashen gray. Her arms are drawn up in front of her, her hands rigid, fingers curled into claws.

I stagger back, and my stomach turns over. Collapsing on the road, I feel the muscles under my tongue seize as I vomit. Nothing but a foul-smelling liquid comes up. I refuse to believe it. She can't be dead. Not my Liv.

Men's voices sound again in the distance, and I wipe my mouth with the back of my hand, stumbling into the trees, where I slide down onto the ground and cry. Noiseless and aching, I double over and clutch my cloak, pressing my face into it as the rumbling of wheels sounds on the road behind me.

I watch as the guards return on foot, pulling a small wagon with an open top. They situate themselves along the road, and together, they pull Liv's body up the embankment, placing her atop the wagon's bed. I am going to vomit again.

"Do we have a blanket?" one of them asks.

"Oh, you're worried about her decency?" another asks.

"No, I just don't want to see her ugly face. It's terrifying." He pretends to shake with fright, and they all laugh. "I'd have offed myself, too, with a face like that."

One of the guards, an older man, steps forward. "Cover her and shut your mouth. This is someone's child."

The younger guard doesn't look moved, but he quiets himself and covers Liv's body with a blanket. They pull away and head back toward town.

I sit in the shadowy grove of oak trees, put my head in my hands, and weep. I can't see through the torrent of tears. I gasp for air and cry out. Lying down in the dirt, I press my face against the ground. I want to crawl into the earth, to disappear, anything that will make me forget about what I've seen.

14

The sharp refraction of the sun through the branches above me stings my blinking eyes. I'd fallen asleep as visions of Liv tumbled through my head. The cold wetness of the ground soaked into my clothes, chilling me to the bone. The tears rise again, and I angrily push them away. My body aches as a heaviness settles in my chest. I stumble out of the trees, my legs like lead working against me.

The sun is low in the sky, and darkness is descending. I'm not even halfway to the place where Constance said I should meet her. I hope she will still be there. I hope it's not too late to find her, now that there is nowhere else I can go. I push forward in a daze. Over my shoulder, the sound of horses and people talking startles me. I scurry down the embankment and press myself into the dirt to avoid being seen when the carts come barreling past. When the sound moves off, I carefully stand and look down the road. A cart full of heavily armed palace guards disappears in the distance.

Liv's face stays in my mind as I walk. I can't help but feel as if I've failed her. When Luke told me he would claim me to give us a way out, I thought I could bring Liv and Erin along. I thought we could save each other. Her absence resounds in every breath I take. The weight of her loss crushes me.

Her parents must be in agony. The thought brings a new kind of sorrow.

As the sun sinks lower and lower, I'm exhausted and unable to keep track of the minutes as they tick by; the distant bell tolling is my only clue as to how much time has passed. The road from town is paved with stones for much of the way before it turns to dirt. The farther I walk, the less there is to see. Trees sprawl out in every direction, their leaves yellowing. Even they know winter is coming.

As the sun dips below the horizon, I come to a place where the road splits off into two distinct forks. The left path is covered by dirt and gravel, pressed flat by carriage traffic. The right path looks as if it hasn't been traveled on in years. Overgrown weeds push in from all sides, and the ground is littered with large stones nearly as high as my waist.

"Decisions, decisions," says a voice.

I stagger back, tripping over my own feet and falling hard onto my side. From the embankment on the opposite side of the road emerges a familiar face.

Constance.

"You scared the hell out of me!" I scream, stumbling to my feet and trying to keep my heart from pounding out of my chest. "What are you doing here?"

"Waiting for you," she says, smiling.

"How did you know I'd come?"

"I didn't. But I hoped you would." Her red hair, which she wears in a long braid down her back, looks like twisted flames in the orange haze of the setting sun. Walking closer, I see a constellation of freckles across the bridge of her nose and planes of her cheeks that I hadn't noticed before. Her smile quickly fades as she looks me over. "Are you all right?"

I fumble with my words while recounting the horror of that morning's events. I can barely bring myself to speak Liv's name aloud.

Constance sighs, and her shoulders slump down. "I'm so sorry. Truly I am." She walks over to me and slips her arm around my waist, propping me up as my legs threaten to give way.

"The way she looked," I say, wiping away the tears. "Something was wrong."

Constance's body stiffens. "The way she looked?"

I struggle to find the words to describe what I saw. "Her

hair was white, like snow, where it had been brown before. All her color drained away, and her skin was wrinkled and gray."

"Come with me," she says.

I look around. The road is empty. No houses, no buildings. The watchtowers loom in the distance, and beyond them, the great expanse of forest known as the White Wood. "Come with you where?"

"Are you always so suspicious?" she asks.

"Are you always so vague and mysterious?" I ask in return.

"I try to be," she says, smiling gently. I allow her to lead me toward the head of the path that is completely overrun. We make our way through the trees and underbrush, before we come to a towering wrought-iron gate. Its ten-foot bars are festooned with vines and bougainvillea, whose incandescent pink blooms are shriveled and falling to pieces in the late-autumn air.

We go through the gate and up a long twisting drive lined with ancient overgrown oak trees, each of their branches draped with curtains of moss, their knotty trunks as wide across as the broad side of a carriage. The setting sun illuminates the hazy outlines of the velvety red and orange petals of the poppies that grow wild and abundant, their black seedy centers dotting the landscape like a million pinpricks.

"Shouldn't they be dead by now?" I ask, looking out over the flowers that color the otherwise brown and dying landscape.

Constance gazes at the poppies. "I hadn't really thought of that, but I think you're right."

We round a bend, and a large house comes into view. One wing has collapsed, and vines have overtaken almost all the rest of the visible sides. Boarded windows line the lower floor while the ones above are open to the elements. The paint, which might have been white at one point, is cracked and peeled, and the front door is half off its hinges.

"Do you know what this place is?" Constance asks.

"Should I?" I glance up at the house. We are miles from town, and unlike the eastern border, which is the most fortified because beyond it are the Forbidden Lands, the far western side of Lille is largely abandoned. It's not butting up against a great expanse of territory that leads straight to the place where the potential new kings of Lille are born and raised.

"Cinderella lived here with her family. This is where it all began."

I look at the house again. It's identical to the illustrations in my copy of Cinderella's story. "I thought it was on the other side of the Gray Lake in the south of Lille? And didn't it burn down in a fire?"

Constance shakes her head. "Lies. It's always been here.

It's not much to look at anymore, I'm afraid," she says, a ring of sadness in her voice.

She helps me up the front steps, and we go inside. As we stand in the entryway, I care less about how it looks and more about whether it's even fit to stand. There's a large hole directly over the foyer. Leaves and debris litter the cracked marble floor, and a wide staircase with broken and missing steps leads up to the second level. The banister has fallen off and lies in pieces on the floor.

Constance sees me eyeing the stairs. "Don't worry. We don't have to go up there."

I follow Constance into a room just off the main hallway, my legs still knocking together. It is a small parlor with a fire already burning in the hearth. Some tattered furniture is scattered about, but it's dry and warm, and a pile of neatly folded blankets sits in the corner. It looks like Constance has made camp here for several nights.

She gives me a large basket with a tall handle. I flip open the lid and almost faint from pure excitement. Inside are grapes, a small wheel of cheese, a loaf of bread, and a small carafe of milk closed with a cork stopper.

"Take as much as you'd like."

A half loaf of bread disappears before I stop myself. "Are you sure you don't want any?"

"No. Finish it off."

She doesn't have to tell me twice. I keep eating, and

the heaviness that comes with a full stomach settles over me.

"I can't thank you enough."

"It's no trouble," Constance says. She grins, and I am taken with her all over again. But guilt rushes in and chases those feelings away.

"I didn't have a plan when I left the palace. I just ran." Sadness crashes over me again. "I don't really know what I'm doing here."

"You're here with me," she says.

"And who are you exactly?" I ask. "I know your name, but—are you from Lille? What were you doing in Cinderella's tomb?"

She pushes her hair behind her shoulder and clears her throat. She speaks in a way that reminds me of someone reading a story aloud.

"The sisters were no better than their mother," she says. *"Common and uniquely cruel, they taunted Cinderella without end. The oldest stepsister, Gabrielle, had hair like the fiery flames of hell and a face only the devil could love."*

I hold my hand up. "I know the story. And I don't mean to be rude, but I don't want to hear it again. Look where it's led me."

"Yes," Constance says. "Look where it has led you." Light from the fire flickers across her features, and the hair on the back of my neck stands on end. Constance pushes out her chin and angles her head to the side. "I've always taken umbrage with that portrayal of Gabrielle. There are many generations between us, but her blood is strong. I've always been told I look just like her."

I am dumbstruck. "You—you're related to Gabrielle? The wicked stepsister?"

"Wicked? No. Stepsister, yes."

I step back and run right into the wall. My head swims with fragments of the story. The stepsisters are said to have been exceedingly cruel to Cinderella, and their descriptions make them out to be monstrous aberrations. None of the stories mention either of them having children or families of their own.

"That makes you kin to Cinderella," I say, trying to put their family tree together in my head.

"A sixth great-niece," Constance says.

I can't even think straight. "If you're serious—"

"I am," Constance says.

I slowly sit down. My thoughts turn back to the more immediate issue of the king's men. "The guards are looking for me, and I don't want to put you in a bad situation. They'd kill you just for helping me."

"They would try," she says, looking thoughtful. She turns slightly, showing me the dagger hanging from her belt. "And where can you go that King Manford won't find you?"

I haven't thought it through. All I know is that I need to get as far away from Lille as possible. "I planned on walking until my legs gave out. I'm not really sure where."

"That's a terrible idea." Constance crosses her arms.

"It's a good thing I don't need your permission then, isn't it?"

She blinks repeatedly, smiling a little and nodding. "I don't have a better suggestion. I don't think you'd be safe in any city in Mersailles. He could never allow you to defy him and get away with it."

"If I stay away, maybe he'll let it go," I say.

"He won't."

"How do you know so much about what he would and wouldn't do?" I ask.

She sighs, and her shoulders slump down. "Because I keep the stories no one else is allowed to hear, the things Manford and his predecessors don't want anyone to know, the true history of my family."

"The true history?" I ask.

She drags a chair over and sits directly across from me.

"Have you ever thought about what kind of a person would have a child and name it Charming?"

"I've never really thought about it," I say. And now that I think about it, it seems kind of ridiculous. "Are you saying that wasn't his real name?"

"No one knows what his real name was," she says.

I laugh but she doesn't. She is dead serious, and I still myself, allowing her to continue.

"Did you know Cinderella's father was the highest-ranking adviser, the closest person to the old king who ruled Mersailles before Prince Charming took over?"

"No," I say in utter shock. "I've never heard that."

"He was. But Prince Charming came to Mersailles in a time of drought and famine so devastating it was unlike anything the people had ever seen before. They were desperate, and Charming told them he could save them if they made him king. In the beginning they refused, putting their trust in their king. Charming bided his time, and when things got worse, he offered his help yet again. This time the people agreed and deposed the old king, making Charming their ruler."

"And he did what he said he would," I say. I know this story, too. The founding of our kingdom by the benevolent Prince Charming.

"The crops once again flourished; the rivers ran through drought-stricken lands. There were rumblings of magic, of curses somehow broken, but the people of Mersailles knelt at his feet." Constance shakes her head. "As soon as Charming had the people in the palm of his hand, things began to change. Cinderella's parents spoke openly of how the laws Charming was implementing were unfair and dangerous. While Cinderella's father tried to rally political support to overthrow Charming, her mother tried to rally local people, to get them to organize and protest. When Charming got word of her efforts, he sent his guards to arrest her. She would not go quietly, and they executed her in the driveway."

I look toward the front of the house. Had I walked over the spot where Cinderella's mother had died?

I turn back to Constance. "My grandmother spoke out against King Stephan, Manford's predecessor," I say, measuring my words, trying not to cry. "She was taken, arrested. Executed."

Constance hesitates for a moment. Her eyes fill with tears, and I look away.

"Then you can understand all of this," she says.

I nod.

"Cinderella's father remarried, and his new wife, Lady Davis, was just as disgusted with Charming as Cinderella's mother had been," Constance continues. "But she thought the best way to fight him would be to train, to learn to fight, to carefully plan his downfall. She passed messages to others who were willing to fight, a sort of underground network of resistance."

"I've never heard anyone speak of Lady Davis as a good person," I say, questioning everything I've ever thought was true about the tale. "She's the villain of the story."

Constance shakes her head. "She vowed to keep her

girls safe no matter the cost, but I don't think she had any idea what that cost would be. Prince Charming ordered Cinderella's father to the palace for questioning, and he was never seen again."

"Prince Charming killed him," I say. It's not a question as much as harsh realization. Of course he killed him.

"There was no proof, but Cinderella's father loved his family. Lady Davis believed he would have come home if at all possible. By this time, Cinderella was eighteen. Prince Charming held his very first ball, and everyone was required to go and well . . . you know that part of the story."

"But the story—Cinderella's story doesn't say anything about that. That's not how it goes."

"It is a lie," says Constance.

We sit in silence for several moments.

"Do you want me to continue?" she asks. "The truth is tricky. People want to know it, but when they do, sometimes they wish they didn't."

I think carefully about this. Everything that happened in the palace plays in my head. "Yes, I want to know. Tell me everything."

She takes a deep breath and continues. "Shortly after Prince Charming married Cinderella, the laws surrounding the ball and the treatment of women and girls in Lille became so much worse than they had ever been. Some people rebelled, but he put down any and all resistance."

She reaches behind her and pulls her braid forward over her shoulder. She twists the end, which reaches down into her lap, between her fingers. The firelight glints in her brown eyes as she glances at me. She catches me staring, and although I am a little embarrassed, I don't look away. The corners of her mouth creep up in amusement.

"When Prince Charming died, I think the people of Mersailles actually thought they might be able to bring about some change, but that never happened because his successor, King Eustice, was worse than he was," Constance says. "I have a letter from my great-grandmother to her daughter telling her of the horrible things King Eustice did."

"The kings of Mersailles have all followed the same tenets Prince Charming put forward," I say. "People are so afraid that they would rather stay quiet than say or do anything." As I try to take in everything I've learned, one thing sticks in my mind. "Cinderella went up to the castle willingly. Even after everything Prince Charming had done? Why?"

Constance clasps her hands together in front of her. "That is the question, isn't it?" She lowers her tone. Anger and frustration color her voice. "It's something that's haunted my family through every generation between Gabrielle and me. They couldn't understand it, and neither do I. You traipse up to the castle to see the man who destroyed your family? Who does that?"

"What does your family think?" I ask.

A gentle sigh escapes Constance. "My mother suspected the fairy godmother may have had something to do with it."

"The fairy godmother was Cinderella's friend," I say. "She helped her."

Constance shakes her head. "You have to set the story you know aside, Sophia."

My name from her lips sounds like a song. I look down. When I gather the courage to look up at her, she is fighting back tears, a mask of pain stretched across her face.

"You don't have to go on," I say. "I can see that it's hurting you."

"I want to tell you. I need to tell someone." She sighs heavily, and sorrow pours out of her. "The prince shackled them to wooden stakes just beyond the towers, Lady Davis and Gabrielle and her younger sister, and left them there to die. Gabrielle was able to free herself and the others after three days. They were starving, half-frozen, but they escaped. Prince Charming said they were exiled to save face. I imagine he was furious when they got away."

"Where did they go?" I ask.

"Out into the country, past the White Wood. They moved constantly, afraid they'd be hunted down."

"What became of them?"

"Lady Davis died twenty years after their escape."

Constance tugs at the ends of her hair again. "Gabrielle and her sister made a life for themselves far from here, but they never gave up on Lille. Through the years, their descendants have trained and fought and died trying to fix what is broken here, carrying on the legacy of Cinderella's mother and of Lady Davis, but it has all come to nothing. I tried to take out that statue in the square a few nights ago, but the charge wasn't powerful enough."

I remember the burned circle of grass. "That was you?"

She nods. Then suddenly her face falls and she leans toward me. "I am the last. The last one who knows the truth."

"I'm so sorry, Constance." I don't know what else to say.

"He'll be after you now." Her knee presses into mine on purpose. Testing her boundaries a bit. I don't move away. "He won't stop."

"No, he probably won't," I say. "But neither will I."

She presses her lips together and lifts her chin a little. "You'll just stay on the run forever?"

"Not exactly what I had in mind," I say. A wild thought takes shape in my head. "Maybe I get to him before he gets to me."

15

The fire dies as the evening hours creep up on us. I had expected Constance to laugh in my face when I told her maybe I'd go after the king before he could get to me, but she sits quietly, studying me. After a few minutes she leans forward, crossing her bare arms over the plane of her legs. I try to refocus.

"My mother told me that Gabrielle received a letter from Cinderella shortly before her death, asking her to meet here, at this very house, under the cover of darkness, but when Gabrielle showed up, Cinderella was being dragged away by the king's guards."

"What did she want to meet her for?" I ask.

"Gabrielle heard her screaming about . . ." She trails off.

"Screaming about what?"

"She said that the prince was the curse upon Mersailles and that to save us, he had to be stopped."

"But he's dead now," I say. "And nothing has changed."

Constance sighs and pushes her hair, which is now completely loose, over her shoulder. "You can't go home. I don't think it's worth it to ride back to my family's cottage, but I'm not sure where we go from here." She stands and goes to the little fireplace, poking at the kindling until the fire burns bright and hot again.

Her body, backlit by the flames, is like a vision. She is tall and strong. She's got her sleeves pushed up; a wide, jagged scar runs over the muscles of her upper arm. They flex as she stokes the flames. I imagine how they might feel wrapped around me, and I wonder if she can tell how enthralled I am with her.

"Can I ask you something?" I say, trying to put my mind elsewhere.

"Of course." She stares down at the fire, and I can only see her face in profile; the apple of her cheek lifts, smiling. She's seen me watching her.

"Do you believe in curses?"

"I don't know. And what does that mean anyway? Who could even do that?"

"Someone powerful," I say as an idea completely takes hold of me. "Maybe someone who could turn a pumpkin into a carriage, someone who could enchant a pair of glass slippers."

"The fairy godmother?" Constance exaggerates every syllable. "Are you saying she might have known more about the curse Cinderella warned Gabrielle about?" She looks doubtful.

"Maybe," I say. "And think about it. All that fairy godmother business was probably just another lie. What kind of a woman has the power to transform objects and make a gown materialize out of thin air?"

Constance stares blankly into the fire. "A witch."

A chill runs through me and I stand up. "A witch?"

In Mersailles, a belief in magic is almost bred into us. Woven into the Cinderella story are the fairy godmother's fantastical abilities. But I don't know anyone who has ever truly seen magic. I think of Liv and her prize at the bicentennial celebration, her replica wand. She believed unquestioningly, as do most people, in even the most unbelievable parts of the tale.

Witchcraft is something different. I've never heard anyone suggest that the fairy godmother might have been a witch.

"Do you know what happened to her?" I ask.

Constance shrugs. "When Cinderella died, the godmother disappeared. There were rumors she went into the heart of the White Wood to live out her days."

Luke's plan for our escape had included venturing into

the White Wood. I think of his face as the guards took him away. My heart breaks all over again. "I want to try to find someone who knew her," I say. "She was there, and after everything that happened, especially if it happened the way you say, there's got to be some kind of record. Maybe she knew people in the area?"

"We're talking about a woman who lived almost two hundred years ago," Constance says. "Anyone who knew her would be dead."

"You've kept your family's story all this time. Maybe something similar happened with her. I think we have to go to the last place she was known to be."

"The White Wood? You want to go looking for answers there?" Constance asks, her voice creeping up.

"We have to try. Or I suppose, *I* have to try. You don't have to come with me, but I'd like your company. If there are others like you and your family, people who have kept a history, maybe we can find them and they can help us understand this curse."

"You'd like my company?" Constance asks.

I nod.

"I can't say no to that," she says softly. "I don't think we'll succeed, but who wouldn't want to be alone in a creepy forest with you?" Constance struts over and stands in front of me. "I've had people on my side before but none quite as headstrong as you."

"Is that a good thing?" I ask.

She gently nudges my shoulder with hers as she brushes past me and speaks in a hush, very close to my ear. "I guess we'll find out."

A rush of warmth spreads over me. In my mind, I see Erin's face and again feel guilty. I step away from Constance, ashamed of how I've behaved. Constance wrings her hands in front of her and shakes her head as if she's done something wrong.

"We'll leave tomorrow," she says.

I nod. "If she was in the heart of the White Wood, I say we just head for the center and see what we find."

"So we have no actual plan then? No map. Nothing."

"Not true," I say. "I know the general direction, and my plan is to make it to the center of the White Wood alive, with you at my side."

"All in a quest to take down the king and bring his entire kingdom to its knees?" Constance asks.

"More or less," I say, laughing.

She grins so wide I can see a chip in her bottom front tooth, her eyes creased at the corners. I want to spend the rest of the night talking to her, finding out every little detail about her.

"Well in that case, we'll need some rest." She strips off her trousers, and I fuss with the blankets to avoid staring at her.

Constance takes up a spot on a pile of blankets next to

the fire, and I hear her breathing fall into a slow, steady pattern while I struggle to quiet my mind. As I lie awake, the moon with its mournful face shines its ethereal light down on me through the sitting room window. Liv will never again see something so perfect and beautiful.

I try to sleep. My body aches and my mind is tired, but every time I close my eyes, I see Liv lying in that ditch.

Sleep is something I can do without for a while.

❧

I sit anxiously on the edge of my seat, watching Constance sleep. I want to get moving, but I don't have the heart to wake her. She stirs and rolls over, eyes still closed, lips parted, her hair a tangle of tight ringlets spread out under her head like a crimson cushion. Her eyes flutter open.

"Morning," I say.

"Morning." She rubs her eyes, sitting up. Her bare legs jut out from under the blanket. She gives me a once-over. "You haven't slept at all, have you?"

I shake my head. "I'm eager to get going."

She stands up and stretches. "We should go into town for supplies." Constance lets her gaze pass over me from head to foot. I'm still wearing the pants and tunic she gave me in Cinderella's tomb. She smiles. A little shudder of excitement pulses through me. "You're already dressed. I just need a minute."

Constance rummages through a large burlap sack in the corner, producing a wadded-up ball of clothing that she tosses onto a chair. She turns back to her bag and retrieves a pair of boots to add to the vests and tunics.

"Where did you get all this?" I ask.

"You know how people can be. They go swimming, want to show off a bit, so they strip down and dive in. They almost never put their clothing in a safe spot, and more than once, I've come across a perfectly good pair of britches."

I raise an eyebrow and laugh. From the look of her stockpile, there are at least six or seven people naked in the woods somewhere. She picks out a pair of tan trousers very similar to mine, except hers can only stay up with the help of a pair of leather suspenders.

"Well, what do you think?" she asks.

I can't keep from grinning. "You look lovely." Her immediate frown makes me worry I've offended her. "No, it's just— I meant you look good. You look just fine."

"Not really what I was going for. Two women traveling alone would bring too much attention," she says, pulling on a shiny black pair of riding boots. She tosses me a wool-lined coat.

"This clothing is our best shot at getting out of town without anyone noticing," she says.

I look down at my chest. "I'm not going to fool anyone dressed like this."

She doesn't try to hide the little smile that creeps across her lips. "Just keep your shirt loose in the front, and don't tuck it in."

My cheeks flush hot.

"We'll braid back your hair, and if you keep a hat on and your head down, we should be okay."

Constance nudges me toward the chair in front of the fire. She stands behind me and pulls her fingers through my hair, parting it, and braiding the loose pieces so they lie flat against my head. My mother sometimes braided my hair this way when I was little, decorating the ends with little glass beads, singing songs to herself as she worked, and tugging at my scalp a little too tightly when I nodded off or tried to scoot away. The memory stings.

Constance repeats the process from ear to ear, gathering the tails into a tight bun at the back of my head. As she finishes up, her fingers brush over the sensitive skin at the nape of my neck and send a shiver down my back.

The final touch is an oversized wool cap, fitted snugly over my head. Constance produces a small mirror from her bag, thrusting it at me as she looks on, proud of her handiwork. I understand why she's so confident in this disguise. Anybody passing me on the street might think I am just another young man.

"I may need your help getting my hair in order," she says. She sits down and sections off a piece. "If you could just hold the rest back while I braid this part." I stand and gather her hair, nearly a foot longer than mine, behind her shoulder. It's soft and thick, smelling of rose water, and I let my hands linger in the tangle of curls. I'm drawn to her, and I keep waiting for her to tell me the same things Erin had—that I am longing for something impossible—but she doesn't, and I'm dizzy with the excitement of it and torn by the guilt I feel.

When she finishes braiding her hair, she can't fit the tail ends under a cap, so we settle on tucking them down the back of her shirt. She then winds a thick scarf around her neck.

"Look at us." She does a full turn. "I like this outfit more than any dress." She shoves her hand in her pocket and smiles.

"I like dresses," I say. "But I'd like to wear this sometimes, too."

Constance smiles, and I can't get past how stunning she looks. I shake my head. I need to get ahold of myself.

"We'll head to the market," says Constance. "I have a small cart. The horse should be able to handle it for us."

I follow her around the outside of the house where her horse is tethered. As she loads her belongings into the cart, I notice that the house is built in a square arrangement, the middle of which opens to a courtyard. An enormous tree, a type I've never seen, stands in the center, its branches resting on the roof of the house. Its massive trunk is as wide as the ones that line the drive, but this tree has a distinctly different color. Instead of the faded shades of brown that mark the trunks of the others, this one is a silvery gray with patches of yellowish gold along the underside of its branches. Moss hangs from it like a curtain. The chirping of sparrows that have taken up residence in its wide canopy filters down.

"That's where Cinderella's mother is buried," says Constance, gesturing to the tree. "In the story, she doesn't even have a name."

As if on command, the wind gusts, sweeping back the moss to reveal a small marble headstone at the base of the tree. Constance walks to the side of the house and pulls up a handful of wild lilies. She arranges them in a bouquet as I follow her to the headstone that reads: Alexandra Hochadel, Beloved Mother, Wife, and Friend.

"I wish I knew more about her," says Constance, placing down the bouquet.

"Why do you think she was left out of the story?" I ask.

"Because she was determined? Smart? Willing to die for her family? Take your pick. Any of those reasons are good enough to warrant suppression." Constance stands and stares up at the tree. "It's beautiful, isn't it?"

"It is," I say.

"Apparently, it sprouted the evening Cinderella escaped to the ball."

I am overcome by the notion that the tree is watching, listening, like a living, breathing thing.

"Strange," I say.

"Strange indeed," says Constance.

A strong gust makes me pull my coat in around my neck. My fingers brush against the necklace my father had given me, and his callous words replay in my head. I take it off and place it on the headstone. If remembering Cinderella's mother is considered an act of defiance, I'm happy to do it.

16

We're a mile outside the city center, settled in next to each other. With every passing bump in the road, my apprehension grows. What will happen if the guards in town find out I'm the girl they've been searching for? I'd be arrested for sure, but maybe my punishment will be worse. And what will happen to Constance? I've made my decision that any existence is better than the one I've been living, but I don't want Constance to have to suffer for it.

"You look like you've got a lot on your mind," Constance says, glancing at me from under her hat as she steers the horse toward town.

"I do. Everything feels different to me now. I didn't intend for all this to happen, you know. When I left the ball, I just wanted to get away from the madness."

"That's how things happen sometimes," Constance says thoughtfully. "Something small. A choice we make because, in the moment, we needed to make it. But that doesn't mean it's any less important. I believe that things happen for a reason, Sophia. If you hadn't left the ball when you did, we never would have met."

"Must be fate," I say. She nods. It is comforting to know she's on my side. "Since I've been here with you, I've gotten a glimpse of what it's like to not have to watch what I say or pretend to be something I'm not." I want to be open, but I feel terribly exposed, like I'm showing her the most delicate, guarded parts of myself.

She reaches over and squeezes my hand, causing that familiar little spark to course through me again.

"My mother taught me that I am a whole person with or without a husband," she says emphatically. "Who I am inside and how I treat others are the only things that matter. The same goes for you. Don't let anybody tell you different."

"Yes, ma'am," I say, smiling. Another question pushes its way to the front of my mind as the cart bounces along the road toward town. "You'd like a husband, then? Or at least, you'd consider that an option?" I try to sound curious to hide how incredibly nervous I am to hear her answer.

Constance pauses for a moment. "No. That's not for me."

I don't press her, even though my mind races with a dozen questions.

"Can I be honest with you?" she asks.

"I thought that's what we were doing here," I say.

"I don't just want equal footing in Lille. I want much more than that."

I look at her, confused. "Equal footing sounds pretty good to me."

"It's a start," she says. "But you know what will happen? We'll have to force people to give us what we're asking for."

"When you say we, you mean you and I?" I ask.

"Yes, but there are others," Constance says. "At least, there were."

I sit straight up. "Others?"

"Not many, but yes. Others. People who have slipped through the king's fingers, mostly women who feel like they have nothing left to lose. You've heard of the incident in Chione?"

"That was you too?" I ask in utter disbelief.

"No. It was Émile, an ally of mine. But she's gone now."

The flyers the king had handed out made it clear that the people responsible were executed. I can tell by the look on Constance's face that she saw them, too.

"The watchtowers guard every border," I say. "No one in or out without the king's say."

"Not all of Lille's borders are guarded so heavily. The western edge that butts up to the White Wood has only two towers and the guards are complacent. They think fear of the wood is enough to keep people from crossing into it." Constance huffs loudly. "The palace underestimates the resourcefulness of women forced into a dark and dangerous place."

I remember the seamstress's husband, and how he was so completely offended by the thought that she'd kept one cent of the money she'd earned. I think of her terrified son and the bruise on her neck. Those things might be enough to make someone risk an illegal crossing.

"What do you think needs to happen in Lille?" I ask.

She stares at me, her brown eyes glinting, a deadly serious look on her face. "I think we need to burn the whole thing to the ground and start over. The entire system, the ideals that have been woven into this society. It all has to go."

"That feels like an impossible thing to do," I say.

"If I had told you a week ago that you would flee the ball on foot and discover Cinderella's tomb, what would you have said?"

"I would have said it was impossible." I turn to her. "But a week ago I didn't know you. If it wasn't for you, I might not have even made it out of the tomb."

"And if it wasn't for you, I might not be going to the

White Wood to find some remnant of the one woman who knew the whole truth about why Cinderella went up to the palace that night, or about what curse afflicted Prince Charming and what that has meant for us over all these years." She smirks. "It's you and I together that will make the difference."

I've never been very good at making myself small, and with Constance maybe I don't have to. I want to knock our king off his throne, and she'll help me do it.

17

We ride into town and wind through the streets, keeping our heads down. People are going about their business as if only a day ago their daughters hadn't been snatched away from them, as if Liv hadn't died. I resent being back here.

The market is bustling and crowded as usual. Shouting from the livestock auction mingles with the mundane chitchat from the other marketgoers, and it grates on me. Even with the throngs of people milling about and almost none of them looking in my direction, I fear that my disguise won't be good enough. That someone might recognize me. Constance backs the cart into an alley between two shops and climbs out.

"We'll need a sack of rice and root vegetables, things

that will stay good for a few days or longer." She puts a handful of silver coins in my palm and reaches up to adjust my hat, letting her fingers brush over my ear and down the side of my neck. A ripple of delight surges through me. "Meet me back at the cart in thirty minutes. Do not stop. Do not talk to anyone if you can avoid it. Try to blend in." Constance squeezes my shoulder and rushes off.

The market is set up in the town square, where all remnants of the bicentennial celebrations have been cleared away. Larger booths ring the outer edge of the area, and smaller stalls and tents crowd the inside. The smell of animal dung wafts through the air, and this warmer-than-usual morning makes it particularly pungent.

The merchants yell, advertising their wares, none of them paying attention to their surroundings. I watch a young boy pocket a silver spoon from a table as the man attending it bargains with one of his patrons. My first thought is to alert the merchant, but when he makes a comment about the length of a young girl's skirt and how her legs are simply too inviting to resist, I stop in my tracks. He deserves to have his things stolen.

Winding my way through the crowd, I catch bits and pieces of people's conversations.

". . . went up there in her mother's dress. They found her in a ditch. Killed herself, she did." The man speaking is chuckling so heartily that his cheeks are ruddy and a thin sheen of sweat covers his forehead. I look away. Familiar anger creeps up and heats my face.

". . . they were beautiful, best lot in a few years. I heard a baron from Chione took two brides."

"Is that allowed? Two at once?" I hear a woman ask. Slowing my pace, I look up again. Her husband shoots her a dagger of a glance and turns his back to her.

"I'd have taken two if I had thought of it at the time, but now it's just you I have to deal with." Her husband and his friends laugh while the woman smiles one of those fake smiles, all mouth and no eyes. I know the smile, and a little piece of me dies every time I have to use it.

I turn sharply to head away from them. Constance is right. Even if we can find a way to end Manford's reign, men won't suddenly start keeping their hands to themselves, or allowing women the same rights that they have. We'll have to fight for it, and I cannot help but wonder what the cost will be.

I push forward and find the stall selling grains. Sacks and barrels of everything from rye and buckwheat to milled flour and rice are all stacked on top of each other. A small boy swats mice away from the sacks as an older man sits at a wooden table near the front of the stall. He doesn't look up as I approach.

"Excuse me," I say, before stopping short. My voice is

sure to give me away. I pretend to cough, covering my mouth with my hand and using it to muffle my voice. "I need a sack of rice."

"Five or ten pounds?" asks the man, glancing up.

"Ten," I say. We'll need as much as we can carry. I continue to feign a cough.

"You all right?" he asks.

I kick myself. I'm trying to avoid suspicion, and I've only managed to pique his. I clear my throat. "Yes, I'm fine."

The man stands and leans across the table. I take a step back. "Your voice—it's all singsongy like. You always sound like that?"

Now he's just being nosy. The boy lugs over the sack of rice as I toss four coins onto the table. I pick up the sack by its fabric handles, give the man a quick nod, and hurry away. I look back to see him scratching the top of his head and craning his neck in my direction. He knows something is off.

I haul the sack to the bed of the cart and lean against the wall, waiting anxiously for Constance to return. If the man has followed me, I can't make him out anywhere among the many faces. The crowd ebbs and flows, women carrying their children, men chatting away with their friends. My mother might be here somewhere. I scan the crowd, and a familiar face appears.

Erin.

I haven't even considered that she might be here.

I catch myself in the act of calling out to her, a habit I no longer have the luxury of indulging. I stare at her through the web of unfamiliar faces, and she turns toward me as if answering my silent signal. When she meets my eyes, she seems confused, but I'm horrified.

Erin's left eye is swollen, her bottom lip is puffed out, and she has a purple bruise on the right side of her neck. I step forward, trying to get a better look. Confusion melts into recognition, and she smiles. Even in this disguise, she knows me. She whispers something to the man who stands next to her and quickly zigzags through the crowd toward me, positioning herself at the corner of the wall. She pulls the hood of her cloak up around her neck and looks down as she speaks.

"I thought you were dead," she whispers. "I was so worried. I can't tell you how happy I am to see you."

"Erin, what happened to your face?"

"I'm betrothed now, Sophia. Isn't that wonderful?" She chokes back tears.

"You were chosen?" I ask. Of course she was. She is everything I have ever wanted. That someone else sees her this way doesn't surprise me. I just don't want to believe that someone who chose her would hurt her.

"Yes, first round. My father is ecstatic."

How could her father possibly be happy? Has he seen her face? "What did he do to you?"

"Don't worry about me," she says, fumbling with her purse.

"You've been betrothed for little more than a day and already your face is—"

"Shh!" Erin puts her back on the corner of the wall, her shoulder nearly touching mine. "Get away from here." She looks at me, and my heart breaks open. "Even in those clothes you're beautiful, Sophia." She is trying to change the subject.

Tears sting my eyes. "Come with me. We're leaving. You can come with us."

"I can't. My father would disown me. Did you hear about Liv?"

I nod.

"She is in a far better place than you or I, or—maybe just me." Erin forces a smile through a torrent of tears. She buries her face in her hands, and I reach out to touch her arm. "I wish things could be different, but I know that they can't be. He paid a high price for me."

"What? Who?"

"My betrothed. He paid half a year's wages to make sure he could claim me."

"Erin, I—" I can't speak.

"If I don't stay with him, I'm certain he'd complain to

the king, and my family would be held responsible. I can't do that."

"Do you know what happened to Luke?" I ask. "Where they might have taken him?"

"Probably to the execution block," Erin says, staring off. I bristle and her face softens just slightly. "I'm sorry."

Silent tears trail down my face, and then quite suddenly, that sadness turns to a white-hot rage in the pit of my belly. I move toward her and take her hand; she shakes free from my grasp and backs away. I don't care if her family falls into ruin. I don't care that her fiancé will complain. I look for him in the crowd and wonder if I might be able to run him over with the cart and get away before someone notifies the palace guard.

Erin shakes her head. "This place will break you if you stay. If you can escape, you should. Please, Sophia, please go."

She disappears into the crowd, reemerging a moment later beside her fiancé. He slips his arm around her waist, and in this moment I realize I know him, too. It is Édouard. And the men turning their faces away from Erin, as if they can't stand to look at her, are Morris and his friend. I feel sick.

Constance appears at my side. She's procured a short dagger and several other items, all held in a small leather pouch. She dumps it out in her hand and shoves the items gleefully in her pockets. She follows my gaze out to Erin.

"You know her?" she asks. I quickly wipe my face.

I nod, and Constance puts her hand on my shoulder, studying me carefully. "You're angry. I understand, but we can't make a scene here. We'll be arrested on the spot."

"He did that to her." I point to Édouard, who is now nuzzling Erin's neck in a predatory way. I want to break his pointy, arrogant face.

Suddenly, a blaring of trumpets cuts through the din of voices. Constance pulls me back against the wall as a line of royal guards marches into the market, pushing people aside and upending tables to make room for the procession. Behind the phalanx of guards, King Manford rides in on a snow-white steed. He sits atop it, his chin raised high. Everyone bows. Constance yanks me down, and the horns blare again. Is he here for me? No, that can't be. I glance back at the cart. We can make a run for it, but Constance holds tight to my arm, shaking her head no.

"If we run, we die," she whispers. "Don't move. Don't make a sound."

I keep my head down as the king dismounts and paces in front of the crowd.

"I am so disappointed," he says. "The ball is a sacred tradition. But, as I'm sure you've heard by now, the night's festivities did not go entirely according to plan."

My heart crashes in my chest.

"There are consequences for defiance. I thought you were all well aware of that." He sets his hand on the hilt of his sword and glares at the crowd. "It seems you need a reminder."

18

A hush descends on the crowd, and as he turns in my direction, I quickly bow my head and stare at the ground.

"Do you not respect the rules that have been set forth for you?" the king asks. He clearly isn't looking for an honest answer, but someone in the crowd pipes up.

"We do!" A woman pushes through to the front of the crowd and bows low in front of the king. "Your Majesty." As she stands I see the king smile in a way that catches me completely off guard. He seems happy to see her.

"Lady Hollins." He takes her hand in his and kisses it.

"We are thankful for your benevolence," says the woman. "We are outraged that someone among us has defied you so blatantly. We will not have it."

I don't know why she feels the need to make such a public display, but she is falling over herself to pledge her loyalty to him, and he soaks it up. As I watch her, it becomes clear that she absolutely believes what she's saying.

"Our traditions are sacred," says the king. With a flick of his wrist he dismisses Lady Hollins, and she takes her place in the crowd. "Our ways are absolute," he continues. "Prince Charming saved Mersailles from devastation, saved your beloved Cinderella from a meaningless existence, and we honor him by continuing to follow the example he set. My predecessors and I have put rules in place for your own good, and how do you repay this kindness? By defying me." His voice takes on a raspy darkness that sends a shudder straight through me. "One of your number left the ball without permission. She has been located and dispatched."

Constance glances at me.

Liar.

"However, it has come to my attention that one of you fine people may have aided this girl in her escape. And that, my humble subjects, simply will not do."

From behind him, a cart appears. In the back is a woman in a tattered dress, tied at the wrists with a hood over her head. The guards forcefully remove the prisoner and bring her down to kneel before the king. He reaches out and snatches the hood off, revealing the tearstained face of the seamstress beneath. I take a step, and Constance nearly breaks my arm trying to hold me in place. What is this?

"This woman's husband informed me that the girl who left the ball came to his shop to seek the services of this seamstress," he says angrily. "And he, being the diligent and loyal subject that he is, noticed that the funds collected by his wife were light. It is my opinion that she intended to aid the runaway by giving her money to fund her travels."

The seamstress shakes her head frantically. "It's not true!" she sobs. Her eyes are rimmed with red; she trembles violently.

"Are you calling me a liar?" the king demands.

The woman hangs her head, defeated. "No, Your Majesty. I would never do that."

But he is. He is a liar.

"Was there a young girl in the shop or not?" the king asks.

"There were many young girls in my shop, Highness."

"*Your* shop?" The king looks perplexed. "Your husband is the owner of the shop, is he not?"

The seamstress nods.

"Those who would aid a fugitive are just as guilty as the runaway herself," the king bellows, glaring into the crowd as the people of Lille cower in fear. "How can I make you see that it's simply not worth it to try to defy me? You cannot win."

He walks up to a young girl near the front of the crowd, maybe ten or eleven years old, and slips his hand under her chin. "Smile. You're so much prettier when you smile." I can't see her face, but she must acquiesce because he grins down at her in a way that makes my skin crawl.

A hulking man in a black hood comes to stand behind the seamstress. He holds a shining ax, its blade as wide as a wagon wheel, and though the sky is overcast, it glints in the light.

"Keep your eyes there," King Manford says to the girl, pointing to the man.

I recall a memory, so faded I can barely see it in my mind. My mother, me as a young girl, a crowd gathered in the square. My mother stood stoically as a man in a black hood walked through the crowd. Her hand slid down to cover my eyes as gasps erupted all around us.

This is an execution.

"No—" The word is almost silent as it leaves me, as if it knows better than to make itself heard.

A murmur ripples through the crowd, and Constance's face freezes in a mask of horror and disgust. A guard rolls a stump in front of the seamstress and pushes her head onto the makeshift chopping block.

The king glares at her. "Tell me, woman. Was it worth your life to help some stupid peasant escape her fate?"

I can't catch my breath. She didn't do what he is accusing her of, but what can she say?

"If my life could serve a purpose," the woman begins, raising her head a little and looking directly at the king, "then let this be it. I would die to give even just one person the chance to be free from you."

There are gasps from the crowd. People look back and forth between one another.

The king's face twists into a hideous scowl. "And so you shall," he says. He gives a flick of his wrist, and the man in the hood lifts up the ax. It balances at the apex of its arc, hesitates, and then swings down in one clean motion. The seamstress's head rolls into the dirt.

A choked scream escapes my throat, but the sound rises and dies in the same breath. There are more gasps from the crowd, the sounds of someone being sick, sobbing. The king mounts his horse and stares out at the gathering of people. "Remember what you've seen here. Her life was pointless, and she died because of her own recklessness. Your lives are a gift from me. And I will allow you to keep them as long as the rules are obeyed." He digs his heels into the sides of his horse and races off with his guards in tow.

I fall onto my knees and look at the sky.

This is my fault. I went to the woman's shop to get the ribbons, and I let my stubbornness, my hatred of the king's laws, get in the way of that one simple task. I only wanted to help her and her son. Her son. Will his father now turn his heavy hands to the boy, if he hasn't already?

Constance wraps her hand around my waist and pulls me up. I can't even feel the ground under my feet. I just stare at her in silent, abject horror.

"We have to get out of here right now," she says.

This is the reason no one speaks up. Manford has no qualms about killing someone on a whim. It could have been any of us. We are too busy trying to survive to worry about anything else. We rush to the cart, and I start to climb in.

"Just a damn minute," a voice snarls. I'm yanked backward and land hard on the ground. A searing pain shoots down my side. My hat falls off, and the braids at the back of my head come loose.

"I knew you was a woman." The man from the grain stall stands over me, glowering. He picks me up by the front of my coat and slams me against the wall of the alley. My head hits the brick, and my vision goes blurry.

"You're a pretty thing, ain't you?" The man whistles, blowing his rancid breath into my face. "Why are you dressed like a man?"

Passersby look at us, but no one stops. My head throbs with every heartbeat.

"Get off me," I say. I dig my fingers into his arms, but he doesn't budge.

"Women aren't allowed to keep no money. Where'd you get them coins? You stole 'em, didn't ya? Didn't you just see what happened? Gotta be some kind of fool to—"

Suddenly, his body goes rigid. A glinting blade pressing up against his neck convinces him to unhand me. While Constance proceeds to back him against the alley wall, I put my cap on, tucking the loose ends of my braids underneath. I'm dizzied by the stabbing pain at my side. The man's eyes dart between Constance and me.

"What are you two playing at?" he asks. A small trickle of blood runs down his neck.

"What makes you think you can put your hands on her?" Constance's voice darkens, every single syllable taking a beat of its own. Her hand doesn't waver.

"You gonna kill me, woman?" the man asks incredulously. He doesn't think she will do it, but I'm certain she will.

"I could do it," she whispers, her mouth close to his ear. "And not even bat an eye. Slit you open like a fish and let your guts spill out on the ground. I suspect even the dogs would leave your entrails alone, you disgusting little man."

As she leans away from him, the man notices something in her eyes that makes him take her seriously for the first time.

"Come now," he says. "You don't really want to hurt me. A beautiful lady like yourself wouldn't do that."

The corner of Constance's mouth twitches. "That you try to flatter me when I have a blade at your neck makes me want to slit your throat and spare the world your ignorance."

I hear a sound like water dripping on the cobblestones and look down to see that he's pissed his pants. Constance wields her power like a sword, a power that I didn't even know we could have. I'm in awe of her.

"Let's go," I whisper. I am sure someone is going to spot us if we stay too much longer.

Constance pulls her knife away. "Wouldn't want to dirty up my blade." She steps back, and the man takes a deep breath.

"Good on you, miss. I dare say when the constable hears about this, he'll hang you, but—"

Constance raises her knife and brings the hilt down on top of the man's head, sending a loud *crack!* echoing through the alley. He falls face-first onto the ground, muttering something incoherent. We scramble into the cart and nudge the horse forward to the main road.

"Do you think he's dead?" I ask, trying to figure out if I care.

"No." Constance sounds severely disappointed by that.

I'd never seen anyone so skillful with a knife, and if she was afraid while she threatened the man, she didn't show it.

"I hope the headache he has when he wakes up never goes away," she says. "And who was that woman from the crowd? Lady Hollins?"

"I've never seen her before," I say.

"She would have betrayed any one of us in a heartbeat," Constance says. "People like her are more of a threat than almost anyone else."

We stop a quarter mile from the western edge of the town's limits. The watchtowers stand waiting for us. This is the first time I've approached them with the intent of sneaking by.

"How will we get past?" I ask.

Constance reaches down into the saddlebag and produces a small, bulbous container made of clay. The top tapers to a dull point with a length of cloth, coiled like a rope, stuffed inside the opening.

"We'll need a distraction," Constance says, smiling in a way that would be funny had I not been so nervous about getting past the guards.

We come to a small rise in the path. Trees on both sides create a corridor that leads straight to the border and into the nearly impenetrable darkness of the White Wood. Two palace guards patrol the flat land between the two towers. There is no cover, no place to hide.

"I'll light this at the base of that tower," Constance whispers as she points to the one farthest away to our left. "As soon as it goes off, we'll steer the cart straight through."

"As soon as what goes off?" I look again at the little clay container.

"The bomb." She holds the container up, giving it a little shake like I should know what it is.

"Did you make that?" I ask.

"Of course," she says flippantly. "My mother taught me."

"My mother taught me how to make bread."

The corner of her mouth turns up. "Well, that has its uses, too."

"They'll follow us," I say, my heart galloping in my chest.

"No, they won't," says Constance. "They won't even see us, and even if they do, they're afraid of what's out there, so they won't follow."

"That doesn't make me feel better."

"Stay in the cart," Constance says. "Get ready to move. The fuse will burn for five minutes, which should give me enough time to get back here to cross with you."

I've imagined escaping Lille a million times in my head. At no time did I imagine how afraid I'd be if I ever got the chance to actually do it.

"It's risky," says Constance, reading my expression. "But sometimes that's the only way to get things done. Take the risk, light the fuse. Onward." Her tempered optimism has faded a bit, and I see a side to her that is so determined and fierce that I'd be frightened if I wasn't so inspired. She hops up and disappears into the trees beside the path.

I grip the reins while studying the path in front of me. It's a straight shot into the White Wood. I glance behind me. There is nothing back there for me other than a long list of reasons why I need to find a way to end Manford.

Onward.

19

I'm sick and tired of these patrols," a man's voice says.
"No one is coming this way."

I freeze. The voice comes closer. I can see the figures of
two men passing by the head of the trail. I quickly climb
down into the shallow gutter at the side of the road and
press myself into the damp earth, trying not to breathe.

"We're out here because the king doesn't think we're
good enough at the other posts," another man says.

"What's this?" I hear the first man ask.

"A cart," the man answers. "No passengers. You let
anyone through?"

"No," says the other man.

I shrink closer to the ground to keep my body from
shaking as the footsteps come closer. The musty smell of
earth fills my nose and mouth.

"Over here," says a voice that sounds like it is directly above me. I brace myself, ball up my hands, and prepare to fight.

A noise like the firing of a cannon erupts in the distance. A rumble ripples through the ground, and the men standing by the cart shout as they race toward the sound. Suddenly, a set of arms pull me up out of the dirt. I struggle to get my hands around the person's neck.

"It's me!" Constance shouts. "Move!"

We jump into the cart, and I grab the reins, giving them a quick, sharp snap. The horse bolts straight ahead. Constance glances back as the guards stand at the base of the tower, shouting and tripping over themselves. She grips the edge of the cart to keep herself from tumbling out as we disappear into the White Wood.

The ground turns uneven, and the horse slows a bit.

"We have to keep moving," says Constance.

A feeling of foreboding permeates the forest as the light in the sky fades, ushering in shadowy darkness all around us. Constance stares behind us as we descend farther into the trees. When she is certain we're not being followed, she whips her head around.

"Were you trying to choke me back there?" she asks.

"I thought you were one of the guards," I say, heat rising in my face. "I'm so sorry."

"You can't choke a full-grown man. You have to stab him or run him over with your cart. Come on now, Sophia."

She straightens her jacket and leans back on the seat, grinning.

Something wings out of the trees, swoops over the cart, and lands on a branch just off the side of the road. It's the biggest crow I've ever seen. Its midnight-black wings stretch nearly as wide as I am tall. Its beady black eyes shine in the dark. I cringe. "I don't even want to know what other kinds of creatures are in these woods."

"Me either," Constance says. "Unfortunately for us, our destination is at least another four days' travel into the heart of the forest."

That is not what I want to hear. "Four days? We can travel that far in and not come out the other side?"

"It seems impossible, I know. But that is where the heart of the forest lies. The last place the fairy godmother was thought to be. If that's where she went, she picked a perfect spot. No one in their right mind would have bothered her in there. Except the very desperate."

"And now we're headed out there," I say. "So what does that make us?"

"I'd say we're plenty desperate."

A chill moves through me as a gust of wind splits the air. The trees along the trail shudder, sending a shower of leaves down onto the ground, red and gold and brown, the familiar hues of autumn blanketing the forest floor. But just ahead, the tree trunks turn black, and their branches are devoid of leaves. Constance takes a short, quick breath as we roll past the demarcation in the trees.

"I lost my temper back there in the alley. I'm sorry." She's trying to distract herself from whatever feeling had come over her.

"You don't have to apologize," I say. "Did your mother teach you how to use a knife as well?"

She nods. "She wanted me to be prepared for anything. I can teach you if you'd like."

I've always wanted to know how to use a sword, a dagger, anything that might help me protect myself. My mother might have actually fainted if I was both in love with a girl *and* thinking of learning to use a sword. "So you'll teach me after we survive this little jaunt through the most terrifying place in the land? Seems like I might need to learn sooner than later."

A hoot comes from the trees, and Constance's eyes grow wide. "You're probably right. But you've been inside the palace. This place can't be as bad as that."

She has a point.

A rustle along the path almost makes me jump out of my skin. I peer into the darkness ahead of us. "When we need to go back, how will we get into Lille?" I ask, trying to keep my mind occupied. "I don't suppose you have another bomb lying around."

"I do, as a matter of fact." Constance grins mischievously.

"But I don't think it's wise to set off an explosion every time we cross the border. We'll stay hidden, but next time, it'll be in plain sight."

Constance reaches back into the bed of the cart and rummages through her burlap sack, pulling out a small envelope. She hands it to me.

"Is this what I think it is?" I've never held, or even seen, an official pass from the king. A part of me thought they were just a myth, something parents tell their children to give them hope that there is something beyond Mersailles's borders, far from the king's oppressive rule. Constance takes the reins as I turn the letter over in my hand like it's made of glass. The envelope is similar to the one my invitation to the ball had come in. I open it and remove the folded piece of paper. The words are written in the same billowy black script, and they list two names: Martin and Thomas Kennowith. Details of their approved course follow. They left Lille to pick up a new cart and will return at a later, unspecified date. At the bottom, a sentence in very small print reads, *"Failure to adhere to the parameters of this pass will result in imprisonment and a fine."* Two boxes are next to it, the red wax stamp of the royal crest in one and nothing in the other.

"We can use this to get back in. Save our bombs for another time," says Constance.

"Where did you get this?"

"I stole it," Constance says rather flippantly.

"You've got everything covered," I say.

"Well, not everything," she says. "I haven't figured out how to make you look at me the way you did when I was standing by the fire back at the house. I don't know that anyone has ever looked at me that way." She bites her bottom lip as if she's said too much.

My heart speeds up. I guess I've been more obvious than I thought. I avoid her gaze. "I doubt that no one has ever looked at you that way. You must know how other people view you."

"I don't care how I seem to other people," she says, leaning in very close to me. "But I would very much like to know how *you* see me."

She is direct. I don't feel like I'll be risking anything by being honest. The warmth of her body so close to mine makes me forget where we are, what we've witnessed. "You're smart. Funny. You knocked out a man with one blow—"

"A shining example of who I truly am," she says in a half-serious tone.

"I think you're the most interesting person I've ever met."

"Interesting?" She sits back, a little smirk drawn across her lips. "Care to elaborate?"

Now it feels like a game. A little push and pull between us. "I feel like you looked at Lille's decrees and decided to do the exact opposite."

"That's not quite true, but not so far off. What about you? Is that what you did?"

I shake my head, taking back the reins. "No. I tried to go along with what everyone wanted. I guess I just wasn't very good at following the rules."

"Looks like we're the same in that way," Constance says. "Maybe in a few other ways, too." I almost steer the horse right into the ditch.

❧

As we head deeper into the woods, it is as if we have entered a windowless room. The trees become so tightly packed that the only way through is to stick to a path that barely accommodates the width of our cart. The wheels ride up onto the embankment, and we almost tip over several times, causing us to have to back up and realign with the road. My teeth chatter together, and I stare straight ahead, fearing that if I look to either side, I might see some nightmarish creature. Constance hands me a lamp and a small box of matches. The light illuminates only the area of the cart where we are sitting and does nothing to penetrate the curtain of blackness in front of the horse.

"At least if something attacks us, we won't see it coming," Constance says.

I turn to stare at her, but she only shrugs.

We clip along at a steady pace for hours until the growls—not from a bloodthirsty creature in the dark, but from our own stomachs—force us to stop. We make camp the first night right in the middle of the pathway. Constance is certain no one will be coming this way, and I refuse to go into the woods. She builds a small fire while I make a terrible gruel in the small cast-iron pot we've brought with us. Constance manages to ladle spoonfuls of it into her mouth without gagging. She smirks up at me.

"We're camping on a road in the middle of the White Wood. The very least of my worries are your cooking skills."

As we sit by the fire, I think of Constance and her family, living on the fringes of society, just out of the king's grasp, and how they've preserved the truth, hoping they'd have the chance to help the people of Mersailles. I can't keep myself from wondering if I even deserve to be here with her.

"There you go again," Constance says. "Lost in your thoughts."

"I was just wondering if you think I'm some fool," I say with a twinge of embarrassment. "I grew up in Lille, and I've never known any other way of living except by the king's rules. And then here you are, with all these revelations and all your skills, and I feel like I've been living in the dark."

Constance stares at me across the fire, stirring something

foreign inside of me. A fire, but not one made of anger. It is something else entirely.

"I don't think you're a fool," she says. "We come from different places. I grew up knowing all of this. You're just starting to understand it. But it's okay."

"How?" I'm not convinced. I should have trusted my gut about Cinderella's story. I should have known it isn't the whole truth.

"Because I value your perspective. You grew up in town, right in the center of the cruelty and chaos. That could be important when we're figuring out a way to stop Manford." Constance shifts on the ground and lies back against her burlap sack, closing her eyes and crossing her legs. "Give yourself a little more credit. You're beautiful, brave, and you knew something was wrong in Lille before anyone confirmed it for you."

Again, her candid conversation comforts and intimidates me at the same time. I haven't missed that she called me beautiful either.

I wait to see if she is going to say anything else, but the slow rise and fall of her chest tells me she's drifted off. The fire starts to die, but I can't settle my head enough to sleep, so I replay Constance's words in my mind, hoping they'll keep the images from the market away. As I wait for morning to come, the crow returns and sits perched in a tree just off the trail. While it's there, I don't sleep.

20

Constance is much more adept at knowing when the day is done, so I follow her lead for three days. Sleep had eluded me the first night, but in the nights that follow, I'm lost in a deep slumber, sometimes unable to wake on my own. In the mornings, Constance gently nudges me awake, and hours have passed when it feels like only seconds.

On the fourth day, the path we've been traveling ends abruptly, its continuation nothing more than a narrow trail disappearing into a twisted wall of trees.

"The cart can't go any farther," Constance says. "We'll have to walk from here."

"And the horse?"

"We'll bring him with us. If we leave him alone, the wolves will be on him in no time. He can traverse the terrain better than we can."

The trees are more densely packed than any I've seen up to that point. I can fit through if I stand sideways, but I can't imagine making the rest of the trip that way, and as much as I want to bring the horse, I don't think he'll fit.

Constance climbs down from the cart to transfer a day's worth of supplies, a large book, and several stacks of paper bound together with twine into two leather satchels. I unhitch the horse, preparing myself to push through the massive wall of trees in front of us, even though everything in me is telling me to turn and run. I hold tight to the reins and take a step forward. The horse doesn't budge.

"It's all right," I say to him, rubbing his nose, trying to comfort him with a lie. Just then, my inner ear pops the way it does when storm clouds rush over the mountains. The pressure in the air around me changes, muffling all sound. My skin prickles as the horse rears up, huffing and snorting. I try to pull him back down, but the reins tighten painfully around my hand.

The horse rakes his hooves across the ground and whinnies, eyes wide, puffs of moist air spurting from his nostrils. He jerks his head away, and my hand folds inside the tangled rope. I cry out. Constance grabs her dagger and cuts the rope. Once it's severed, the horse breaks free.

"Are you all right?" Constance asks as she takes my hand in hers and examines it by the light of the lamp. A ragged swath of skin has come away from the outside edge of my palm, and blood trickles down my arm. Constance rips a length of cloth from the bottom of her tunic and quickly binds the wound. The blood soaks through the makeshift bandage. I steady myself against a tree trunk and take a deep breath. Constance grasps my arm, a look of genuine concern on her face.

The horse circles in front of us, huffing and whinnying. "What's wrong with him?" I ask.

"Something's spooked him," Constance says, an uneasy ring in her voice. "We'll have to leave him if he won't come willingly."

As I pick up the satchel, a long, low, almost sorrowful howl cuts through the air, sending a chill straight through me. I angle my head to the side as another call—this time from a different direction—echoes the one that came before it.

Constance's hand moves to her dagger, and I kick myself for not insisting on having a weapon before we came into the forest.

"They've caught his scent," says Constance. She turns to me, her brown eyes gleaming in the dark. "The wolves."

I saw a wolf in town once. It wandered in with a broken leg and was put down in the street. Seeing it lying there, I was sure its paw was the size of my head, maybe bigger. If the wolves in this part of the forest are even half the size of that one, the horse doesn't stand a chance, and neither will we if we run into one.

Branches snap just off the pathway. Constance brandishes

her dagger. I search for something to use as a weapon and spot a large branch that has been broken off at the end, creating a jagged point.

A hulking figure emerges from the tree line to our right. Growling and snarling, it slinks along the ground. It is a wolf, twice the size of the one I'd seen in town. The top of its head is chest height, and even in the dark I can see its mouth open just enough to show its yellow teeth. My breath catches in my throat. I hold the branch up, gripping it with both hands.

From the left, another wolf emerges from the trees. This one is smaller and gray in color. It snarls loudly and the horse rears up. The wolves circle him, snapping and snarling. The smaller wolf swipes at the horse's leg, opening a gash. He huffs. Clouds of white steam puff out of him; his eyes grow wide. I lift the branch and bring it down hard on the back of the smaller wolf, and it yelps like a hurt dog. It whips around and snaps at my foot. Constance pulls me back, and we tumble between the closely packed trees. She kicks the wolf in the snout as it bears down on us.

The larger wolf has opened a gash in the horse's side, and blood spills onto the ground. The gray wolf turns and joins the other in bringing the horse down in a chorus of howls and grunts.

"Move!" Constance shouts.

She slings her bag over her shoulder and grabs the lamp

as I scramble to my feet. We rush forward. The trees are nearly touching in all directions. Their branches intertwine with one another like interlaced fingers. The thorny, low-lying underbrush scrapes at my ankles and tears at my pants. The snarling of the wolves fades, but I still risk glancing behind every few minutes to make sure nothing has followed us.

Constance holds the lamp up, but it's constantly snuffed out by strong gusts of wind that come from nowhere. The air smells of rotted leaves and dirt. I try to ignore the new sounds I hear—not from animals or insects, but whispers, so faint that I think maybe I am imagining them.

"Constance, how much farther do you think we have to go?" I say, trying to quell my increasing sense of dread. "I thought I heard—"

"I don't know. We should be approaching the heart of the forest but—" Constance stops and holds up her hand in a plea for silence. The wind brushes past me, and in it, a faint noise. A melody. I look at Constance, who presses her finger to her lips. The sound comes again, and this time, I hear something like words.

"Who could be singing out here?" I whisper. The sounds of the night creatures have ceased altogether, leaving only the haunting melody in the wind. The trees move high over our heads, their naked branches twisting around each other to form an impenetrable canopy. I cling tightly to Constance's jacket for fear that if we are separated, we will not be able to find each other again. The song wafts in and out as we push on. Again, I lose track of time. My legs ache, and my hand throbs.

"How long do you think we've been walking?" I ask.

"I—I don't know. Maybe hours, maybe . . ." Constance's uncertainty unsettles me even more.

The melody suddenly echoes and becomes louder, building to a crescendo before ceasing altogether. Movement in the shadows catches my eye. Grunts surround us on all sides.

"The wolves," I whisper.

Constance grabs my hand and takes off. We can't run, but we move forward as fast as we can. Something pulls at my shoulder, and an earsplitting cry erupts from my throat. Constance slashes at the dark just behind me with her dagger, then yanks me forward through a thick clump of trees where my foot catches on a root, causing us both to fall. Scrambling to my feet, I pull Constance up beside me and we stumble into a large clearing where the night sky is visible. Someone has felled the trees in a perfect circle. In the center stands a small house. I take a deep breath. Relief washes over me. We are out of the woods, but fear rushes in again as I realize we are not alone.

21

A woman emerges from the shadows of the covered porch. She stands on the stoop like a ghost, melding with the dark. The enormous crow that has been following us sits on the broken porch rail next to her. She runs her hand down its back, and it takes off, winging its way over the treetops. Constance steps in front of me, hand on her dagger. The old woman hums the haunting melody. Her eyes, black as coal, move over us. Her withered skin creases as she smiles wide.

"You're a long way from home," she says, her voice raspy and low. "I can always tell when someone is close by. The wolves begin to howl. They're quite hungry this time of year."

Neither of us move. The woman walks to the edge of the porch. She keeps her eyes on me. Something rustles in the trees behind us. At any moment, the wolves might burst from the tree line and tear us to pieces. Snarls and snaps in the distance draw closer.

"Are you coming in or not?" the woman asks. "You're more than welcome to stay out here, of course." She looks past us into the woods. Her fingers twitch as she whispers something under her breath. The grunting and snarling move away from us. She turns and disappears through the doorway. Constance motions for me to follow her as the howl of the wolves fades to nothing. We quickly mount the steps and go inside.

The cottage is in a precarious state. The roof slants downward at a steep angle, and when the wind whips by, the entire structure shudders. Dozens of herbs hang in bushels from the beams under the ceiling, and the rear wall is covered, floor to ceiling, with shelves of jars filled with all manner of strange things—dried herbs, liquids, and even different parts of small animals suspended in a viscous liquid.

A black cauldron hangs over the roaring fire, bubbling with some delicious-smelling concoction. Candles cover every available surface, some lit, some melted into nothing more than little mounds of wax. The air is hazy and thick. The minute I step over the threshold, an odd sense of calm envelops me. My fear of the wolves, the uneasiness of the White Wood—it all fades away.

"You've come a very long way," says the woman. "Venturing this far into the White Wood means only one thing—you're either very stupid or very desperate."

"We're looking for information about the fairy godmother," I say.

The woman bristles and gives an annoyed huff. "Sit." She gestures to a wooden table in the kitchen area with a set of mismatched chairs crowded around it.

"Forgive us if we're hesitant," Constance says. Her hand never stops hovering over her dagger.

"You're afraid," says the woman. "And I don't blame you, but if you draw that dagger it will be the last thing you ever do." She settles into a seat by the fire, her gaze steely. "When you say you're looking for information about the fairy godmother, what you really mean is you're looking for her magic. What is it you need? A philter to persuade a lover? An elixir to make you beautiful? Need someone dead?"

A chill runs up my back. "You do that?" What have we found in these forsaken woods?

"I do a great many things," says the old woman.

"And who are you exactly?" Constance asks.

"Oh, come now," says the woman in a much more serious tone. "You act as if you didn't know you'd find me here." She taps her foot on the floor and hums a little tune.

I glance at Constance, who stands stone-faced, her lips parted.

"There's been a mistake," I say. "We're looking for information about the fairy godmother."

"My dear girl, I don't know who in this cursed forest would know me better than I know myself, and if you have questions, I suggest you start asking before I throw you out into the dark."

"It cannot be," Constance whispers.

I step around the side of the woman's chair. She studies me silently. Her hair, a wash of gray that melts into a midnight black near the ends, is gathered together in dozens of tight bundles, all of which are pulled behind her and twisted into a single braid. Her frame is solid, round, her skin the color of the deepest, richest sepia. She wears a plain cotton dress with a long gray shawl.

"The Cinderella story is two hundred years old," I say. My mind races as the woman nods.

"It is indeed," she says.

"What am I missing?" Constance asks, an edge of anger in her voice.

"A great many things, apparently," says the woman.

Constance stomps around the woman's chair and looks her dead in the eye. "We didn't come through the White Wood to be mocked. We came here for answers about Cinderella, about why she betrayed her family by marrying

Prince Charming, about how the kings of Lille have kept such a tight grip on this land."

The woman slowly looks up at Constance. "Why does any of that matter to you?"

"Because Cinderella's family is *my family*," says Constance. Her hand still sits on the hilt of her dagger.

The woman stares at Constance as if she is seeing her for the first time. Her eyes grow wide, and the corners of her mouth turn down. She presses her arms across her chest. "You look very much like Gabrielle." She gazes up at a small portrait hanging by the hearth. A young boy with dark eyes, maybe six or seven years old, stares back at her. "I suppose that means she was able to make a life for herself somewhere in the world."

Constance balls up her fists. "If you call scrounging for food, living in constant fear, and being one of the most hated women in the land a life."

The woman looks Constance over again. "I never thought I'd see the day when kin to the evil stepsisters would be here in my humble abode."

Constance clenches her jaw, and I move to her side.

"Gabrielle was many things, but she was neither evil nor cruel, just as I'm sure you've never been a wish-granting fairy, godmother, or otherwise." Constance and the woman exchange angry gazes.

"Anyone with eyes can see that's not the case, but do you have any idea what I really am?" the woman asks.

"You're a witch," Constance says. It is accusatory, almost mean.

"I'm not much for labels, but I like that one. It doesn't have quite the same ring as fairy godmother, but I suppose it will do." She tilts her head and stares at me.

I would never have guessed that this was the fabled fairy godmother. The woman in the story is a nymphlike creature, with wings and a wand that spews magical dust. This woman's face is crisscrossed with lines, the folds around her mouth and eyes deep.

"We need information, not spells," I say.

She clasps her hands in her lap and rocks back and forth in her chair. "It's a strange request. Most people seek me out for something more material."

"People still look for you? They know you still exist?" I've never heard even a whisper of her.

"They do," she says. "Sometimes I help them, sometimes I don't, but when they return home, they tend to forget where they've been and why."

"What do you help them with?" I ask. "Dresses? Carriages? Glass slippers?"

"That story has taken its toll on you, hasn't it?" she asks. She looks at me as if she pities me. "Anything they think will give them an edge at the ball." The woman stares into the fire, settling back in her chair. She measures her words and movements, as if she is adept at controlling something that lurks just beneath the surface of her calm exterior.

"Do you know that the Cinderella tale is a lie?" I ask.

The old woman bristles and then smiles. "Which part?"

"I want to know what role you played in getting Cinderella to the ball that night," says Constance. "I know the story isn't true."

"What do you know of truth?" The woman sounds amused. "You think because you're related to Gabrielle that you're owed something?" She scowls at Constance.

"I know my family's history," Constance says angrily. "We know you worked for the royal family when Cinderella was alive."

"See there?" says the woman. "You're already wrong. I'm not now, nor have I ever been, in the employ of anyone in the palace." She turns her nose up and scoffs. "I was there of my own accord, but I don't see how that's any of your business."

"The king is after me," I say. "I ran away from the ball. I put my entire family and everyone I care about at risk, and I want to destroy him before he has a chance to hurt me or anyone else."

Constance's posture changes, and she stands a little taller and presses her shoulder into mine.

The woman shakes her head. "Lofty ambitions, my dear." She turns and stares so intensely into my eyes that I take a step back, my heart racing. It is like she can see inside me.

"Do you know what it's like in Lille?" Constance asks. "Do you understand the damage the Cinderella fairy tale has caused to the women and girls who live in town?"

I gather myself. "My friend died after attending the king's ball." Constance and the woman look at me. "And my other friend, Erin, is suffering a fate worse than death. We just watched a woman be executed because the king thought she helped me escape."

"People make their own decisions," says the woman. "You can't blame the king for all of your problems."

I step closer. Constance cautions me with a little wave of her hand, which I ignore. I look down at the woman. A palpable energy emanates from her, but I steel myself. "When the leader of this kingdom treats women as property, it sets an awful precedent. People think it's okay to do the same."

"I've never understood why people follow along so blindly," she mumbles. "Even when they know something is wrong, they do it anyway. Maybe you all should start thinking for yourselves."

Constance moves toward the door. "This was a mistake, coming out here. She can't help us."

"Wait," I say. I kneel at the woman's side. "What's your name? Your real name. None of that fairy godmother nonsense." I haven't been almost devoured by wolves to walk away with nothing.

She looks away from me. "It doesn't matter."

"It matters to me," I say. "As hard as the king tries to make us nameless, we aren't."

A faint smile flits across her lips. "My mother called me Amina, but I've not heard that name spoken aloud in many, many years." Something softens in her. Her defiant attitude is just a mask. Even out here in the darkest part of the White Wood, this woman is fearful.

"Please, Amina, we need to know anything you can tell us about Cinderella's true story, the kings who have ruled over Mersailles—especially Prince Charming, his past, where he came from, anything."

"And what would you do with this information?" she asks.

"We would use it to end the reign of men like Manford," says Constance, whose tone remains firm. "Forever."

Amina sighs heavily, her shoulders slumping. She runs her hand over her forehead and allows her fingertips to rest on her lips. "Even if I told you the truth, you wouldn't believe me. I sometimes find it hard to believe myself. Do you truly think men like him can be stopped?" Her tone suggests she has thought long and hard about this very question.

"Yes," I say. I don't know if that's true, but I want it to be. "Maybe if you tell us what you know, you can help us." While Amina is icy with Constance, I see a softness in her eyes, a willingness to open up to me.

"I will never be free from this burden, no matter how honest I choose to be," Amina says, looking me directly in the face. "I will carry it with me into the next life as penance for what I have done."

"Whatever it is, it can't be any worse than what the kings of Mersailles have done."

"You can't be certain," Amina says. Her eyes bore into me, and a primal rush of fear sweeps over me. This woman, delicate as she seems, is powerful, but she takes great care to mask it in our presence. "I have done things you cannot fathom. I have been more wicked than you can imagine." This is not a warning. This is not a threat. It is an admission.

"Tell us what you know," Constance urges again. She moves to a chair and sits down.

Amina leans forward and sighs, resigning herself to something. "Very well. But I will not be held responsible for the hopelessness, for the emptiness that you will feel when I'm done."

Her warning echoes Constance's. And if Amina's revelations are anywhere near as life changing as the ones Constance shared with me, there will be no going back. I sit down on the floor and wait for her to continue.

She laughs lightly. "Foolish girl."

22

"The king who sits on the throne today is not a normal man." Amina pulls her shawl around her and walks to the shelves at the rear of the room. She plucks a short glass jar with a cork stopper from the shelf, shuffles back over to her chair, and sits down. She leans forward and takes my hand in hers, unwrapping the bandage. I wince as she pulls the cloth away from the wound and uncorks the jar. A sweet smell wafts out.

"Honey and comfrey," I say, recognizing the scent of the honey and the stringy leaves of the comfrey plant.

She smiles. She dips her fingers, which I notice are each marked with ink in a triangle pattern, into the mixture and smears my hand with the pungent salve. I set my hand back in my lap after she rewraps it. The pain is already starting to subside.

"It's hard for me to say what the king is or isn't," says Amina. "A man, a monster, or some terrible combination of the two."

"What does that even mean?" Constance asks tensely. I shoot her a glance, urging her to be patient, and she clasps her hands together tightly in her lap. I don't want her to be quiet. I only want her to try to keep things calm. We need to know what Amina has to say.

Amina continues, unfazed by Constance's impatience. "Would you prefer the long version or the short one?" she asks curtly.

Constance sits back in her chair, still fuming. I hope she can bring herself to listen to the full story before she loses it completely.

"The long version," I say.

Amina smiles at me and then purposely frowns at Constance, who rolls her eyes. She reaches under her chair and brings out a small rectangular box. She produces from it a long churchwarden pipe. The chamber is elaborately carved with figures of flowers and leaves, and the stem is nearly as long as my forearm. She fills the chamber from a small cotton pouch and sets about lighting it. She takes a long draw, exhaling slowly. "All my life I've practiced magic. My mother raised me in the craft, taught me from the time I was young. You will hear people speak of light and dark, but in my experience you must be well versed in both to find a balance. By the time I was grown, I'd gained quite a reputation for myself. People came from near and far to seek out my services."

She looks toward the shelf. I follow her gaze to a book that is thicker than all the others, more worn, and bound in some kind of leather. For some strange reason, I want to pluck it from the shelf, but I turn back to Amina as she continues her story.

"They also came with accusations and rumors. When a baby was born with a strange mark, when the eggs of the fowls were runny with blood, when the moon seemed too bright, they blamed me. And one day they came pounding on my door and lit a pyre and dragged me out of my home fully prepared to send me to my maker."

"What stopped them?" I ask.

"A man," Amina says. "He drove the village folk from my doorstep, saved my life. He came to me seeking the thing all men seek—power—when he happened upon that dreadful scene. He asked me to aid him in his efforts to persuade a burgeoning kingdom to make him their ruler. He asked me to make the rivers run dry, to make the wheat die in the fields, to make the rain cease to fall."

A dreadful shock of recognition passes through me. I know this story.

"Who was he?" Constance asks. There is fear in her voice, a wavering in her tone. "Who was this man that came to your door?"

Amina rests her pipe on the arm of her chair and stares

into the fire. "The very same man who now sits on the throne."

I hear Constance inhale sharply.

"No," I say. "How is that possible?"

"Lille has had four rulers since the time of Cinderella," Amina says. "Prince Charming, King Eustice, King Stephan, and your current ruler Manford. Charming lived to be nearly a hundred years old, as did his successor, Eustice. But tell me, my dears, do they pass their kingdom to a son? A living relative?"

"All of the successors are handpicked from an annexed city in the Forbidden Lands." Even as I say it aloud, I realize how ridiculous it sounds, how convenient.

Amina grunts.

"The king always chooses his successor," I say. "They do it to avoid infighting."

"And how does it work?" Amina asks. "The kings of this land happen to outlive everyone around them. No one living remembers what the king looked like in his youth. And then what? The king goes into seclusion to wither and die and is buried without pomp or circumstance just before a young man, chosen by the dying king, arrives from the Forbidden Lands and comes to power and seems to know every law, every rule as if he'd authored it himself?"

My hands tremble, and fear rises in me again, but this time I am shaken to my core. I feel like I'm watching the very structure of my life, the thing it is built on, crumble to pieces. "That is how it has always been done."

"Mersailles has only ever had one ruler since the time of Cinderella," Amina says. "There is no city in the Forbidden Lands producing potential heirs to the throne. Charming is Manford. Manford is Charming."

I cannot fathom what she is saying. Constance's mouth is open, her eyes unblinking.

"How—how can that possibly be true?" I ask as I struggle to comprehend what this means.

"He has a power," Amina says. "Something that sustains him. I don't know how, but what is certain is that the prince of Cinderella's tale, his successors, and the man you call King Manford are one and the same."

Constance shakes her head, and Amina eyes her.

"I am sitting right in front of you," says Amina. "A witness to the events I've just revealed, and still you doubt. This is the kind of ignorance the king relies on to keep his ruse going. Just because you don't believe it doesn't mean it can't be true."

Constance opens her mouth to speak, but I interject. "Did you do as he asked? Were you the one responsible for the famine that devastated Mersailles all those years ago?"

Amina shifts uncomfortably in her chair. "I am."

"My grandmother told me stories passed down to her from that time," I say. "People were starving, dying. You did that?"

Amina shakes her head and looks at the floor. "I said I was a witch. I never said I was a good witch. I told you I've done wicked things. Didn't you believe me?" She snuffs out her pipe and puts it back in the box. "When the devastation became too much, the people became desperate. Desperate people do foolish things. They put Charming on the throne, and I provided the magic that brought back the crops, the flowing rivers, all of it. They groveled at his feet and begged him to keep them fed, and he did. He became their benevolent leader."

"And what did you get out of all of this?" Constance asks. "I doubt you helped him without getting anything in return."

"He made me one of his closest advisers," Amina says in a way that sounds almost disappointed. "He continued his cursed reign, and in turn he made sure I never had to worry about who might decide that a witch might make good kindling."

"Cursed," I say quietly. "This has to be what Cinderella meant when she said he was cursed."

Constance nods. "We need to find out how he sustains himself. Maybe if we can figure out that part, we can stop him."

"I can't help you," says Amina. "I don't know how he does it. No one does. It is the thing he keeps only to himself."

"You understand what this means?" Constance asks,

looking like she's come to some terrible revelation. "By doing this, he can continue to hurt people. And he can do it forever if he's found a way to cheat death." Constance stares at Amina. "How do *you* do it? You're still alive. Maybe he's doing the same thing you are."

"No," says Amina sternly. "I age. I do not suddenly become young when it suits me. I use herbs, spells. It is a constant effort, but I cannot go on indefinitely."

"You can't make yourself young, but if you're as old as you say you are—" I don't know how to say it without it sounding like an insult.

"Why don't I look like a rotting corpse?" Amina asks.

I nod.

"It is a glamour, an illusion. I've perfected it over the years, and I use it now so I don't frighten your friend." She winks at Constance, who crosses her arms hard over her chest, glaring back at her.

"Why have you decided to stay all this time?" I ask.

Amina grows still and quiet. "Because I must."

I think of Manford ruling over Lille for the rest of time, finding new and terrible ways to hurt us. I can't let that happen.

"Once a man has tasted the kind of power he now wields, he won't ever give it up willingly," says Amina.

"We'll strip him of that power by force," I say. I sit quietly for a moment before asking a question I know Constance wants answered. "Why did you take Cinderella to him? Why did you help her get to the ball if you knew what he was?"

Constance's angry exterior melts away, and a look of desperation takes its place. She needs answers.

Amina hangs her head. "Cinderella's parents stoked the flames of rebellion after Charming began to implement laws and rules that were so restrictive and damaging to the people of Lille that they began to question his ability to be a fair and just ruler."

"The decrees," I say.

Amina shakes her head. "If you drop a frog in a pot of boiling water, it will jump out. But if you stoke the fire slowly, it will allow itself to be boiled to death. The changes in the very beginning were subtle. A curfew was imposed for the safety of the women. Women were required to wear long dresses to protect their modesty. Men were elevated to positions of power because they knew best." Amina gives an exaggerated sigh. "Everything was framed as being in the best interest of the people."

"And the people just allowed him to do it?" I ask.

"Of course," Amina says. "Why wouldn't they? He was their savior, their protector."

"You didn't seem so concerned with people's well-being when you were causing a famine and letting them starve to death," Constance snaps.

"He saved *my* life. I was indebted to him," Amina says.

For the first time, I see something like regret in her eyes. "After Cinderella's parents were killed, he held the first annual ball. He sent out invitations that instructed young women to present themselves to be chosen. He made death the penalty for not attending. I realized I had to do something to stop him, and that I would have to take extreme measures to do it."

"You tried to kill him?" Constance asks.

"No." She hesitates. "I couldn't, not after what he had done for me."

"So what did you do?" I ask.

"I found someone who wanted him gone as much as I did. Someone who might appeal to his lust for beautiful young women, maybe someone he'd already stolen everything from."

I glance at Constance, and her face goes blank.

"I knew what he did to Cinderella's parents," Amina says. "They were dead because of him. I went to Cinderella, expecting to find a fatherless girl, grieving the deaths of her family, willing to do the impossible out of sheer desperation. Instead I found a stepmother, Lady Davis, fierce as a raging fire, who almost slit my throat upon seeing me. I found three young women, Cinderella being the youngest, who were ready to crush Manford under their boots. They were prepared to move against him. I gave Cinderella everything she needed and accompanied her to the ball in disguise."

"She went there to kill him?" Constance asks, astonished.

Amina nods.

I loop back through the story Constance had shared with me. It is the one mystery that seemed to haunt her the most—why would Cinderella have married Prince Charming after everything he did to her family?

"He's still alive," I say. "Why didn't she do it? What happened?"

Amina lowers her gaze. "When he saw her for the first time, the look in his eyes—he wanted her more than anything and he told me that if he could have her, if I could assist him in this, that he would be a better man, a better king. I thought maybe, if he could love and be loved in return, he could atone for the things he'd done."

"That makes no sense," Constance says. "He's not capable of loving anyone except himself."

"Isn't that what love does?" Amina asks. "It changes people. It makes them want to be better."

Constance leans in. "She goes up there to kill him and ends up his blushing bride? Make it make sense, Amina."

Amina closes her eyes as if she's in pain, furrowing her brow, breathing deeply. "I'm a witch. I used a potion, slipped it to her in a glass of punch before she had a chance to assassinate him. She fell for him as soon as their eyes met, and nothing he'd done in the past mattered anymore."

My mouth hangs open in shock. Constance doesn't speak.

"Lady Davis and Gabrielle tried to drag her back to the house, losing her slipper in the process. They took her home and locked her away, but there was no hiding from him. He came calling, shoe in hand, and made a spectacle of it. He had palace artists record the event, immortalizing it in what would become the first palace-sanctioned version of Cinderella's story. He took her to be his wife, and for a very brief time, it felt as if tensions in Mersailles were eased."

Constance stands up, clenching her fists. "It was all based on a lie. You—you tricked her."

"The law of three says that whatever you put out will come back to you three times over," Amina says. "I'm sure I'll get what's coming to me. Just you wait."

"And you'll deserve every bit of it," Constance says through gritted teeth.

I can't wrap my head around the enormity of his lies, the depth of his deception. Cinderella's story is so much more complicated than I imagined. I never would have thought that this is what the actual truth could be. But what I suspected, that Manford was the monster of the fairy tale, turned out to be true in the most terrible way.

"How do we stop him?" I ask. It's the only question that matters now.

"You can't," Amina says. "You are no match for him. Nothing can be done."

"I don't believe that," I say.

"You have no idea how powerful he has become," Amina snaps. "There is no defeating him. My best advice would be to run, hide, save yourselves if you can."

"You can't be this much of a coward," Constance says.

Amina turns slowly, and a wave of silent rage pulses out of her. I stand up and move between them.

"Please," I say, as much to Amina as to Constance. "We need your help."

Constance speaks to Amina without looking at her. "We can't go back. You need to help us."

Amina glances at me, her face softening again. She looks around the small room, muttering something to herself. She nods at me. "You can sleep by the fire. You"—she eyes Constance—"can sleep outside for all I care. I don't have much extra room, as you can see, but stay, and we'll discuss this in the morning when I've had a chance to clear my head."

Amina shuffles off, and I sink down onto the floor, relieved that she and Constance haven't come to blows. The things Amina told us feel too big, too impossible. Am I just supposed to take her at her word? Believe that magic is real and so much more dangerous than I thought possible?

Constance briefly considers taking Amina's advice to

sleep outside, but changes her mind as the howling of the wolves, along with a blustery wind, picks up again. Amina tosses me a pile of blankets before settling herself on a straw-stuffed mattress in the far corner of the room. The house contains cupboards and closets but no other rooms as far as I can tell.

Constance and I take turns stoking the fire to keep the drafty little cottage warm throughout the night. As we drift in and out of sleep, I keep some distance between us, though I awake several times to find her face very close to mine, her eyes closed, her breath soft and warm. I'm afraid I'm dreaming, that I might reach out and she'll be gone. But I allow myself to think of what it would be like to spend my days with her freely, in a future we create.

23

Constance stirs before Amina. She sits up, rubbing her eyes. Her body suddenly stiffens.

"Are you all right?" I ask.

She groans and rubs her shoulder, rolling her head from side to side and stretching her neck. "The floor isn't very forgiving. Did you sleep okay?"

"Not really." I unbandage my hand to find the wound almost completely healed.

"Look at that," says Constance. "I guess the witch is good for something."

I look to where Amina is sleeping. "Whether she'll help us or not is another question."

I have a feeling Amina wants to help us. She wouldn't have shared her story if she didn't. But she's clearly not a person who does anything out of the kindness of her heart, so I understand Constance's skepticism.

Constance shifts around on the pile of blankets. Her tunic, which is entirely too big for her, slips off her shoulder. My heart speeds up a little, and I look away. When I turn back she is smiling at me, which only makes my heart beat faster. She purses her lips, then lets them part, sucking in a quick puff of air. She smiles again, and I notice a deep dimple in her right cheek. If I had been standing, I might have had to sit down.

"One thing," I say, changing my train of thought.

"All right." Constance raises one fiery-red eyebrow.

"I know you've got a lot to be angry about. And I don't blame you, but we don't have any better ideas." I glance toward Amina. "We need her to tell us what she knows, and I'd like it if she didn't use whatever power she has to obliterate us first."

"We don't even know if she's telling the truth."

I had thought the same thing, but I look down at my almost completely healed wound. Her books and concoctions line the walls, and I'm sure there is something at work here that I don't yet understand.

"I don't know exactly what she is either," I say. "But just promise me you won't provoke her before we figure out more."

"I'll try," she says. "For you. Not because I'm afraid of her."

"Of course not," I say, smiling.

Amina rolls over and sits up. Bits of hay stick out of her mussed hair, and she looks confused for a moment.

"You awake there, Granny?" Constance asks, an edge of annoyance still coloring her voice. I shoot her a glance, and she frowns dramatically, mouthing the word "sorry" to me.

"Unfortunately. It's been quite a while since I've been up with the sun. I have you two chattering away to thank for that." She climbs off the mattress and stumbles to her feet. "Put the kettle and pot on. We'll need something to eat. What will it be—eye of newt, tongue of dog?" Amina cackles.

"That's disgusting," Constance grumbles.

I push the pot over the fire and move the embers around before throwing another log on.

"We were just about to go over a few things," I say.

"I'll need coffee, my pipe, and a moment to wake up before we start on this again," says Amina. She gathers a clay mug and her little cedar box and plops down in the chair by the fire. She puffs on her pipe, then splays her hand out in front of her. "Go on then."

"Cinderella got a message to Gabrielle, asking her to meet in secret," Constance says.

"Is that so?" Amina seems intrigued.

Constance goes to her bag and pulls out her belongings. She unbundles a packet of handwritten notes. Some of them are faded and look too delicate to even touch. She hands them to Amina. "One of Lady Davis's most brilliant ideas was establishing a network of people willing to pass messages in order to organize their efforts. Over time the network shrank, mostly because the king was increasing his stranglehold on the women of Mersailles. These are some of the communications."

I peer over Amina's shoulder.

Tell M I made it.

Meet us in the grove at midnight.

Bring the supplies from the barn.

My skin pricks up. "I saw a note like this at Cinderella's tomb the night I escaped the ball."

Constance hangs her head. "I'm not surprised. The tomb would have been a perfect place to leave a message. So many people used to leave little notes there a message like this wouldn't have been noticed."

Amina shuffles the remaining messages and peers down at a particularly yellowed and curling slip of paper.

Meet me at the place where we grew up, on the day my mother died, when the moon is gone from the sky.

"That one is from Cinderella to Gabrielle five years before Cinderella's death," says Constance. "Gabrielle met her, and Cinderella tried to tell her something, but the guards found her and took her away. She risked her life to deliver a message."

"It's not as if he kept her in a cell," Amina says quietly. "She had her own room in the palace. It was quite lovely, actually."

"A prison is still a prison no matter how pretty the decor," says Constance. Her patience is already paper thin.

Amina remains silent.

"Does it make you feel better to think of her as some pampered princess?"

Constance can't keep her emotions in check, and it's wrong to ask her to. She has a right to everything she feels. I just hope Amina will still be willing to help us.

"Why do you think I've spent these last years of my life in these godforsaken woods?" Amina asks. "It's not for the scenery. I know what I've done, and you could just leave me here to rot like I deserve, but no. You traipsed out here to bother me."

Constance looks at me, and I force a quick smile just to show her I'm not going to stand in her way.

"What happened when the spell wore off?" she asks. "You gave her a love potion. I'm assuming it didn't last forever, so what happened after it wore off?"

Amina sighs. "What I gave her lasted a full cycle of the moon. The spell lost its potency just after they were married, and she began to feel differently toward him."

"Being responsible for the death of her parents seems like a good reason to loathe someone," Constance says.

Amina nods. "He wanted her more than anything. And more important, he wanted her to feel the same way about him. As the potion wore off, it became clear that she would never love him the way he wanted her to, but he couldn't let it go. His pride was too great to let her walk away. He kept her in the palace until she died."

"People said she was sick, bedridden in the last years of her life," I say.

"She was locked away in the palace during the remaining years of her life." Amina opens herself up again. "No one was allowed to see or speak to her except for one servant, some ancient woman who died just after Cinderella. And Manford himself, of course." Amina turns to Constance and speaks directly to her. "I don't know what she intended to tell your Gabrielle. Whatever Cinderella knew, she took to the grave."

Constance runs her hand over her forehead and slumps down in her seat.

"Maybe you should let it go," Amina says. "Cinderella lived and died a long time ago, and what's going on in Mersailles, especially in Lille, is tragic, but what can you do? Nothing has changed in two hundred years. Maybe it never will."

Constance shakes her head. "Coward."

Amina raises an eyebrow and then returns to gazing

into the fireplace. "All the name-calling in the world doesn't change the fact that you can't do a damn thing to stop him." She goes to the shelf, takes down the strange book I'd seen earlier, and opens it on the table in the kitchen. After running her finger over the words written there, she adds ingredients from the jars on the rear wall to the cauldron.

I watch her carefully. "What are you doing?"

"Making myself invisible so that your friend can't keep staring at me like she wants to kill me." She shoots Constance an angry glare.

"Are you serious?" I ask.

Amina laughs. "No, but it is something I have to do, unless you'd like to see me as I really am."

Constance stiffens up. "You mean you're not just a mean old granny?"

Amina pauses, her ingredients bubbling in her cauldron. Suddenly her face contorts, taking on a pale-yellow hue, her mouth turned downward. Her skin droops as her appearance shifts. She transforms into an ancient-looking corpse, haggard and rotting. I cover my mouth to stifle a gag, and Constance rears back, knocking over a pile of pots and clay plates. Amina suddenly reverts to her former appearance and smiles.

"Don't let this façade fool you. I'm not your granny. I'm not to be trifled with. Do you understand?"

"All right!" Constance yelps.

My heart feels like it's trying to escape my chest as Amina fills a cup from the cauldron and drinks the mixture, a slight look of disgust on her face. She stuffs her pipe and smokes like a chimney until her eyes close into slits.

I retreat to the kitchen. Amina grumbles to herself as Constance follows me and slides down to sit on the floor. My heart is still racing as my attention is drawn to the book that lies open on the counter.

I lean close to it. It smells like burned paper and rotted meat. I cup my hand over my mouth as I read the words. It looks like a recipe, but the ingredients are things I've never heard of: the crowning of a rooster, High John the Conqueror, freshly shed snakeskin. I glance at Amina and then reach out to turn the page. Each one is filled with recipes and spells, all hand-lettered with notes scratched in the margins. There are papers and notes stuffed between the pages.

Near the back of the book is an entire chapter that is bound with red ribbons tied in a series of intricate knots and topped with a wax seal. The title reads *Necromancy*.

"What is necromancy?" I ask.

Amina turns her head and looks at me out the corner of her eye but says nothing. Constance looks over my shoulder at the book.

"It's when you communicate with the dead," she says.

Amina chuckles. "You know everything now, don't you?"

"That's not what it is?" Constance asks.

"No," Amina says. "It's not. You can't communicate with the dead. They're dead."

Constance pushes her hand down on her hip. "No. I've heard of this. It's for communicating with the dead. I'm sure of it. She's lying."

Amina stands up and marches over to us, and for a split second I think she's going to pull out a wand and curse us herself. Even Constance looks like she regrets saying anything.

"You have no idea what you're talking about," Amina snaps. "You have to call the spirit back to communicate with them."

At the edge of my thoughts, an idea emerges. I push it aside, but it has already taken root. It blooms and stands in my mind's eye, fully formed.

And terrifying.

"Can we—can we do that with Cinderella? Can we communicate with her to find out what she was trying to tell Gabrielle?"

Constance stares blankly at me.

Amina scowls. "Cinderella has been dead nearly two hundred years. A necromancy spell for her would require—" She stops and stares directly at me, and I worry she has somehow sensed the idea that floods my mind. So horrid and unimaginable I don't want to speak it aloud.

"Require what?" I ask. I wait to see if what's required is as gruesome as I think it might be.

"A corpse." Amina takes a long draw on her pipe; the smoke encircles her head. "*Her* corpse." I stare back at Amina. I mean to ask her to elaborate, but her expression stops me. Her features harden to a mask of stone as she shakes her head and mumbles something to herself. Constance is lost in thought. She raises her head to look at me but doesn't speak. I hope she won't think me a monster for what I am about to say.

"Cinderella is the only one who might know how to stop him," I say, measuring my words. "The only one who might have known what his weakness was."

"I won't help you," Amina interrupts. She glares at me as she speaks through clenched teeth. "How dare you ask me to do such a thing."

"Wait," says Constance, glancing between Amina and me. "Are you suggesting we raise Cinderella from the dead?"

"You don't understand," Amina says. "They don't come back as the people they were. They are living corpses, changed. I won't do it."

"We need to talk to her," I say. "Everyone else who may have been useful is dead. Cinderella was there with Prince Charming in the castle. This is how we find out what she meant to tell Gabrielle. You owe it to us."

"I don't owe you anything." Amina's fingers tremble as she grips her cup and shuffles back to her chair.

Constance walks over to her and bends low to look right in her eyes. "You helped put Manford on the throne. You've seen what he's done, what he's become, and now you have some kind of conscience? Where was it when you were helping Cinderella fall in love with him against her will?"

"I made a mistake!" Amina yells, her voice cracking. "A mistake that cannot be made right because I can't—" She stops and gathers herself. "I can't make it right."

"You haven't even tried," Constance says angrily.

"Stop." I scoop up the book and take it over to Amina. I look her right in the face. She is pained. "We all make choices that we wish we could take back. But we can't change what has already happened. The only thing we can do is try to make things better now. People are still suffering." I hand her the book. "You can help them and us."

A silence overtakes us. Amina stares into the fire for a long time before getting up and closing the book, placing it on the shelf. She tilts her head back and closes her eyes, taking a deep breath like she has resigned herself to something. "We will need to gather and prepare the supplies. The ritual is complicated."

"You'll help us then?" I ask.

Amina nods and my heart leaps.

"Necromancy can be very dangerous, more than you

can imagine," she says, her voice low. "We open ourselves up to another realm where spirits and other inhuman beings dwell. Every precaution must be taken. When you open the door between this life and what comes next, well, I'm sure you can imagine what horrors could arise. And some spirits are not so easily dismissed. We must be cautious."

"Why did you change your mind?" I ask.

"You, Sophia," says Amina. "You're a damn sharp sword. A wildfire."

That catches me by surprise. I don't see myself that way at all. If anything, those words describe Constance better than me.

"She's not wrong," says Constance, nodding like she sees those things in me, too.

"So you two agree on at least one thing," I say.

"Don't go putting too much weight on that, dearie," says Amina. "I don't care for this one too much." She waves her hand at Constance.

"The feeling's mutual, Granny," says Constance.

24

Our preparation for the ritual begins that same evening. Amina leads Constance and me to her garden. Maybe these plants thrive on shadow or moonlight, because even in the late autumn there are blooms and green leaves. She strolls through, counting out what she needs and making a list of the things she doesn't have.

"Do you recognize this?" Amina asks, pointing to a waist-high plant with dozens of amethyst-hued, thimble-shaped blossoms all bunched together like the honeycomb of a beehive.

I shake my head, taking a seat on the little steps that lead down into her garden. Constance sits next to me.

"Foxglove," Amina says. "Helpful for raising the dead or, in the opposite case, stopping the heart. Deadly poisonous.

What about this one?" She points to a short bush with small trefoil leaves and sunny yellow blossoms.

"That's rue," I say, excited that I know at least one of the plants. "My grandmother would make a tea from it if she had a cough or an upset stomach."

Amina seems highly amused with my answer. "Your grandmother was a wise woman. It's also used for protection and divination." She looks thoughtful. "We'll harvest what we need the first night of the full moon. There are some things that we'll need to gather from elsewhere, but I must warn you, it won't be a pleasant task."

I look at her quizzically. "I'm not sure I like the sound of that."

"The spell requires a still-beating heart. It can be from something small. A rabbit, perhaps. We'll have to open its chest while it's still alive." Amina makes a cutting motion with her hand, and my stomach turns over.

"On that cheery note, I'm going back inside," says Constance. She runs her hand over the small of my back as she gets up. A warm shudder courses through me. I watch her as she walks toward the front of the cottage. The feeling stays with me in the chilly nighttime air.

"I don't like her one bit," Amina says.

"I like her very much," I say. I bite my tongue, feeling that familiar stab of shame. I hate that I still feel this way even this far from Lille.

"Obviously." She leans over into a bush and readjusts a tendril of small shoots snaking up a latticework. "She's annoying. You, on the other hand, seem like a sweet girl. How did the two of you come to be allies in all this?"

"She helped me after my parents put me out. It was only a few days ago, the night of the ball, in fact. It still doesn't feel real. It's hard to explain."

"Well, you don't have to explain it to me." Her way of speaking is rough, unapologetic. She and Constance are alike in that way, and I appreciate every bit of it. Too many people have lied to me, spouting the same rehearsed lines over and over. "And there's no sense in feeling sorry for yourself."

"I don't. I feel sorry for them. My parents, that is. They only know how to follow the king. They've lost their way when it comes to knowing how to help me."

"And you're not lost?"

I think for a moment. "Maybe I am. But the difference is that I want to be found. I'm not happy pretending everything is fine when I know it's not."

"And just who is it that you suppose will find you?" Amina asks.

"It'll be me," I say. "*I* will find myself."

She closes the gap between us and sits down beside me. She studies me, looking into me, like she can see every single one of my flaws, my weaknesses, and I am afraid.

"It is so much easier to forget the world when you're alone in the forest. There are fewer opinions, less to consider."

"That sounds like something I could get used to," I say. "But I don't really want to forget what's going on in Lille. I can't turn my back on all the people who are still there, fighting to survive."

There is a rustle in the trees. I jump up and look around frantically. Amina laughs.

"It's all right," she says. She holds her hand out, and from the tree line the crow emerges, swooping down and landing on her shoulder. "He's a friend of mine." The bird nuzzles her and then flies up and settles on the roof. "He's what we call a familiar. He keeps an eye on the path that leads here, lets me know if anything is amiss." A bit of her rough exterior softens. She pats me on the shoulder. "Come. Let's go inside."

Around the front of the cottage, I find Constance sitting on the narrow front step. Amina walks straight past her without so much as a downward glance. I sit next to her.

"This must be hard for you," I say. "Being here, knowing she played a part in what happened to your family."

"It is," Constance says. She sighs heavily and presses her leg against mine. "I knew she was involved, but it was so deceitful. She led a lamb to a slaughter. I've always known that Cinderella would never have stayed with Charming—with Manford—if it hadn't been for the fairy godmother."

"It doesn't change what happened, but she's willing to help us now, and I think she knows exactly how much pain and suffering she's caused. That's why she's out here."

"Hiding is why she's out here." Constance is unmoved.

"Yes, but why?" I ask. "She's exiled herself as a form of punishment. Maybe she didn't know what else to do. You heard her say she doesn't think he can be stopped. Maybe she's given up."

"I think a part of me had given up, too." Constance heaves an exaggerated sigh and turns to me, smiling. "I'm not going to forgive her for what she did, but I won't kill her."

"I guess that's good enough for now."

She looks at me in that way again, and I never want her to stop. She makes me feel seen. Alive. Hopeful.

"You know, if we can stop Manford, you could come back to Lille. You wouldn't have to stay away." Imagining all these new possibilities helps me push away the thoughts of what will have to come first.

"I'd like that," Constance says. "It'd be nice to stay in one place after all this time."

Under the glinting moon, her hair is like a smoldering ember, her face so much like the splendor of the stars in the sky above us that I wonder how she can be real.

"But if we can find a way to end his reign," Constance says, "it doesn't mean that everyone will suddenly change. The people of Lille don't know anything other than Manford's laws and rules. It will be hard to make them see a new way."

We sit in silence for a moment, a swell of sadness rising

in me, and Constance seems to sense it. She lays her head gently on my shoulder, and her hair brushes against my cheek. I breathe in the flowery scent that always clings to her.

"If this doesn't work," she says, "we can run away together. Maybe get our own decrepit little shack in the woods."

She is joking, but it doesn't sound like a bad idea. I feel my face grow warm. "You might get tired of me."

"I might get tired of your cooking," she says, smiling. "That gruel was—"

"Terrible? I knew it!"

She reaches down and runs her fingers over the back of my hand. For a moment I think she might turn her face up and press her lips against mine, and while I want that more than anything, I can't bring myself to slip my hand under her chin and bring her mouth closer. My feelings for Constance grow with each passing second, but my feelings for Erin hang heavy on my heart. I feel terrible for caring so deeply about Constance while Erin suffers.

She shouldn't be suffering, and neither should I. It is this feeling that strengthens my resolve to do whatever must be done to make sure Manford's reign comes to an end, even if that involves raising Cinderella from the dead.

25

The next night, the moon is just a sliver of silver in the black sky, and Constance, Amina, and I have gathered by the fire as a wicked wind gusts through the White Wood.

Constance sharpens her dagger on a flat stone as Amina puffs away on her pipe.

"There's something I'd like to ask of you," Amina says.

Constance scowls, and I nudge her with my shoulder.

"What is it?" I ask.

"We're heading into an unknown future. I'd like to see if, perhaps, we might illuminate our path."

Constance is exasperated. "You clearly have something specific in mind, so why don't you just get on with it."

Amina rolls her eyes and stands up, stuffing a piece of

parchment into Constance's hand. I lean over and read it. It's a list of the herbs we need from the garden, and underneath it is a schedule with little drawings of the phases of the moon and the word "divination."

"Divination?" Constance asks. "Like fortune-telling?"

"It is a tool," Amina says. "For looking ahead."

"You can see the future?" I ask.

Amina sits back down and takes up her pipe. "In a way, yes. Don't you think a little peek into the events to come might be helpful?"

"How do we do that?" I ask, intrigued.

Amina settles into her chair and crosses her legs. "After the harvest, on the full moon, we'll see what can be seen."

"Can you ever just give a straight answer?" Constance asks, throwing her head back and looking at the ceiling. "I'm exhausted trying to decipher your riddles. See what can be seen? What does that mean?"

"It means shut up and stop asking so many questions," Amina snaps.

Constance sits forward and opens her mouth to speak, or more likely to share some choice words with Amina, when the winds whip themselves into a strong bluster.

The roof rattles, and the floorboards creak under Amina's rocker. A stiff draft moves through the room, and the flames of the roaring fire lap at the blackened bricks of the fireplace. A noise is carried in on the wind.

"This place is going to get blown away with the next strong gust," Constance says.

"And hopefully you with it," Amina says without even looking up.

Constance raises an eyebrow. "Listen—"

"Shh!" I say, scrambling to my feet. "Did you hear that?"

"The wind, Sophia," Constance says.

"No. No, there's something else."

There is another sound in the wind. The whinny of a horse. As the wind gusts again, we all hear it. Amina leaps from her chair and stands listening in the middle of the room. She goes to the threadbare rug that takes up most of the floor, grabbing it by its edge, revealing a small door underneath. When she lifts the hatch, I see the unmistakable glint of fear in her eyes. "Get inside. Now. Don't say a word. Don't even breathe if you can help it."

Constance moves to my side, and we crowd into the little opening, which leads to a root cellar. With its low ceiling and dirt floor, it is nothing more than a hole in the ground. We crouch down while Amina drops the hatch and covers it with the rug, knocking a shower of dust onto us.

"What is it?" Constance asks. Her voice is magnified in the small space, and Amina stomps hard on the floor above.

"Shh," I say. "Someone is coming."

I still my breath and try to hear over the rush in my ears. Horses, men's voices, and then a bang at the door.

Amina's boots knock against the floorboards as she makes her way to the front of the house. The groan of the rusted hinges rings out as she opens the door. A heavier set of steps enters the cottage and stops just over our heads.

"Still living in squalor, I see," says a man's voice. It's familiar.

"It suits me," says Amina.

"Indeed it does," says the man. "And tell me again why you've chosen this life? You certainly aren't out here on my orders."

"I prefer it to the city or the palace." Amina's tone is condescending, and the man shifts from one foot to the other just above us. "Why are you here?"

"You know why I'm here."

Suddenly I recognize the voice, and fear washes over me. My heart sputters, and I hold my breath. King Manford.

"You haven't set foot on my doorstep in years, and now you show up because you want something."

"I'm hurt," he says.

"Oh please," Amina says. "We both know it would take more than that to hurt your feelings."

"You know me too well," he says. I hear him laugh. It's the most grating, unnatural thing I've ever heard.

I search for Constance's hand in the dark and find it clenched at her side. She takes a step closer to me.

"You are the fabled fairy godmother," the king says in

a mocking tone. "Making carriages out of pumpkins and shoes out of glass. You belong in the palace. It is you, after all, who has always been on this journey with me."

"Our journey ended long ago," Amina says.

"Is that what you tell yourself?" He sighs.

"Enough," Amina says. "You need to leave and let me continue on as I have all these years, without your interference."

Constance taps me on the shoulder and points down at her other hand. I've been squeezing it too tight. I let go immediately. As she readjusts herself she presses her chest so close to mine that I can feel her heartbeat. It is racing.

"I want the girl, and I want her now. Where is she?"

"Didn't you *invite* her to the ball? That implies she had the right to leave if she wanted to."

The king laughs heartily as more dust rains down on my head.

"You know better than that," he says.

Constance presses her lips to my forehead, and I shut my eyes tight. I wait for Amina to open the hatch and turn us over. There is a rustling above us as Amina takes a step toward the king.

"Leave," says Amina. "And do not come back."

"I'd hoped that time away would have brought you some much-needed focus, but you are still utterly useless. Your magic is flawed, weak. Are you sure you can still call yourself a witch?"

Amina takes a long, deep breath. The longer he stays, the more he'll be able to get under her skin, maybe even make her second-guess her decision to help us.

"You're just as worthless as you've always been," the king snarls. He moves toward the door, then pauses. "Your spells and potions have always been lacking. I've had to take things into my own hands because of your ineptitude."

Amina doesn't respond.

"I do hope you'll keep me informed should you hear anything," says the king.

The front door opens, and a horse whinnies. No sound is made for several moments, and then the hatch pops open. Amina looks down on us, her face crestfallen, her mouth drawn into a tight line. We climb up and stand quietly, waiting to be sure the king is gone.

"What was all that about?" Constance asks angrily. "Suddenly when we're here, he just decides to stop by for a visit?"

"No sense in hiding how you feel. Come right out with it," says Amina, who looks absolutely drained.

"You told him we were here!" Constance runs to the window and peers out, her dagger drawn. Amina appears not to hear her as she slumps into a chair.

"Wait a minute," I say, holding my hands up, my heart still pounding. "Amina could have opened that hatch and handed us over right away, but she didn't."

Constance retreats to the kitchen.

"Do you think he'll come back?" I ask.

"Not if he knows what's good for him." Amina sighs. "My dear Sophia, you may one day find yourself the topic of your own fairy tale. I can already see him turning your escape into a cautionary tale."

"I won't give him the chance to use me like that," I say. "I would die first."

Amina turns to me, sadness in her eyes. "Please don't say that. Because you very well might."

26

We spend the following days preparing for the harvest. Every rustle of the trees or creaking of the boards in the old cottage makes me jump, fearing the king has returned. Constance is so suspicious of Amina that she adjusts to Amina's schedule, sleeping when she sleeps, waking when she wakes, and following her around, which pushes Amina to her wits' end.

When the full moon rises they are barely speaking, but the time has come for us to gather the herbs for the necromancy ritual and to perform the work Amina calls divination.

Amina gathers bushels of herbs from her garden—wormwood, mugwort, bay leaves, vervain, yarrow. Using a mortar and pestle, she grinds them up in different combinations. She makes sachets from white linen and stuffs them with the herbs, stitching the edges closed. The look of concentration on her face is so stern that I dare not interrupt, even though I am curious about the ritual's steps.

She consults her book, goes out and checks the sky, and when she's done, she brews an infusion of rue and serves it in three cups.

I swallow a mouthful and have to stifle a gag, my eyes watering. "It's so bitter."

"Be sure to finish all of it," Amina says. She drinks hers like it's nothing. Constance sips her tea, and when we're done, Amina asks us to follow her outside.

"It's the dead of night," Constance says.

Amina blinks. "And?"

"Do you think it's safe?" I ask.

Amina laughs. "No. It's not safe, but it is necessary."

Constance tightens her belt and runs her hand over her dagger's hilt.

An insidious little smile spreads across Amina's lips. "It won't do you much good. It's not the wolves or bears you should be afraid of. The night creatures, the ones with no name who come alive in the moonlight—those are the things you should be worried about."

Constance pauses in midstep, thrusting her chin in the air. "I'm sure there isn't anything out there as scary as you."

"Let's hope you're right about that," says Amina.

"Can we get on with this?" Constance asks.

"I think you should be more mindful of your tone," Amina says, still smiling. "Lest you find yourself on the wrong side of a transformation spell. It would be a shame if you ended up as some slimy, amphibious creature." She walks out the front door.

"Is she threatening me?" Constance glances at me. "Because it sounded like a threat."

I hear Amina cackling from somewhere outside and shrug, but Constance remains stone-faced.

"I don't think she means it," I say.

"I don't want to spend the rest of my life as a toad, Sophia."

"But you'd be such a cute one," I say. "A beautiful bullfrog."

Constance shakes her head and gives my hand a quick squeeze.

We walk in procession behind the cottage and through a thicket in the bright light of the full moon. As we emerge into a second, smaller clearing, we come upon a pool of water. The space above it, open to the night sky, allows the moonlight in. Devoid of plant life, animals, or even ripples, the flat pond, wide as the cottage itself, seems out of place. It looks like a large round mirror.

My head swims. I feel like I'm floating. I glance at Constance, who has taken a seat on the ground.

"What was in that tea?" I ask.

Amina sways back and forth with her eyes closed. "The rue is quick. Especially in the moonlight." She glances toward the water. "In you go."

"We have to go all the way in?" I ask. The moon seems brighter than I've ever seen it.

"Absolutely." Amina's tone becomes deadly serious. "Long ago, when people wanted a glimpse of what the future might hold, they could look into a body of water such as this, on a night when the moon was full, when the water is calm. I have learned that putting yourself into the pool during divination makes the visions clearer. When you enter the water, empty your mind and see what will be revealed."

"There you go again," Constance says. "You and your riddles."

The air is suddenly quite chilly, and a thought occurs to me. "Do I have to disrobe completely?"

Constance's gaze sweeps over me, sending a jolt down my spine.

"Nudity is optional," says Amina. "But from what I can tell, we all have the same bits and pieces. And even if you don't, there's nothing to be ashamed of, dearie. I've seen my fair share of tallywhackers as well."

Constance scrunches up her nose. "Make her stop."

I stifle a laugh. I feel almost euphoric in the light of the moon.

"I'll go first," says Amina.

Amina disrobes without a second thought and strides into the water. Constance slowly turns to me, covering her eyes with her hands.

"I was right, Amina," Constance says. "There is nothing in these woods scarier than you."

I can't hold it in this time. My laugh rings out like a bell in the stillness.

"Hush," Amina croaks.

She bobs in the water, eyes closed. The moonlight shines down on her. The water beads on her hair. The pond doesn't ripple as she gently sways in the water. All around us, fireflies gather on the branches on the trees, their little yellow lights flickering on and off. Constance and I watch in silence. Suddenly Amina's eyes snap open and she looks at Constance. "So that will be the way of it."

"The way of what?" Constance asks.

Amina wades to the shore and wraps herself in her shawl. "You next," she says to Constance.

Constance turns her back to me and slips her arms out of her tunic, pulling it up over her head and tossing it to the ground. I am unable to take my eyes off her. She removes her trousers and tosses them aside. As she pivots toward me, I have to make a concerted effort to keep my mouth from falling open. A blanket of freckles covers her chest and shoulders and trickles down on to her arms like a sprinkling of stardust. Her hair, a mass of red, luminescent curls, frames her face like a halo. She doesn't look away or try to cover herself. A wave of yearning threatens to consume me. With a smirk, she wades in until the water rests just below her shoulders.

"Close your eyes," Amina orders.

Constance glances at me once more before doing as she's told. My head is still swimming, but now from more than just the rue. Constance tilts her head up, like she's listening to something. She strikes at the water with her hand. Her eyes open slowly. They are rimmed with tears.

"What is it?" I ask.

Constance doesn't answer. She closes her eyes again. Her breaths come in quick bursts; a whimper escapes her. She opens her eyes and climbs out of the water, collapsing onto the ground. I rush to her side.

"I'm fine," she says. I don't believe her. She's trembling, holding herself around the waist. I drape her tunic around her shoulders, and she smiles, but there is sadness there.

"Your turn, Sophia," says Amina.

I'm not wearing a chemise under my tunic and vest, and I think about going in fully clothed. I move to the edge of the water but stop. I've fled the ball, traveled into the White Wood to find a witch, and am preparing to raise Cinderella from the dead. Compared to those things, being naked under a starry sky doesn't seem like such a monumental task.

I unbutton my vest and set it aside. Amina turns completely away, but Constance raises her eyes to the sky. I slip out of my tunic and trousers and wade into the pool. I brace for the chill of the water, but it's like stepping into a warm bath. Constance levels her eyes at me, and something shifts in her. Her mouth opens and then closes, like she wants to speak but can't. And while she looks me over, taking in every inch of me, her gaze lingers longest on my eyes.

"Try to clear your mind," says Amina. "If that's even possible." She gives me a knowing glance. My face flushes hot with embarrassment.

I close my eyes. In the water I am weightless. I tilt my head back and suddenly feel like I am falling. My eyes snap open. I scramble to keep my feet under me. The water sloshes about, lapping at my chest.

"Are you all right?" Constance asks from shore.

"Yes. I—I just—I'm okay." I close my eyes and again feel like I'm falling. The king's face appears in my mind's eye, sneering, a mask of hate and anger. His eyes are black and hollow, and Cinderella stands just behind him, speaking to me, her words muffled. The king reaches for me, taking hold of my shoulders and pulling me close to him. His face transforms into something horrid and rotting—something dead. A ball of white-hot light erupts between us, pulling at the center of my chest. I cry out.

"Sophia!"

Constance's voice cuts through my own screams. She is in the water with me, her arm around my waist, pulling me toward the shore. I cough and gasp, and fetid water spews from my mouth. I'd gone under and hadn't even realized it.

Amina stands very still, staring. Watching. I lean against Constance as we wade out of the pool. I fall to my knees in the dirt, and the cold air stings my damp skin. I'm completely drained, as if I haven't slept in days.

Constance rests her hand on my back. "What happened?"

"I don't know. I saw something," I struggle to explain, glancing back at the pool. "The king—I saw his face. There was a light..."

Constance looks nervously toward the pool as she pulls me up and drapes my clothes around me. The ground seems to move under my feet, and the sky tilts. She lifts my arm and puts it around her neck. "Come on. Let's get you dried off."

Once inside, she helps me into a chair and wraps me in a blanket as my head clears. Amina follows us in and locks the door, a troubled look on her face. Constance kneels beside me, tracing circles on the back of my hand.

"You frightened me," she says softly.

I'm struggling to process what just happened. I saw something out there in the water. It was like a dream, but I was wide awake. A vision? A hallucination?

"What did you see?" Amina asks as she moves to a chair by the fire.

I can't think clearly. Constance answers first.

"I was sitting, reading a book," she says.

"What book?" Amina asks.

"Cinderella's story," she says.

"That's it?" Amina asks.

"No," Constance says, her voice low. "There was a hallway. It was dark and filled with smoke. I saw someone lying there."

"Who?" I ask.

Constance shrugs. "I don't know." She turns to Amina. "What did you see, Granny? A vision of you and Manford skipping off through the White Wood, hand in hand?" Constance is shaken and seems to be trying desperately to take her mind off whatever it was she saw.

Amina turns to me. "I saw my own death."

My heart ticks up. "You're going to die?"

Amina shakes her head and stares down into her lap. "Death comes for us all, doesn't it?"

"Not to Manford," Constance says quietly.

"What did you see, Sophia?" Amina asks.

I take a deep breath and try to think straight. "I felt like I was falling. I saw the king and I saw Cinderella, and there was a pull at the center of my chest and a drop in the pit of my stomach at the same time. His face was smooth but blurred around the edges, and he was just standing there.

He—he smiled at me. And then he changed into a rotting corpse, and then a light engulfed me." I hold myself around the waist to keep from shaking. "It felt like—like dying."

The corners of Amina's mouth turn down and her lips part. I saw this look on her face the night Manford came here. It is terror.

"What does it mean?" Constance asks.

Amina stares into the fire, composing herself before speaking. "I cannot say. I do know that the meaning will make itself clear to you in time."

The images replay in my mind over and over. "I'm scared."

"You'd be a fool not to be," she says. She puffs away on her pipe, a wreath of earthy-smelling smoke encircling her head.

Anger and fear bubble up inside me. "I want to stop Manford. I don't want him to hurt anyone else, but how can I do that if he is the monster you say he is? Who am I to stop him?"

"There is always fear, always doubt," Amina says. "The only thing that matters is that you push forward. And seeing as how that's exactly what you're doing, I would ask you to recognize that you are worthy of this task."

"I don't know if I am," I say. "Constance has been fighting for what's right her entire life. And you, you're *the* fairy godmother."

"Do I look like a fairy to you?" Amina smiles a wicked little smile. She sets down her pipe, takes my hand, and presses it between her palms. "Do you know how many old witches are running around in these forests?"

I shrug. I don't know the answer to that question, but, I wonder, if there *are* other witches and fairy godmothers out there, what are they doing with their powers? Are they hiding? Are they at all concerned with what's happening in Mersailles?

"There's a woman in Lille who runs a shop called Helen's Wonderments. She claims to have all of your recipes, all your potions and powders. Says she's as close to a fairy godmother as most of us will ever get."

"Helen is a liar and a cheat and sells cow piss in fancy glass bottles to unwitting, often desperate people," Amina says disapprovingly. "The only reason she's allowed to continue is because Manford knows she's a fake."

I swallow hard. I drank a half vial of cow piss and gave Erin the rest. That is a secret I'll be taking to my grave.

"Aside from the pretenders, there are more than a few conjure women in this land. I'm not special. I've made mistakes and used my power to hurt people, to do unspeakable things. I am not a saint."

"But you are special," I say. "You have a gift."

"Please." She rolls her eyes. "You don't have to be special or have a gift or anything of the sort. Some people think they are chosen, destined to be great, and do you know what happens while they are basking in the possibility of their own greatness?"

"I don't know," I say.

She narrows her eyes at me. "What happens is that someone with no particular preordained purpose puts their head down, works hard, and makes something happen out of sheer will. That's where we fall."

"And you? You've had your doubts. I wasn't even sure we could convince you to help us."

"That's true. But things change. Even if I don't—well, never you mind that." Amina seems flustered.

We are all shaken by what we've seen: the vague notions of a future beyond our control despite our best efforts to change the present. Constance moves to the piles of blankets next to the fire and stares up at the ceiling.

"Try to get some rest," Amina says solemnly. She puts away her pipe and goes to her straw mat in the corner.

I curl up on a thick blanket next to Constance. We tuck in by the warmth of the crackling fire. Constance dozes off easily while I watch the fire die. I wait nervously for sleep to find me, fearing the king will be lurking in my head.

When I finally drift off, I fall into a dreamless, heavy sleep, but even then, I am thankful to see the sun rise the following morning.

27

The sense of foreboding that shadows me grows stronger as the day comes to begin our journey to Cinderella's final resting place. The larger cart is still parked at the entrance to the footpath, but because our horse was killed by the wolves, we won't be able to use it. We pack everything we need for the trip, including a live rabbit that Constance caught in a snare just behind the cottage. She puts it in a wooden cage and sets it in the back of a hand-drawn cart. I avoid looking at it. I know its fate.

Amina walks around the cart, carrying a stack of books. I glance at the book of spells. The cover is crisscrossed with fine lines that look almost exactly like the ones on my palm. It's not leather at all. It's human skin.

Fear stirs deep inside me, reminding me that Amina is

no fairy godmother. She studies me for a moment and then holds out the book. I don't want to touch it, but she puts it in my hands. A smell wafts into my face—the scent of death. "Amina, how did you make this?"

"I'd tell you, but then I'd have to kill you," Amina says.

Constance's head whips around, and I take a step back.

Amina grins. "Just having a little fun." She takes the book and tucks it in the cart. "That story is for another day."

Constance loads the rest of our things, and we set out on foot. Amina leads us down a narrow but passable pathway that is hidden behind the cabin and snakes around to the spot where we had to leave the big cart.

"I wish we'd known about this path when we showed up," Constance says.

"I bet you do," Amina says.

A rancid odor, like the one emanating from the spell book, hits the back of my throat as we step out onto the main trail. Our horse lies on its side. Buzzards and other wild animals have picked nearly all the flesh from its bones. I look away.

Amina leads us through the White Wood, her crow familiar swooping in every so often and then taking off again. We don't stop to make camp for longer than an hour or two. Just time enough to eat and rest. The ritual needs to be performed on the next moonless night, which gives us only three days to make a trip that normally would have taken at least four on horseback.

Somehow, when we emerge from the White Wood, we have time to spare, and I wonder if the sleepy confusion Constance and I felt when we'd first gone in was some kind of enchantment. Amina stays mum when I ask her, but her little twisted smile is telling.

Three guards patrol the open space between the towers as we crouch low to the ground, watching them. I wonder if Constance might need to bring out one of her bombs, but I don't have time to ask. Amina is walking straight ahead into the clearing.

"What is she doing?" Constance asks, her dagger drawn.

We squat in the dirt, staying quiet as Amina approaches the group of guards. One of them draws his sword, and I start to run after her when her hand juts out in front of her. The guard drops his weapon. It looks like she is speaking to them. She holds her hand near her face and gives a quick, hard puff. A cloud of a shimmering silver powder engulfs them, and they sink to the ground.

Constance turns to me. "What the hell just happened?"

Amina motions for us to join her.

"Did she—did she kill them?" Constance stammers.

I walk out into the clearing with Constance at my heel. The guards are slumped on top of each other, their eyes closed, breathing heavily.

"What did you do?" I ask as we approach Amina, who stands grinning at the foot of the lookout tower.

"A little sleeping dust to send them to dreamland." She holds up a small leather pouch.

"I've had a hard time sleeping," I say. "I could have used some of that."

One of the men shrieks and rolls over on his side, whimpering.

"It brings nightmares," says Amina. "The kind you never forget. The kind that haunt you even in your waking hours."

Constance and I exchange glances.

"Okay, never mind," I say.

"You should have turned them into mice," Constance says.

"Maybe next time," Amina says.

We've reentered the capital's borders, and passing between the watchtowers brings with it a new and terrible sense of dread. We avoid the main road, instead taking a wagon path that loops around the outskirts of the city. As we walk along the road, wagon wheels sound on the gravel right before a horse-drawn cart comes to a stop alongside us.

"Looking for a ride?" asks the driver.

"No," says Constance, sounding annoyed. She doesn't even look up.

I tilt my head, trying to get a look at the driver from under my cap. His face twists into a mask of confusion when our eyes meet.

"It's really dangerous for you to be walking around here, dressed like that." He takes a swig of something from a flask at his hip.

I can't tell if he's threatening us or not.

"Leave us alone," Constance says. She narrows her eyes at him and angles herself between us. I look for Amina, but she has disappeared.

The man holds his hands up. "Now just wait a minute. I'm not saying anything except it's dangerous. I can give you a ride. Just hop in."

Constance's hand moves to her dagger, and the man glances at her.

He scratches the top of his head. He is completely confused. "Do you even know how to use a sword? Women aren't permitted to—"

"The pointy end goes in your neck," Constance snaps.

I catch Amina at the back of the cart, dumping something into the little flask that the man had on his hip just a moment before. She disappears again.

"I hate to be the one to tell you this, but if the king's men see you with a sword, dressed like that, they will arrest you on sight." He smiles, but a look of concern has overtaken him. He reaches for his flask and I tense, worried he'll know it's missing, but it has reappeared on his belt. He takes a long drink. "I'm just trying to—trying to—help."

He is stumbling over his words as his body sways like a tree in a storm. He clutches at his neck, clearing his throat repeatedly, sweat dripping from his forehead. He leans over the edge of the cart as the pupils of his eyes expand into inky black voids. I yank Constance backward just as his eyes roll up into his head, and he falls headlong into the dirt. He groans, rolls over on his side, and sputters before beginning to snore. Amina appears at the side of the cart, holding the man's flask.

"Belladonna." She gives the flask a little shake and tosses it at the man, hitting him between the eyes. He doesn't move.

"Will he die?" I ask. "I don't think he meant us any harm."

"No. I used juice from the berries, not the root," Amina says. "Hear that snore? He'll have a headache, but he'll live. We can't take the chance of him telling someone he saw us. When he wakes up, he won't remember a thing."

"You're sure?" I ask, feeling a slight stab of pity for the man.

Amina looks thoughtful. "If I had a seeing stone, I could tell you for sure, since you seem so concerned." She sighs as she begins to transfer our belongings into the man's cart. "But I haven't come across one of those in ages."

"What's a seeing stone?" I ask.

"An alternative to the kind of divination we used at the pond," Amina says. "An enchanted stone, polished up like a mirror. It can be used to see all sorts of things—the future, the present—but they are exceedingly rare."

"I heard a tale when I was little about a queen in another kingdom who had a seeing stone," says Constance. "A magic mirror, but I think it drove her mad. She became obsessed with her reflection and the visions she saw in it."

"I know that story well," says Amina. "And much like our own tale, it's not exactly what it seems. The reflective power of the glass is a seductive thing. It can show you things that need interpretation, or it can reveal the truth as it is. It can be maddening trying to decipher what you see, but it's important to understand that it's only a reflection. The things shown within it are not always set in stone."

"The story of that queen says she tried to kill her own child. She said the mirror told her to," Constance says.

"But the mirror would not have told her to do so if it weren't already in her heart," Amina says. "It was a shameful turn of events. How did you learn of it?"

"The story about the magic mirror?" Constance asks.

"Yes," Amina says. "It's a very old story."

"I have it," Constance says. She goes to her bag and pulls out the book she'd been lugging around this entire time. The pages are yellowed around the edges, and some of them are detached from the spine and just stuck between the others. Constance hands the book to Amina, and she flips through the pages as we climb into the cart, Constance at the reins.

"Where in the world did you get this?" Amina asks. I've seen nothing that has shaken her to her core quite like this. She's trembling as she looks through it.

"It's been in my family forever," says Constance. "Handed down by Gabrielle herself."

I suddenly feel like I'm looking at a relic, a magical object not unlike the enchanted slippers or even the remains of Cinderella herself.

"It's a collection of peculiar stories," says Constance. "Put together by two sisters who spent the entirety of their lives traveling the world in search of strange tales. The story of the queen with the magic mirror is there, so vain she could not suffer anyone to be prettier than she. 'The White Snake,' 'The Two Brothers'—they're all here in these pages. Of course Cinderella's story is there, too." She points to a piece of parchment stuck between the pages at the back. Amina turns to the story.

I haven't read the story since before the ball, but as I peer down at the book, something catches my eye.

"The drawings," I say. "They're so different from the palace-approved version of the story."

"Indeed," says Amina. She studies the images and then glances up as the cart bounces on the uneven dirt road. She inhales sharply, and I follow her gaze. The palace comes into view over a sloping hill. As much as I hate looking back at Lille, seeing the castle ahead is worse. Trepidation looms over me as we ride closer.

Amina tucks the book into the bed of the cart as Constance brings us to a stop near where I emerged from the woods on the night I escaped from the ball. Constance unhitches the horse, and we push the cart into the brush on the side of the road where no one will see it. We tie the horse to a tree a little farther in.

"We'll cut through this way," says Constance, ducking into the tree line.

Amina follows her in, carrying her supplies, but I hang back for a moment. The sun nestles into the horizon, casting an orange-yellow glow through the sky. That familiar movement of the setting sun is the only predictable thing that still holds any sense of wonder for me. Everything else in my life that was meant to be predictable has irrevocably changed. One decision and a turn of miraculous events have set my life on a new and uncertain path.

Out the corner of my eye, I see Amina standing so still she might have been mistaken for a shadow by a passerby. She doesn't speak, doesn't move. She simply watches intently as I honor the feeling inside myself that told me to wait, to watch the sunset, and to realize that something is shifting.

We navigate the woods by the dying light; long

shadows cast in the confines of the forest make ghosts of the trees, and we come upon the tomb, shrouded in complete darkness. Constance guides us here with barely an upward glance, which makes me wonder how many times she has made this perilous trek.

The grand marble structure looms large in the dark. My life had been forever changed the last time I was here, and I hope that the same will be true of this night. I try to calm the racing of my heart as we slip inside.

Amina walks to the rear of the tomb, to the little alcove where the glass slippers are housed. "It's been so long," she says in a whisper.

The glow from the enchanted shoes dances across the walls of the tomb like sunlight reflecting off the surface of a pond. The entire enclosure is bathed in a soft blue-white light, much brighter than when I'd been here the first time.

Amina takes the sachets from her bag, along with several small jars, and hands them to me. Red ochre, burned myrrh, wormwood juice, and powdered evergreen leaves. I spoon them out in the proper proportions and mix them together in a glass jar. Constance fumbles with a piece of parchment that has been folded into a makeshift envelope where a single flax leaf is stored. I gently take the paper from her hands.

"I'm sorry," she says. "I'm shaken up all of a sudden."

I put my hand on her arm. "It's going to be okay."

Amina walks up to the marble coffin, and we gather around her.

"We'll need to push the lid back," says Amina, looking at me questioningly.

I place my hands on the lid. Constance sets her still-trembling hands beside mine, and the three of us push. It doesn't budge.

"Again," Amina says.

"It's not going to work," says Constance. "It's too heavy."

"We have to open it," says Amina, and a sense of urgency fills her voice. A little stab of panic. We are forbidden to be here. I don't know if the king has his guards anywhere close by, but if they find us here, we're dead.

"We have to lever it," I say. I run outside to search for a large, sturdy branch. I find one thicker around than my arm and bring it back inside. "We'll need to break a piece of the marble off and wedge this inside, and then we can slide it open."

Constance hurries out and returns with a stone the size of a small melon. She holds it up and brings it down hard at the corner of the lid. It breaks off, sending a shower of chipped pieces to the floor. I put the stick in the jagged hole, and we all lean on it. Groaning, the lid slides completely away from Cinderella's head, so it sits at an angle across the coffin. In the dim light emanating from the glass slippers, particles of dust float all around us, and the smell of lavender and jasmine permeates the air.

Constance leans in to look at what remains, gasping sharply. I peer in, afraid of what I might see. A mass of ringlets, silver to the point of shimmering, peek out from beneath a silken shroud, which has decayed around the edges. The outline of a body lies underneath. This is all that is left of the fabled princess.

"Remove the burial shroud," says Amina, glancing at Constance.

Constance hesitates, her hands trembling at the edge of the open coffin. She slowly reaches in and pulls the cloth away. I clasp my hand over my mouth. Amina's eyes grow wide, and her mouth opens into a little O.

Constance shakes her head. "This can't be right. What is this?"

28

Cinderella was thirty-eight when she died, and she's been in this coffin for almost two hundred years. She should be bones and dust, but Cinderella lies, hands crossed over her chest, as if she is sleeping. Decay hasn't touched her, but something else has.

Her hair is so white it is nearly transparent. Her face is crisscrossed with a road map of lines, and her eyelids droop down in paper-thin folds. Her hands are withered, the nails yellowed and cracked, and every inch of her skin is a pallid gray color. Her appearance is almost identical to Liv's the morning the palace guards hauled her up out of the ditch.

"It's not right," Constance says, shaking her head. "Why does she look like this? This isn't what a body should look like at all."

I cover Constance's hand with mine. I don't know what to say.

Amina reaches into the folds of her cloak and takes out a bundle of mugwort held together with twine. She lights the end, and a thick, earthy-smelling smoke clouds the confines of the tomb. She then tucks her sachets all around Cinderella's body. "Sophia, prepare the ink."

Giving Constance's hand one last squeeze, I add a vial of rainwater to the jar where I'd mixed the powders. After stirring the contents, I hand it to Amina, along with the flax leaf. Constance grips the side of the coffin. She doesn't look away from Cinderella. Amina carefully writes on the leaf with a quill and the freshly prepared ink.

Arise and speak

Reaching into the coffin, Amina gently pulls Cinderella's mouth open, placing the leaf inside. Turning and kneeling at the foot of the sarcophagus, she motions for us to join her. I take Constance by the arm and guide her away. She seems to be in some kind of trance.

"Come," says Amina. "Sit down here. It will be all right." It is the most comforting thing she's ever said to Constance in my presence, and still it is a bit gruff. We kneel at Amina's side.

She takes out the grimoire and, using a pair of silver shears, clips the ribbons that hold the pages together near the end of the book. The book falls open along a crack in the wax seal. She runs her fingers through the pages and stops when she comes to what she is looking for.

Scrawled across the two open pages are ingredients, the phases of the moon, and the instructions for the spell. There are sketches of a freshly opened grave, a flower, its petals pressed flat by the pages, crumbling and rotted. At the bottom of the page there are words written in red ink.

The conjurer is bound to the raised corpse until death.

Amina's hands tremble at the edge of the page. This magic scares her.

In the little wooden cage, the rabbit runs around in circles. Amina reaches in and takes it by the scruff of its neck. In her opposite hand is a small knife. Its blade glints in the light of the glass slippers.

"I can't watch," I say. All I can think of is the seamstress's head rolling into the dirt.

Amina sighs. "Then don't."

I close my eyes and hear Constance groan. When I open them again, Amina holds the small, still-pulsing heart in the palm of her hand.

"Quickly, each of us must speak her name once. Clearly and with the intent that she should rejoin the living." Amina pauses and closes her eyes. "Cinderella."

A shock of energy pulses through me, and I look around

wildly, my heart racing. The hair on my arms and at the back of my neck stands straight up.

"Say her name," Amina says.

"Cinderella," I say. Another pulse of energy and a chorus of whispers, like people are having a discussion somewhere nearby.

The air grows heavy, and a low, resonant hum rises from the ground. My skin pricks up as I look at Constance. Her eyes are closed. She takes a deep breath.

"Cinderella."

A muffled noise comes from inside the coffin. My heart leaps into a furious rhythm, as does the one that Amina holds in her hand. I shut my eyes tight, afraid to look. There is a noise like the rustling of leaves and then a long, slow exhale.

"Please," says an unfamiliar voice. "Please help me."

I open my eyes, looking not ahead but straight down at the floor, my heart still thudding. Constance stands up, and so does Amina. I rise slowly and level my gaze with the coffin, where a figure is sitting upright. In the flickering light, her eyelids flutter open, revealing the milky-white orbs beneath.

"Who's there?" Cinderella asks, her voice hoarse and crackling like the sound of burning paper.

Constance stands in an unblinking haze at the side of the coffin. Amina holds the rabbit's heart. It withers and crumples into a ball of dust before my eyes.

"I'm not meant to be here," Cinderella whispers.

"I have summoned you," says Amina. "I would not have done so if it weren't absolutely necessary."

Cinderella's snow-white hair hangs down her back, and she looks from me to Amina and then to Constance. A shower of dust shakes free from her as she cocks her head to the side. "Gabrielle?"

A literal ghost is speaking to us, and it takes everything I have not to give in to the little voice in my head that is screaming at me to run.

"No," Constance says, stepping close to the coffin. "Gabrielle is gone. They . . . they're all gone."

"Who are you?" Cinderella asks, studying Constance carefully.

"My name is Constance. It's been generations since Gabrielle was alive. She was my grandmother many times over."

"You—you look like her." Cinderella's breath rattles out of her. "My Gabrielle."

A knot forms in my throat. Gabrielle's name from Cinderella's lips sounds as if nothing but love remains in her memory, faded as it must be.

"Something is—wrong. Very, very wrong," Cinderella says.

Constance ventures closer. "I need to ask you something. I need to know what you were trying to tell Gabrielle the night you went to see her."

"The night I went . . . to . . . see . . ." Cinderella gazes off. "I can't . . . remember. Everything is faded."

"Give her a moment," says Amina.

"And you—I know you." Cinderella stares at Amina. "I know you."

"Yes," Amina says, shaking her head as if she doesn't want to be reminded. "I helped you get to the ball all those years ago."

"The ball?" Cinderella asks. "Oh—I—I remember that. Yes. The ball."

"Please," Constance says. "Try to remember. You went to see Gabrielle, but they took you away before she even got to speak with you. Were you trying to tell her something about the king? She heard you say he was cursed. What did you mean?" Constance reaches into the coffin and gently takes hold of Cinderella's hand. I am, for the hundredth time, in awe of her bravery.

"We don't have much time. How do we stop him?" Constance presses.

"Stop—him?" Cinderella shifts in her coffin. "Stop him . . . stop him . . . STOP HIM!" She screams so loud the entire tomb reverberates, and recognition flashes in her eyes. She is suddenly alert, focused, and afraid. She reaches up and takes Constance's face in her hands. "Look at me. He did this to me."

I step closer to the coffin. "What did he do?"

Cinderella holds Constance tightly.

"He ... takes," Cinderella stammers. "He takes—he was always taking. And the sadness—I was so alone."

Constance rests her hands on Cinderella's outstretched arms. "What do you mean? What kind of magic does this?"

"What does he take?" I ask.

"I don't know," says Cinderella. "I don't remember. There was only him, and the light, and then there was nothing."

The light. My vision. They are connected.

"I saw something in a vision," I say to Cinderella. "I saw the king, and I had a feeling in my chest like I was being pulled into a void."

"I can't remember." Cinderella sighs and slumps against the side of the coffin. We are running out of time.

"Is there anything else you can tell us?" Constance asks.

Cinderella tips her head back, closing her eyes.

My thoughts go in circles. What is Manford doing to these girls? What kind of dark magic does he wield? I have to go back to the palace. "I'm going to find a way to end him. I promise you."

"She's fading," says Amina. "She doesn't have much time." She quickly takes out a long piece of string that has two knots in it. She holds her shears up and clips it in half.

Cinderella begins to sink back into her coffin, and Constance struggles to hold her upright.

"What was that for?" Constance asks. "What did you do?"

"She doesn't belong here," Amina says quietly. "We have to let her rest, and I will not be bound to a living corpse for the rest of my days. I cut the connection between us. You have to let her go."

Constance nods, lowering her eyes. "We'll stop him. I swear it." She sounds determined enough to march right up to the king and try to kill him herself.

"Don't let him hurt anyone else," Cinderella says, her voice nothing more than a whisper. "I took the little book—the journal—to Gabrielle. I—I couldn't give it to her before—before they took me away. Find it." She closes her eyes, and Constance lays her down inside the coffin.

Cinderella's chest rises and falls a final time before she stills like the marble statue. Constance places the burial shroud over her and arranges her hands across her chest. We stand in complete silence for a long time. I wait for one of them to move or speak.

"Help me put the lid back," Constance says.

After heaving the lid into place, we go out of the tomb and Constance and Amina sit on the step. I pace in the overgrown grass.

"What do we do now?" Constance asks. "We still don't know how to stop him."

"No, but we know Cinderella was trying to give Gabrielle some kind of journal," I say. "Whatever was inside was important to Cinderella. And the light—what light was Cinderella talking about?"

"She said it was only him and her and the light," Constance says. "And then nothing. He was there when she died, and she said he did that to her."

I nod. I still don't know where this leaves us, and I sit down at Constance's feet.

"You need to stay hidden," says Constance. "The king is looking for you, and I think he may have some idea of where you are. You said his guards came to your home, and I don't think it's a coincidence that he just showed up in the White Wood." She shoots Amina an angry look. "He's tracking us."

"For all his cruelty, he is a highly intelligent man," Amina says. "I think we sometimes make the mistake of thinking monsters are abhorrent aberrations, lurking in the darkest recesses, when the truth is far more disturbing. The most monstrous of men are those who sit in plain sight, daring you to challenge them. He's calculating and manipulative, and believe me when I say he will not stop until he finds you."

Her ominous tone sends a shiver straight up my back. "Where will we go?"

"We should go back to Cinderella's childhood home," says Constance. "Just for the time being. Until we can make a better plan."

"That place is still standing?" Amina asks.

I nod, but I don't like the idea. "We just run and hide then?"

"I think we need to make a solid plan," Constance says. "Let's go somewhere safe and then sit down and figure all this out."

"We have time to plan, but do they? The women of Lille, I mean," I say. I stare in the direction of the palace. "How many girls will he hurt before we have a chance to stop him? How many women are being hurt right now in Mersailles because of the rules he made?" I look back. "And what about the young boys who will never have a chance to be decent people because they are taught from the cradle to be despicable? And we're going to hide? I want him dead. Right now." I say those words and wonder if it's too much, if I've gone too far. No. That is exactly what it will take to stop him. Nothing short of death will do.

"We need a plan, Sophia," Amina says. "We cannot make a single misstep."

The weight of all we have learned presses down on me. But isn't this what I asked for? To find a way to make a difference?

"My entire family has been sacrificed to this notion of stopping the king," says Constance. "We've hidden, lived in the dark, made ghosts of ourselves. Waiting, training, hoping that one day the time would come for us to end him, and I had lost any real hope that a change could be made.

But now we have a real chance." She looks up at me. "I'm with you. To the bitter end, if that's what it takes."

"A life of running, hiding, and being afraid every single day is no life at all," I say. I look Constance in the eyes. "We'll put the pieces together, and then we'll destroy him."

29

We gather our cart and horse and travel the long road around the outskirts of Lille. We take the forked road to the run-down house where Constance and I took cover a few short weeks ago. The path is still overgrown and impossible to navigate with the cart, so we leave it in the ditch, covered in branches.

Amina slows as we approach the house. I watch her eyes move over the façade, pausing on the broken front door and the partially collapsed roof.

"It's been a very long time since I've been here," Amina says, her tone soft. She turns and looks over the poppies that still color the landscape orange. "I see a little of my magic still lingers here."

"Your magic?" I ask. "It makes the flowers bloom like this, even in the winter?"

"Not purposely, but so much magic was worked here, on these very grounds, I'd think the land cannot help but be changed by it."

"We won't be here long," I say. "A few days, a week at the most. Just until we've figured out what to do next."

We mount the front steps and stand outside the door. Amina draws a long, deep breath and lets it hiss out from between her pursed lips. We walk into the parlor off the main hallway, and Amina sets to work lighting a fire as I help Constance bring in our supplies from the cart. I put the horse in the small stable near the rear courtyard, glancing at the grave under the giant tree.

Once we're finished, Constance and I join Amina in the parlor. She's making herself a little nest of blankets by the fire.

"Getting comfy?" Constance asks, shooting Amina a disapproving look.

"Quite," Amina says curtly.

"Can't you bibbidi-bobbidi-boo the place back together?" I ask as a gust of wind whips through the room, rattling the bones of the house.

Constance laughs, and even Amina cracks a small smile. "It doesn't work that way." She takes out her pipe and puffs away. "I'm going to take a walk. Clear my head."

"Don't you want to get started on a plan now?" I ask.

"This very night?" Amina asks. "I admire your tenacity,

my dear, but we can't rush into this. We'll start first thing in the morning."

Amina gets up and shuffles out of the room. I feel like we're not doing enough, like we're not moving fast enough. I turn to Constance to complain, and she's smiling.

"She'll come back," she says. "I wouldn't be sad if she didn't, but I'm sure she will."

"I know, but I feel like we're not doing enough."

"We just raised a corpse from the dead, Sophia."

"Still," I say.

Constance pushes the kettle over the fire, and we sit down. I am suddenly aware that she and I are alone together for the first time since before we found Amina in the White Wood.

Constance angles her body toward me, winding a lock of hair around her finger. "Do you think about your friend Erin often?"

The question catches me off guard, though I know it's something we have to talk about eventually. I've been avoiding it because I don't know what to say. I decide to be completely honest. "I do. I think about her all the time."

Constance looks down as if that isn't the answer she wants.

"I never thought I could feel the way I feel about Erin toward anyone else," I say. "But when I met you, that changed."

Constance studies my face, her brow furrowed. "But you still care for her."

"I think I'll always care about her. I want her to be safe. I want her to be okay, even if she and I can't be together." It hurts to say that out loud. For so long, there was only Erin. But with Constance, I see another path, one where I'm not constantly fighting for her affection or struggling to convince her that it's okay for her to care for me.

When the firelight dances across Constance's face, all I want is to tell her how I adore her, how she makes me feel like I don't have to be afraid, but Erin is always there at the back of my mind.

"I would never try to come between you and her," Constance says. "I just want you to know that I care for you, and it doesn't matter what anyone else says or thinks."

I inch closer to her, leaning toward her. "With Erin, it's mostly me chasing after her, trying to force her to understand that . . ." I trail off. It's not fair to say anything bad about Erin. I know what living in Lille has done to her, and it's not her fault.

"Understand what?" Constance asks, her tone gentle.

"To understand that I'm worth it? That *she* is worth it? I don't know." I struggle to find the right words. "For a time, I'd convinced myself that we could make things work. If we could just hold on, if we were willing to fight for it."

"And did the two of you fight for it?" Constance looks down.

"She didn't want to." The words stick in my throat. They make me angry and sad and hurt all at the same time. "She wanted us to follow the law, to obey our parents. And I think, more than anything, she believed that what we felt for each other was wrong." I pause, choosing my words carefully. "I realize now that she wasn't ready to risk everything to be with me and that I shouldn't have pushed so hard."

"You cared for her, so you pushed. I would have done the same thing for you." She glances up at me, her deep-brown eyes soft, questioning.

My heart races. I don't know what to say or do. All I know is that I want to be close to her. I lean in and she reaches up, running her fingers down the side of my neck, tracing my collarbone. My stomach twists into a knot. Before I have a chance to overthink it, I press my lips to hers. Her hands move to my neck and face. A surge of warmth rushes over me as she presses herself against me. There is an urgency in her kiss, like she's trying to prove to me how much she cares, and I yield to her, unconditionally.

The fire in me that has smoldered for her bursts to life in a way I never knew was possible. I'm lost in the tide of her breathing, the sweet smell of her skin, the push and pull of our bodies against each other. Each touch sends a shiver straight through me. In this moment, nothing else matters, only the surrender to the feelings we share.

❧

In the late hours of the evening, Amina returns from her walk.

"Where did you run off to?" Constance asks, straightening out her tunic and working her hair into a curly bun on top of her head.

Amina sits down in the chair and prepares her pipe. "I took a stroll. And I have something interesting to share."

"Something about the king?" I ask.

"In a way, yes. It seems we won't have to wait too long to have our chance at a confrontation with him." Amina reaches into her cloak, pulls out a folded piece of paper, and hands it to me. I show it to Constance.

"He's plastered these flyers all over town. Nailed one to every door," says Amina. "Every girl in the kingdom will be required to attend a cotillion on the midwinter solstice."

"Your walk took you farther than you let on," says Constance, eyeing Amina suspiciously.

"He's looking for me," I say. "He doesn't want to wait until the next ball. He thinks this will draw me out."

"And he's right," says Amina, puffing away and gazing off. "We have less time to prepare now, but this is our chance." Her tone is strained, almost sad. I wonder if she's changed her mind about wanting to help us.

"Then we should get to it," I say, glancing at Constance, who only nods. "I think we should start by trying to find the little book Cinderella spoke of."

Constance nods. "She said it was a journal, and if she

risked her life to try and give it to Gabrielle, then it must be important."

"And if it still exists, if she took it back to the castle, there's no telling what became of it," Amina says. "But we're talking about an object that existed two hundred years ago. It could be dust for all we know."

I shake my head. "We have to try. The cotillion is our way in."

"And what will you do then?" Amina asks. There's a solemn tone to her voice again. I worry there is something she's not telling us.

Constance straightens up. "We'll kill him. That's what we'll do."

Amina sits back, sighing heavily, but says nothing.

30

We spend each night leading up to the cotillion in the parlor over a pot of stew and a kettle of strong black tea, reviewing every aspect of what we know so far about the king, about the palace. We make plans, scratching out the details on parchment, but each one of these plans turns to kindling in the bottom of the fireplace when a flaw is noticed. There will be little room for error, and nothing we come up with seems good enough.

Amina has taken several more trips into town and heard a rumor that the king has increased security at the border because of an uptick in disruptive incidents. Constance thought they may have been staged by the other escapees she'd spoken of, but she had little hope that enough of them remained to pull off an uprising. Amina thought they might be people who were still trapped under the king's thumb, resisting because of my escape. I can't imagine how angry that must have made him.

In addition to making the cotillion mandatory, King Manford has made it clear that anyone who willfully disobeys his orders will be considered a forfeit, their property seized and their family members executed. They are the words of a desperate man.

Our planning comes to a grinding halt when we try to figure out what will happen once we're inside the palace.

"We've come to the most important part and still nothing," I say one evening as we sit racking our brains. We're running out of time.

"We know we can get in," says Constance. "But once he realizes who you are, that you're the one who escaped, you'll be a target."

The visions I had in the pond haven't stopped since we came to our new residence. I still dream almost every night of the king and the light. "I need to find Cinderella's journal. That is the key. I just know it."

Amina rifles through her belongings and pulls out a book I recognize immediately. It's the palace-approved version of the Cinderella story.

"I don't even want to look at that right now," I say.

She flips through the pages and then stops abruptly, looking up. "Constance, I'd like to have another look at that book of fairy tales, the one you said was passed down to you."

Constance rolls her eyes and goes to get the book, handing it to Amina.

"Let's start at the beginning, shall we?" Amina asks.

"We don't have time for this," I say.

Amina ignores my protests and opens Constance's book, running her hand over the first page, a scene of Cinderella as a toddler, standing on the front step of her house and holding her father's hand. Amina glances back and forth between the two versions of Cinderella's tale.

"Exactly like the palace-approved version," I say.

Amina shakes her head. "Look again."

I lean in. She's right. The larger drawing is the same, but in the backdrop there is something on the ground, a heap that almost bleeds into the intricate rendering of the foliage that lines the pathway to the house.

A shiver runs up my back.

"Didn't you say Cinderella's mother was executed in the driveway?" I ask Constance.

She only nods. The little heap of ink looks like a person slumped on the ground.

I take the book from Amina and lay it on the floor, setting the palace-approved version right next to it. "The next drawing should be one of an older Cinderella bowing in front of her new stepmother."

It is, but in Constance's version, Lady Davis is leaning forward, her hand extended, her face gentle, her eyes full of sorrow, and Cinderella isn't bowing as much as she is kneeling, like she's just collapsed, her fingers rigid against the floor.

"Her father's imprisonment and execution," Constance says. She glances up at me. "What is going on here?"

"I think this book may be closer to the truth than anything I've ever seen," says Amina. "Whoever recorded it this way, with the drawings telling the real story, would have put themselves at great risk by doing so."

We flip through, and I spot another difference. "In the palace version, it says that after Cinderella's wedding, Gabrielle's and her younger sister Isla's eyes were pecked out while their mother was forced to watch, and then they were sent into the woods to remain in exile until they died. In Constance's book, they are exiled without all the gory details."

"They were left out there to rot, but they didn't," Constance says. "They got away."

I read over the words. "The color of the dress is different in your version, Constance. Also, it says that the stepsisters simply tried fitting the glass shoe, but in the palace text it says they cut off their own toes to try to make it fit." I glance up at Constance. "People hate them. I saw a little girl at the bicentennial celebration break down in tears at the thought of being like them."

Constance draws her mouth into a hard line. "He made

them monsters to keep the attention off him. He is the real monster."

"And now look," I say. "All these years later, people take it as fact. It's as if repeating the lie over and over makes it true."

I reach down and turn to the last image. It shows Cinderella and Prince Charming sharing a passionate kiss against the backdrop of the royal palace.

"The last drawing in the palace-approved story is of Cinderella sitting on her throne beside her prince," I say. "His throne is golden with rubies, and hers is plain. And his throne sits on a platform nearly two heads above Cinderella."

We study the last picture in Constance's book. Cinderella's curly hair is worn in a plait that hangs down her back. She stands face-to-face with Charming, his arms wrapped around her.

I run my hand over the picture. "The prince's arms, one around her waist, one around the back of her neck." Cinderella's arms hang at her sides, her fingers curled into fists. "This is supposed to be the beginning of their happily ever after. And she doesn't embrace him? Her hands are balled up." I hear Amina's breaths coming in quick succession as she stares down at Constance's book. My fingers tremble at the edge of the page.

Constance leans in. "They're kissing."

"No," I say. "They're not."

I snatch up the book and stand with it in the middle of the room. A bright light, like a small, luminous cloud, hangs around their heads in the space where their faces come together. Their lips parted but not touching. The cloud of light looks as if it is passing between them. Cinderella's eyes are open and blank, staring straight ahead. I push the book away from me, fearing that the king will come out of the picture right before my eyes. My vision from the pool and this picture are almost identical. The king, the ball of light. "This is what I saw in my vision."

Constance runs her hands over her face and lets her arms fall heavily to her sides. "You're awfully quiet," she says to Amina.

"Am I?" Amina asks, rolling her eyes.

"You must know more . . . It is your fault Cinderella fell head over feet for Manford in his guise as Prince Charming." Constance's tone is sharp, angry. "What really happened to Cinderella?"

Amina shakes her head. "There are a great many things I should have done differently."

Constance is fuming. "You were hiding out there so you didn't have to face what you've done. You spent years following Manford around, helping him ruin people's lives. You've had all this time, time that isn't granted to anyone else, and what do you do? You hide."

"My life's purpose was unclear until I met you, my

sweet," says Amina, her tone mocking. "Now I know I'm meant to follow you around, ruining your life, maybe for all time. How does that sound?"

Constance's hand moves to her dagger.

"Try it," says Amina. "See what happens."

"Just stop," I say. I move between them. "Both of you. The cotillion is days away, and we are no closer to a plan." I stare at the picture again. "I'm the one who's sparked those little rebellions we've heard about. I'm the one he's been hunting. And I'm going to have to let him get close to me, so I can put a dagger in his neck."

Amina shifts in her seat, and Constance crosses her arms hard over her chest.

"The neck is a small target," says Constance. "You should aim for something bigger, the chest or belly, first."

Amina slowly turns her head to stare at Constance.

"That's—helpful," I say.

Amina gets up and walks out of the room.

Constance turns back to me. "I say we practice our knife skills on her."

She is only half joking.

&

Constance makes a target out of an outfit she has in her burlap bag: a pair of trousers and a tunic, the sleeves and legs sewn closed and stuffed with dead grass and leaves.

The head is a gourd, half the size of a normal human head, and Constance has painted on a set of eyes and a mouth, turned down into a frown. It's horrifying.

She props it against one of the trees that line the drive and gestures to it.

"Stab it."

I glance at the blade in my hand. "Just anywhere or . . ."

Constance laughs. "Let me show you."

She steps behind me and slides her right hand down my arm. I know I'm supposed to be focusing on training, but I can already tell it's going to be difficult with her so close to me.

"There are three things you have to do when you're using a blade," she says. "You have to be able to hold on to the dagger; you have to be able to strike whatever, or in this case whoever, the target is; and you have to have all your fingers when you're done."

"Sounds straightforward enough."

She nods. She'd sharpened and polished her dagger, and as I stand with it in my outstretched hand, I can't help but feel a little more confident.

Constance puts her hand over mine. "Holding it this way, point up, is good for thrusting. Quick, sharp movements." She pushes my hand forward. "It doesn't take much force to puncture the skin."

I swallow hard. She is very good at this, and I wonder how many times she's had to do it. She puts her opposite hand on the small of my back and leans close to my ear. I think she'll speak some other bit of useful information, but instead she lets her lips brush against the side of my neck. I drop the dagger.

Constance's laugh is like bells. I could listen to it all day. She scoops up the dagger and puts it back in my hand. "That was my fault."

Constance shows me how to angle my arm to make the cut. I copy her movements. I stab the stuffed target.

"Good," she says. "Now flip the blade so the tip is pointing down."

I do as she says.

"This is a kill stroke," she says, plunging her dagger into the rind of the gourd. It splits in half and falls off the top of the target's shoulders. "That probably won't actually happen if you try to stab him in the head, but here's hoping, right?"

"Right," I say, a little shaken. She presses the dagger's handle into my palm. I raise up the blade and bring it down, right into the target's chest.

"Good," Constance says, smiling. "I'm not as good a teacher as my mother was, but we'll manage." She looks at the ground.

"I think you're a great teacher," I say. "Look." I stab the target a few times, and Constance laughs. "What else did she teach you?"

She hesitates a moment.

"We don't have to talk about it," I say, resting my hand on her arm.

She looks at me. "My mother was the fiercest woman I've ever known. She taught me everything I know. Her mother before her was a fighter, too. Once, when I was eleven, we moved as far north as we'd ever been. A small regiment of the king's men tracked us through the mountains, snuck up on us in the night. One of them put a knife to my throat."

The thought of anyone hurting her makes me so angry I can barely contain myself.

"My mother ran him straight through, and his knife tore open my arm as he fell away from me." She runs her hand over the scar on her arm. "She killed two more of them and escaped with me on one of their horses."

"Your mother was a hero."

"I don't think she would have liked that title at all, but she really was." Constance's eyes mist over. "My family may have been forced to leave Lille, but they never forgot." Her voice catches in her throat. "I only wish there were someone left to witness this moment."

"You will witness it," I say. "You and I together. We'll make them proud or die trying."

There is a pause. I've said out loud the thing that's always at the back of our minds. No matter how much we laugh or joke or try to find the good in our situation, there's a very real possibility that we won't make it out of this alive.

Constance looks at me. "Have I told you how amazing you are?"

"Not today," I tease.

We practice with the dagger, restuffing and redressing the target when we've torn it to shreds, and steal moments alone, which feel fleeting. I long for her, even when I'm right by her side. I feel a pull to touch her, to speak to her, to know her every thought, but still, I can't get out from under this heavy feeling.

I must kill the king.

It's the only way to make this work, and I ask myself if I'm up to it. Can I take his life? Am I capable of that? I think of what is at stake and all that has already been lost, and the answers are clear.

I have to put him in the ground. That is our only hope.

31

Three nights before the cotillion, I dream of Liv and Erin, of Luke and Constance, and of the seamstress. I see Constance's face shining like the sun, and Liv and Luke standing far off under a juniper tree. Liv smiles as Constance and I dance happily in the poppy field just past the orchard. The flowers in vibrant reds and pale yellows surround us as I feel the warmth of Constance's skin and catch a whiff of her lemon verbena perfume. We spin around and around, our hands locked together.

And then Erin appears. Her clothes are tattered, her face bruised. She cries silent tears as she watches me with Constance. She yells out to me, and I run toward her. Constance calls my name as I stand between them. I'm being pulled in both directions, like I'm being torn apart. Then a man appears at Erin's side. Édouard. He grabs her by the wrist and drags her away as she screams my name. The seamstress steps forward, a gaping wound encircling her neck. She reaches out for me, and I shrink back.

"I'm sorry!" I scream. "I'm so sorry!"

A stifling darkness falls around me, and everyone is gone. In the darkness, someone laughs. A deep, throaty sound that begins low and distant, then swells until it's deafening. I cover my ears but can't block it out.

I wake in the small hours of the morning; my bed-clothes cling to my sweat-drenched back, and my hair sticks to my damp forehead. I sob harder than I have in weeks. Constance's hand finds mine under the blankets.

"What is it?" she asks, brushing my hair away from my face.

I don't want to hurt her, but there's something I must do. "I need to see Erin to make sure she's okay."

Constance gives me a pained smile. "She's not okay, Sophia. You know that."

"Yes, but I need to go," I whisper. "If we can't stop the king, I may never see her again. I need to do this. Please understand."

Constance hangs her head. "It'll be dangerous, but I can see that you've already made up your mind."

"When I saw her in the market before we left Lille, she was already being hurt. I can't imagine what these past weeks have been like for her."

"The king's looking for you. You can't just waltz into town and knock on her door."

"I know but I have to go." I take her hand, but she pulls away from me.

"Why?" Constance asks, her face hardening. "Why do you have to go? What has she ever done besides hurt you?"

"It's not that simple," I say. "You don't understand how things are for us. The king pushes us into these roles that we don't want."

"You think I don't understand what it's like? I don't need to be there to know. I was born in exile, lived my whole life that way. My family died out there while everyone back here was told they were monsters. All I have left of them are their letters and their stories and my memories. That's the only place they exist for me anymore." Tears spill over.

"And do you know who's responsible for that?" I ask, gripping her hands and pressing them to my lips. "It's not you or me or Lille. It's Manford. He's the reason Erin is in the situation she's in, and I left her there." My voice cracks as the tears come in an unstoppable cascade.

Constance takes my face in her hands. "I'm sorry. I didn't want to upset you. I trust you, and even though I don't want you to go, I can't hold you hostage." She looks like she might be considering it.

I glance at Amina, who snores loudly on her pile of blankets. "Do you think she will understand?"

"No. She won't. But it's not her decision. Please promise me you'll be cautious. Stay out of sight and do not, under any circumstances, go home to see your parents. I'm sure the king has eyes on your house, just in case you turn back up."

"Of course," I say. "I need to see her, to tell her that things will be different, and, well, to say goodbye."

"Goodbye?" Constance asks, confused.

"It feels like all I ever did was cause her pain. I never wanted that. She chose to do what was expected of her, and can I really blame her? Maybe I was selfish for trying to get her to change her mind."

"You weren't selfish," Constance says. "You saw a future for yourself that she couldn't imagine. You wanted her to believe that the two of you could find a way through all this. That's what happens when you care about someone. And when you're brave enough to imagine a different life." She brings my hand to her lips and kisses it gently, letting her mouth linger there. "Be careful."

I take a moment to look at her, to see if there is anything I haven't already memorized about her face. If I stay another moment, I'll change my mind, so I leave, not daring to look back.

I ride into town in the early morning hours; the lamplighters are making the rounds, snuffing out the lamps with their hooked poles. An air of melancholy hangs over the city like a gathering of storm clouds, ready to split open and wash the land in a torrent of pain and sadness.

As I make my way through town, dead set on finding Erin and telling her things are going to change even if I have to die trying, I realize I have no clue where she lives now. Probably with Édouard, and not with her parents in the little house with the wide porch on Strattman Street. I decide to go to Liv's house first to see if her parents know where Erin is.

I tether my horse and go to Havasaw Lane on foot. I hang back along the row of houses across the street from Liv's. Her younger sisters, Mina and Cosette, are sitting in the front window. They look very much like Liv. An ache grips me so tightly I lose my breath. Nothing, not time or distance or distraction, has numbed the pain of her loss.

I cross the street and walk toward the house. As I approach the front step, I can hear the girls reading the passages of Cinderella's tale. They spot me and disappear from the window.

"Papa! There's a strange man outside!"

At least my disguise seems to be working. I hear footsteps barreling up to the front door, and when it swings open, Liv's father stands there, his face ruddy, his eyes narrow.

"Who are you?" he asks, blocking the doorway. "What do you want?"

He stares at me in confusion before his eyes widen and his jaw goes slack. He looks up and down the street and motions for me to come inside. Locking the door behind us, he turns to me as he draws the curtains closed. "Were you followed?"

"No. I was very careful," I say. "I'm so sorry to show up like this, but—" Liv's mother appears in the living room. She seems smaller than the last time I saw her, more delicate. I take off my cap. "Oh, Mrs. Preston, I—I'm so sorry I—"

"Sophia?" She rushes forward and puts her arms around me. "You're alive! We didn't know where you had gone. We thought the king had taken you away or—or worse." Tears stream down her face, and I'm miserable that she is crying for me when her own daughter lies cold in the ground.

"I'm fine, really I am." I wipe the tears from my own eyes. "I know about Liv. I'm so sorry."

"To your room this instant," Liv's father says to her sisters.

The girls scurry up the stairs, and I follow Mrs. Preston into the kitchen, where she takes a seat at the table. She's one of those women who wears every ounce of heartache on her sleeve. Her small frame seems like it might collapse under its weight at any moment. Mr. Preston pours her a cup of tea and sits it in front of her, gently touching her shoulder.

"We did everything exactly as we were supposed to," Mrs. Preston says. "We recited the verses, knew them all by heart. We served the king, followed the rules, and two years in a row we've been denied a visit by a godmother. I wish I knew what we did wrong."

I clench my jaw. She believes, as Liv did, that the stories are real, and while I now know there was real magic involved, it wasn't something you earned by being faithful to the palace or reading Cinderella's story a million times over.

"You didn't do anything wrong," I say. "Please understand that."

Mrs. Preston shakes her head. "I wish you could have come to the funeral. It was lovely, and you were such a good friend to her."

Tears fall again, and I turn away. "I'm sorry I couldn't be there."

"No, no. Don't apologize," says Mr. Preston, shaking his head. "You managed to get away. I'm sure your parents miss you, but you shouldn't go back."

"Marcus," Mrs. Preston interjects.

"I don't mean to give the impression that I'm speaking ill of your parents," he says. "But it's my sincerest wish that you never have to be a part of that terrible ball ever again. And now that he's ordered a cotillion, he'll have another opportunity to ruin our lives." I turn to look at him. He gives me hope that there are still good people in Lille.

Mrs. Preston pats the air with her hands, urging him to quiet his voice, which he does immediately.

"I have two more who will have to—" Mr. Preston stops short. His face contorts into a mask of pain. "They're just eleven and thirteen, but the thought never leaves my mind that very soon I'll be forced to send them off to the palace." He fights back tears.

Mrs. Preston stares out the kitchen window. "Everyone wants to be chosen, but they don't think about what that really means. Have you seen what happened to Erin?"

My heart almost stops. "I saw her in the market. I saw the bruises. Her fiancé, Édouard, had—"

"Husband," says Mrs. Preston, as if she knows what I am going to say. "He's her husband now. It would have been better if she hadn't been chosen at all."

"Where is she?" I ask.

"They'll be living in Eastern Lille, behind the gates, but Erin's parents couldn't come up with the dowry they'd promised, and so Édouard and Erin have been staying about a mile past the orchard until the money is paid in full," says Mrs. Preston. "I've gone to see her twice and was turned away at the door each time. He didn't even let her come to Liv's funeral. I think he resents having to stay so close to us commoners and takes it out on her."

"I want to put an end to it," I say. "The ball, the laws, the traditions. All of it."

Mrs. Preston glances toward the stairs. "People will not let go of those things so easily. I sometimes think they don't even understand that they are doing anything wrong."

"I don't pity their ignorance," I say. "They see what's going on. We all do. We have to show them a better way."

Mrs. Preston covers my hand with hers. "You'll change the world then, Sophia?"

There is no hint of sarcasm, of doubt. She is sincerely asking me what I aim to do.

"I don't know about the world, but we can start with Lille," I say. That's enough for right now. "I should be on my way."

I tuck my hair under my cap, and Mrs. Preston hugs me tightly. "Erin doesn't want to be married to that man— or any man." She looks up at me. The love and gentleness she has for her own girls has always extended to me and to Erin, but I didn't know exactly how much until this moment. "She tried so hard to pretend to be happy about the match. She wanted to make her parents proud."

"I know." How being married to a man like Édouard, who beats her, could make them proud is beyond me. Why was that an acceptable price to pay for being chosen? She's worth more and deserves better.

"Perhaps it has always been you who was meant to save her," she says.

"There's still hope," I say, although I'm not sure I've

fully convinced myself of that. She holds me for a long time before going upstairs. Mr. Preston walks me to the door.

"I won't ask you what you plan to do or where you're going," he says. "It's best that I don't know, but you know where to find me if you need anything."

I nod, take his hand in mine, and give it a squeeze. "Thank you."

I hug him and leave without looking into his eyes for fear that I won't be able to see through the tears. I stand on the stone pathway in front of the house and breathe in the chilly air. It allows me to refocus. Erin.

Just down the road from the orchard, I find Erin and Édouard's temporary residence, a large house with a tiled roof and large stained-glass windows that sits apart from the others on the street.

I leave my horse tethered to a tree close by and walk up to the house, my heart pounding. Will she even want to see me? And what can I say to her after all this time?

Just as I'm thinking of chucking a stone at one of the upper windows, the front door opens, and Erin comes out. I stop, frozen where I stand. I wait for her to notice me, the anticipation tying me in knots. She pulls her shawl in around her neck as she looks up into the sky and exhales long and slow, the way she does when she's exhausted. She levels her head and steps forward.

"Erin," I say, just above a whisper.

"Sophia?" Her voice sounds thin and raspy as if she's been crying. I wonder for how long and if any of those tears are over me.

"I had to see you," I say.

She sweeps down the front steps, and I think she's going to embrace me, but as I reach for her, she stops.

"What are you doing here?" She glances back at the front door.

"I came to see if you were all right. After I saw you in the market—"

Erin huffs loudly. "Leave the past in the past, Sophia. That's where it belongs." Her eyes and words are like ice.

"I thought you'd—I don't know—I thought you might want to see me. I wanted to see you."

"Really? Why would I want to see you? You left. You think you're better than us because you got away?"

I'm struck silent. She is seething, hatred dripping from every word.

"I don't think I'm better than anyone," I say. "Why would you say that? I asked you to come with us. I wanted you to come."

"Come with you where?" She looks back at the door again. "Where did you go?" She shakes her head. "Don't answer that. I don't care. I don't care that you feel sorry for me and came to see how pitiful I am."

"That's not why I'm here. Erin, what happened to you? Why are you acting like this?"

She marches up to me and sticks her finger in my chest. "You left! You left me here to deal with this alone. Liv is dead, and you're gone, and I have no one."

All the time I spent trying to be there for her flashes in my head. How many times had I tried to comfort her, to help her in any way that she would allow, and now this is my fault?

"I tried to tell you how much I cared for you. I tried so hard and you—you pushed me away." This isn't my fault.

"You tried to make me believe that this would work when you knew damned well that it never will," she says. "Not here in Lille or anywhere else. I've accepted my fate. Something you could never do because you're too busy daydreaming. If my husband finds you here, he'll turn you in."

"It doesn't have to be like this," I say after a moment. I'm desperate to give her an out. "I've found another way."

"I won't risk being disowned by my parents all because you have some new plan that will get you executed like that poor woman in the marketplace, like your own grandmother."

My stomach turns over. "I don't care."

"Of course you don't," she snaps. "Your parents have already disowned you. And you have no husband, nothing to lose." Her words cut me to the bone, rip my insides out and stomp on them. "Not even you, with all your wishful thinking, can change things. You're not special, Sophia. You're just a silly girl like the rest of us."

Holding my tears at bay, trembling with frustration, I shake my head. "You're wrong. I lost myself in caring for you. I cared for you so much I forgot that I deserve to be happy too. I'm sorry you don't believe in me." She bristles. "I'm sorry I couldn't save you."

"I don't need to be saved," she says as she weeps silent tears. "I need you to leave me alone. Forever."

"You're afraid. I know what that's like. But you're going to have to decide what you're willing to risk to change things." This is goodbye. It has to be. I know what the king's laws do to the women of Lille, but what they've done to Erin is more than I can stand.

Giving me one last look, she turns and goes inside.

After staring at the closed door for a moment, I mount my horse and ride straight back to Constance, who is waiting for me on the front step. I climb down as she comes toward me, her eyes worried.

"I only wanted to tell her that there was another way, but she still can't understand that."

Constance slips her hand into mine. "I'm sorry, Sophia."

"No," I say. "I'm sorry. I never should have risked going back there, and I don't want you to feel like I was trying to make a choice between you and Erin. I made that choice before I left. I choose you."

Constance presses her lips against mine as she winds her arms around my neck.

"Ahem." Amina clears her throat, standing on the front step with her arms crossed. "Went out for a little stroll this morning? I hope you enjoyed yourself. Are the palace guards on your tail?" She splits a pointed look between me and the driveway.

"I wasn't followed."

"You went into town," Constance says to Amina. "Don't be a hypocrite."

"I can blend in seamlessly, thank you very much, while Sophia just looks like a very beautiful man," Amina snaps.

"And what's wrong with that?" Constance asks playfully.

"Did you accomplish whatever it was you were trying to do?" Amina asks.

I nod. The answer isn't simple. Nothing is simple anymore.

32

On the morning of King Manford's winter cotillion, snow blankets the land. The air is frigid, and the cold has stripped the trees of their leaves. Lille looks like a page right out of Cinderella's fairy tale.

I can't sit still, choosing instead to pace back and forth in front of the hearth. Amina sits in a chair near the fireplace, hovering over a piece of golden parchment.

"It's disturbing how easily I was able to nick this from the mail carrier," she says. "They really should be more vigilant about keeping an eye on their parcels."

Constance took the horse and cart before the sun came up; as soon as I hear the faint sound of wheels on the road, I run out to meet her. She climbs down, takes one look at me, and pulls me into an urgent embrace. She's as nervous as I am but shows it in subtle ways—a fervent kiss, a look of sadness in her eyes when she holds me.

"The town is abuzz, but I didn't see a single smile. People are nervous. Kind of like you." She winks at me. "Are you ready?"

"No. But if I wait until I'm ready, I may never go."

Amina nods a greeting to Constance as we go inside. They've come to an unspoken understanding that there will be no bickering, not on this day, at least.

In the early afternoon, clouds move over the hills, turning the day gray and gloomy. I'm sitting quietly with Constance, holding her hand and studying every angle of her face, when Amina stands up. "You'll need time to travel to the palace, so it's probably best if we get started now."

My heart races. The moment has come.

Constance and I follow Amina outside into the small clearing behind the house where the giant tree sits. Constance drapes a cloak around us, and we huddle together in the chilly winter air. Amina looks to the sky and holds her hands up in front of her. As she mutters something unintelligible under her breath, a shudder runs through the ground.

Suddenly, a light, like liquid starlight, flows from Amina's fingertips to the trunk of the massive tree, snaking out onto its branches. I crane my neck to look up at the canopy and watch the tree burst to life, wide green leaves sprouting from every branch. In the dead of winter it shouldn't be possible. Amina steps back as the light from her hands fades away, but the tree remains luminescent.

"Ask of it what you will," Amina says. "It will provide anything you should need, but you must understand that the magic is only temporary. All that the tree provides, it will take back at the stroke of midnight."

Constance stares in amazement. "Is this what you gave to Cinderella?"

Amina looks away. "It is. On this very spot, on a night very much like this one."

I slip out of Constance's embrace and approach the tree, looking into the shimmering canopy. "A dress." Do I need to ask it for a certain kind of dress? A specific color? I glance back at Amina, but a rustling sound draws my attention up as a pocket of warm air wraps itself around me like a blanket. The same strange luminescence that clings to the tree now clings to me. I hold my breath as a dress of shimmering silver materializes around me. Constance looks on, her eyes wide, hands clasped tightly together.

Amina whispers something into the branches. There's a gentle tug at the back of my head, and a tingling surrounds my feet. I can barely see anything through the silvery haze. As it dims, Amina smiles. Constance looks back and forth between the glowing tree and me.

"It worked?" I ask.

"Like a charm," says Amina.

The light is fading from the tree branches, so I quickly whisper one final thing to it. "Please help me find a way to defeat the king."

Amina's smile fades. "It can't help you in that way, I'm afraid. This spell is very good at creating fancy frocks and unique baubles, but what truly matters is you, Sophia. You must use your head and your heart."

"You can't blame me for trying."

Amina reaches into her cloak and pulls out something wrapped in a piece of cloth. She hands it to me. I unwrap it and find she's given me a dagger.

"Just a little something," Amina says.

The blade is long and slender and glints in the light of the enchanted tree. The handle is intricately carved, and set directly in the center is a shimmering pink stone.

"It's quartz," Amina says, tapping the stone. "I charged it during the last full moon. It should offer you some protection."

"Thank you," I say. "It's beautiful."

"I gave it to Cinderella the night of the very first ball. She didn't get a chance to use it because of my cowardice, my willingness to believe that there was another way to stop the king."

I look down at the weapon again, grasping its handle,

feeling the weight of it in my hand and on my heart. Amina tries to give me a reassuring smile.

It's hard for me to reconcile my feelings for her. She reminds me so much of my own grandmother in some ways: her quick wit, her knowing little smile. But Amina helped Manford ascend the throne, costing the people of Mersailles their lives. And how many have been lost since the time of Cinderella? How many have had their lives ruined because of Manford? She helped him. But she is helping me now. And like she said, we cannot go back.

"Don't worry about me," I say. "I'm going to be okay."

She takes my hands in hers and sighs. Doubt creeps in. Are we all just kidding ourselves by thinking we can make this work? Amina won't meet my gaze. Her vision in the pool revealed her own death; had she also seen this moment? Does she know how this will end?

Amina helps me tuck the sheath for the dagger between the folds of my dress and walks into the house, dabbing her eyes with the sleeve of her cloak, leaving Constance and me alone. Her eyes move over me, taking in every part, and I don't have to ask her how she thinks I look. It's written in her eyes, in her smile.

"I don't know what to say," Constance says.

"That's a first," I say. I close the gap between us. "I've never seen a dress like this." I reach down and give the gown a little tug. It looks like it is made from the moonlight itself.

"It's nothing compared to you," she says.

My heart breaks at the very real possibility that I might never see her again.

"Promise me something," Constance says.

"Anything."

"Promise that you will come back to me." Constance wipes tears from her eyes. "If you tell me you'll come back, I'll believe you."

I press my forehead against hers and close my eyes. "I promise that I'll do everything I can to come back to you." That's all I can say without lying to her.

I lean forward and kiss her, wrapping my arms around her, breathing her in and hoping that this isn't the last time.

Amina stands in the doorway. "It's time, Sophia."

Constance loops her arm under mine, and we walk toward the front of the house. We pass a row of windows, mostly broken fragments still hanging in their frames, and I catch a glimpse of myself. I peer into the glass and reach up to touch my hair. My natural curls hang down around my shoulders, held away from my face by tiny silver butterflies made of glass set on silver pins. My skin shines, brown and beautiful, free from rouge or powder.

"You're stunning," Constance says. She plants a kiss on my cheek and lets her lips linger there. Her touch sends little sparks of fire straight through me.

My ride waits for me in the front drive. Two elegant

stags, black as night and fitted with red bridles, are hitched to a shimmering black carriage with a domed roof, decorated with red ribbons and matching curtains.

"Is this real?" I ask.

"It's real in this moment," says Amina. Suddenly, a ball of light engulfs her, and I step in front of Constance, totally unsure of what is happening. When the light fades, a squat little man in black coattails and a red bowtie stands where Amina had been.

Constance grabs her dagger and raises it up.

"Wait a damn minute!" Amina's voice comes out of the little man. "It's me, you fool!"

Constance's eyes grow wide, and she holsters her dagger. "Maybe give us some warning next time?"

"Maybe don't try to stab every man you see," Amina shoots back.

Constance looks to me and shrugs. "It's a habit."

Amina climbs up to take the reins. "Let's get moving."

"That look suits you," Constance calls to her.

"You like it? Then I'll have to make sure I never look this way again," says Amina, scowling. "Let's go, Sophia."

Constance puts her hands on my shoulders and kisses me gently.

"I'll go on foot," she says, "and approach the palace from the mausoleum. I'll try to find another way in."

We've decided that, while I walk through the front

door, Constance will try to gain entry in secret and make her way to the row of cells where I'd heard a voice from behind the locked door.

I climb into the carriage and Amina snaps the reins. We lurch forward and begin our journey to the palace. As we cut a path through the freshly fallen snow, I look back only once to catch a glimpse of Constance retreating into the house.

33

The castle comes into view, much as it had before, except this time, I'm not at all impressed by the opulent show of excess. It's a façade put up to entice the girls of Lille, and once they're inside—Liv's face flashes in my mind, and I can almost hear the king's patronizing tone as he degraded her in front of everyone—they can't escape.

We join the long line of carriages that extends up the drive to the main road. When we're directly in front of the palace, Amina hops down and opens the door for me. We exchange glances as I step out, and she leans in to close the door behind me while whispering in my ear.

"I'll stay as near as I can and find Constance once she's close."

I nod and file in with the other girls. Murmurs surround me. Some smile warmly. One young woman tells me she likes my dress and that my hair is beautiful, but the compliments are tinged with fear. I catch a snide comment about what I must have done to earn such a dress. While the insinuation stings, I let it go. I didn't come here to care about what anyone else thinks. I have a job to do.

I hand my invitation to the guard, who studies it thoroughly before pausing. My heart gallops in my chest. Does he know the name doesn't match the face? He looks me over slowly. After a few more moments of scrutiny, he files the invitation away and crosses off a name on his list.

"Go on," he says.

By taking the invitation that was meant for another girl, whoever she was may be at home right now, wondering why she wasn't invited. A stab of panic. I hadn't thought about what position I've put that girl in. She is supposed to be here; the cotillion is mandatory. If she's found at home, something terrible could happen to her and it would be my fault. I feel an even greater need to find the king and stop him.

I walk into the main entryway, keeping my eyes focused straight ahead. There are fewer oohs and ahhs than there had been in October. These girls are being forced back to the palace because of me, and I see the fear in their faces everywhere I turn.

I have a plan, and I try to keep that foremost in my head as we move toward the main ballroom. I make a note of where all the doors in the main hall are located and tally up the number of guards. There are more of them this time around.

The guards herd us into the ballroom, where the doors clang shut as the trumpets blare. My palms sweat as we form a line. I run my hands down the front of my dress and gently touch the hilt of my dagger.

The trumpet blasts again, and I look up to see men flood into the ballroom. The Viscount of Chione is back, and so are many of the land barons. I watch the procession in confusion. Will there be another choosing ceremony? Most of the girls in attendance have probably already been selected. The royal anthem plays as the king comes in and takes up his place atop the platform.

"I am honored by your presence," he says. His eyes are wide. He scans the room with a frenzied sort of haste. He looks unnerved. "I am sure many of you are wondering why I've called you to this event, and the answer is quite simple. There are people in this kingdom who think that the rules don't apply to them. I've brought you here as a reminder that every man, woman, and child in Mersailles is beholden to me. For your lives, the food you eat, the clothes you wear. You can have those things because I allow it, and I am very disappointed that you are not more grateful." He shakes his head. "Henceforth, in addition to attending the annual ball, you will also be required to attend the winter cotillion. Anyone not chosen will immediately be considered a forfeit."

Shock befalls the room, and I hear a whimper. Some-one starts to cry. The viscount shifts uncomfortably from one foot to the other. Even he seems shaken by the king's proclamation.

"If you were chosen at the annual ball, form a line to your right," orders the king in a monotone voice. As I sus-pected, most of the girls rush off and stand against the far wall. Several dozen of us stay in line. "All of you who were chosen will be escorted back to your carriages. You have served your king well, and I expect that you will serve your husbands unquestioningly. The rest of you will have an opportunity to be chosen tonight."

The girls are escorted out by the guards, while those who are left stand quietly in line. "As we gather this evening, I'd encourage you all to remember the reason you're here. Cin-derella wanted every girl in her kingdom to be the bride of a deserving man, to have her own fairy-tale ending." I stifle the urge to throw up as he continues to lie to us. "You are all worthy of that honor. I hope you have studied Cinderel-la's story. I hope that you have let it show you the way."

The king smiles wide as laughter rises up among the suitors. A man who looks like an older version of Luke's schoolmate Morris stands on the tier closest to the king. It must be his father, and I wonder if his latest wife has had some accident or has been given up as forfeit. I wonder if my face conveys every bit of rage I feel. I hope so.

The king gazes down the line of girls and stops when

he comes to me. Something animalistic flashes across his face. He quickly looks from side to side to see if anyone has noticed. He claps his hands twice to signal the band. The remaining girls scatter while the men on the platform come down and start to mingle.

I fight to keep calm. No one will be permitted to leave. He'll make these young women pay for the choice I made to abandon the ball. Just then, a man appears in front of me, and it takes me a half second to register who it is.

King Manford.

From his smell, a mixture of wine and smoke, to the predatory look in his eyes, everything about him repels me. I have a feeling that if we weren't in a room full of people, he'd show his true nature immediately. I watch the corners of his mouth twitch as he struggles with something inside himself. I stare up at him, and he smiles. "It is customary to bow or curtsy when in the presence of royalty."

I don't move.

He narrows his eyes, which are a shade of such deep brown as to be almost black. His angular jaw is set hard, and his mouth is a straight line. "You are not what I expected."

I can feel the eyes of everyone else in the room on us as he hovers over me.

"A waltz!" he shouts, startling me. The band plays a

melody, and he takes my arm, dragging me to the center of the ballroom. He slips his hand behind my back and pulls me into the dance. "You're very beautiful," he says. He spins in a circle, practically lifting me off the ground. "What's your name?"

"You already know the answer."

"Clever girl," he says. "I didn't think you would return. I thought I would have to hunt you to the ends of the earth. You are either very brave or very stupid. Tell me, which is it?"

"I'm here so no one else has to suffer for what I did. I left the ball. You can take that up with me. Leave everyone else out of it." The weight of my dagger presses against my leg. He has a vise grip on my hand, and I can't reach for it. He holds me close as we spin. I look up at the portraits of our former kings, and while each of them differ, I realize now that the eyes are the same.

They are all Manford.

Did he put up the paintings to taunt us? The truth has been in plain sight this entire time, but no one understands what it means. I lean in and put my mouth close to his ear. "I know what you are."

He stops as the music carries on, and couples around us continue their dance. He crushes me to him, and I wince. People are watching us, whispering among themselves. His jaw clenches and then goes lax several times in a row. He steps away from me. I judge the distance to his neck. He bows slightly and turns on his heel, leaving me alone in the middle of the floor.

Something is wrong.

The music stops, and Manford's voice calls out again. "If you would, please move to the rear courtyard." The room clears out almost immediately, but even that isn't fast enough for him. "Hurry!" he barks.

People trip over themselves in their haste. As the last of the guests file out, a tall young man with sandy-blond hair and kind eyes stops to stand next to me.

"Will you be joining us outside?" he asks. "Your dress is lovely. Can I get you something to drink?"

As I turn, a guard sweeps in and strikes him on the top of the head with the hilt of his sword. The man collapses in a heap. Before I can speak, the king appears, scowling down at the man like it's his own fault he's just been knocked out cold.

"Get him out of here," the king orders. The guards drag the man away, and the king turns to me as if nothing has happened. "You'd like to see the rest of the castle, wouldn't you?"

He extends his hand to me. Everything in me screams to run, but I can't. He reaches out and takes my arm, tucking it tightly under his. From the ballroom, we proceed down a long hallway lined with mirrors and more paintings of the king. A chill emanates from him, his arm is stiff, and his grip iron tight. No warmth. I wonder if his heart still beats in his chest.

"You're very fond of your own image, aren't you?" I can't contain my resentment.

"I have every reason to be, don't you think?" he asks, holding his chin up and sneering.

I let my gaze sweep over him. I think about flattering him, playing to his vanity, but I cannot bring myself to do it. I stay quiet.

He stops abruptly and opens one of the many doors that dot the hall. I peer inside and see that the walls are lined with shelves filled with books. A fireplace big enough for a person to stand up in sits at the back of the room.

"Do you like to read?" he asks.

"I do," I say, which sounds like an act of defiance.

"And you've read Cinderella's tale, as all girls are required to do?"

"I have, though I'm not a fan of such outrageous works of fiction."

He pulls the door shut harder than necessary and looks down at me. "You have a very free way of speaking. It may get you into trouble." He leans over me, and I take a step back, even as he holds tight to my arm.

"It's not in my nature to lie."

He wrestles with something inside himself again,

readjusting his jacket and taking long, slow breaths. "You think I am disingenuous?"

"I know you are. You claim to be some benevolent leader, but your treachery shines through. You can't hide it."

"Is that so?"

"You think any of the girls who come here for the ball are happy about it? You think they look forward to it?" I wonder if maybe, after all these years, he's begun to believe his own lies.

He looks thoughtful for a moment and then turns to me. "I don't care if they do or not. They come because I tell them to. I hold this annual ball because I can, because I want to. It's not nearly as complicated as you're making it out to be."

"I didn't think you could be any more of a—"

He tightens his grip on my arm. "A what?" He glares at me. There is an unnatural echo in the timbre of his voice.

I stare up at him. His face is completely blank, devoid of any emotion. Even the twitching at the corners of his mouth has ceased.

"A—a monster."

"There it is again. That fire. It will be stomped out completely when I'm done with you." He stops to rein in his emotions yet again. He still grips my arm as we continue down the hallway. "I used to know someone very much like you."

"I doubt that," I say.

He digs his fingertips into my arm. It hurts, but I won't give him the satisfaction of knowing how much. I bite the inside of my cheek instead.

"Do you know where she is now, the woman you remind me of?" He puts his face so close to mine that I can smell his sour breath. "Dead." A shiver runs through me. Realizing he's rattled me, he laughs softly. "She loved me deeply. But not once she found out—" He stops short. He could be speaking of no one other than Cinderella.

"Found out what you really are?" I ask. I imagine what must have gone through her head when she saw him as I am seeing him, with the fairy-tale exterior chipped away, with the reality of his monstrous deeds laid bare.

He clears his throat and looks away from me. "The rules I have set forth are meant to keep troublemakers like yourself out of the way. A girl like you is simply too disruptive to the natural order of things."

"A girl like me? And yet you've taken me aside, planned this grand event to lure me in. You can barely control yourself in my presence, so really, who has power over whom?"

His face changes into a mask of pure amusement. He raises an eyebrow. "Do you have no fear of death? Are you that stupid?"

"You've brought me here to bully me? You're pathetic." Anger wells up like water behind a dam. He's repellent, and I can't stand to be so near to him. He angles himself in front of me, my back to the wall.

"You say you know what I am and yet . . ." He leans in close, staring me in the eye. "I think you have no idea."

I push away the fear that has crept in, and I stare back at him, which seems to catch him off guard. He blinks repeatedly as if I've startled him. He's probably never had someone detest him as openly as I do.

"Cinderella didn't love you the way you wanted her to," I say. "She rejected you, and you've spent all this time punishing every woman who reminds you of her? How very pathetic."

He leers at me and leans forward, pressing his forehead into mine so forcefully it hurts. His jaw clenches up as he balls his fists. He hisses air between his teeth and then relaxes, leaning back. "I am going to hold you up as a shining example of how no one should ever think they can disobey me without consequence. Your name will be scrawled in the history books as the girl who tried to defy me and was destroyed."

He would use my fight to end him as fodder for another book of lies. I think of people whispering my name as a curse, fearing to walk in my footsteps. I can't let that happen.

My heart crashes in my chest. I take a deep breath. I straighten up and plant my feet. I reach into the folds of my dress and grasp my dagger. In one quick move, I plunge it into his neck. I twist the blade the way Constance showed me. He blinks. Standing upright, he staggers, clutching at his throat. I jump back, pulling the blade out. I smile at him. I've done it. I've ended him.

Constance said that if I killed him, he would probably collapse in a heap.

King Manford doesn't move.

She told me blood would rush from the wound.

Manford does not bleed.

Constance said when people die, sometimes they groan and sputter.

Manford does neither.

The sound echoing off the walls is something I hadn't expected to hear, something that makes my blood run cold, something that makes me realize I've made a terrible mistake.

A laugh.

34

I stumble back as Manford laughs himself into a fit. He snatches my knife away.

"That was your plan?"

The hole in his neck is gaping. I didn't miss, and yet he is still alive, taunting me.

"Take her away," he says.

A flurry of activity erupts on my right. Palace guards appear from out of nowhere and drop a hood over my head. Someone yanks my arm so hard it feels like my shoulder might come out of its socket. Pain shoots into my fingertips. My hands are bound in front of me, and I am pushed down the hallway. Someone grabs my elbow.

"Get off me!" I scream. I swing my arm up as far as I can before thrusting it backward, hitting the soft flesh of what I picture is somewhere in the person's midsection. A yelp rewards my effort. Laughter and a snide remark from the others let me know I've hit the guard in a far more sensitive place.

The cloth covering my face shifts so I can see the floor. The guards lift me as we descend a set of stairs, and the ground below transforms from polished wood to gravel and dirt. I struggle against the hands that hold me but can't make contact again. A door clicks open, and a guard drops me onto a cold, damp floor. My hands still roped together, I pull the hood from my head as the door clangs shut. I throw my entire weight against it, only to lose my balance and fall to the floor again.

"Let me out!" I scream. I hear the murmur of voices.

"Be patient," the king's voice hisses through the door. "You'll have me all to yourself soon enough."

Bells toll in the distance. It's eleven o'clock.

"See you at the stroke of midnight," the king whispers.

A swell of anger courses through me as I drive my foot back into the door as hard as I can. He laughs before his footsteps recede down the hall.

The room I'm in is no bigger than a pantry. Stone walls, no windows, and the ceiling slopes low enough that I can touch it with my outstretched arms. A steady drip of water leaks from one of the creases where the wall meets the ceiling. The stub of a candle sits on a rock in the corner, along with flint and a thin, twisted piece of linen. I use the rock to ignite the flint, and a shower of sparks briefly lights up the room. It takes me several strikes with my bound hands to finally set the linen aflame to light the candle with it. It casts shadows all around me, making the space feel even smaller.

I can't believe what I've witnessed. My dagger went straight into his neck and still he lives. Amina told me he was not a normal man. We assumed he couldn't die, but we hadn't considered that he couldn't be killed. Now I'm unsure if he can be stopped at all, but I know for certain he'll be back for me soon and I need to find a way to escape.

Gathering my resolve, I set to work wriggling my hands out of the restraints. The rope digs into my wrists, causing a deep gash. Pain shoots up my arm with every tug. The pain becomes too much to bear, and I search for something to cut the rope with. The bricks and stones that make up the wall are uneven and jagged, and some of them have cracked clean in half. I find a piece of one that looks sharp enough and twist my hands around, sawing at the rope until, after several minutes and several more cuts to my hands, the rope frays and I wriggle out.

I rub my wrists as I look around the room. In the corner, the tattered remains of a book lie on the ground. I pick it up and leaf through the pages. It's Cinderella's tale.

Of course this would be here.

I toss it back into the corner and bend to look through the keyhole. I see the wall opposite my cell, the darkened hallway. The smell of damp earth fills my nose. I know exactly where I am. I'm in one of the little rooms where I heard a woman's voice on the night I escaped the ball. I go to a wall and knock on the stones.

"Hello? Is someone there?" I wait. The steady drip of the water is all I hear. I call out again, louder this time. "Hello? Is anyone there?"

"Be quiet," comes a hushed voice.

Grabbing the candle, I try to look through the little hole where the water trickles out, but it's too high.

"Hello?" I call again.

"There's a loose brick at the bottom of the wall," says the voice. "Take it out and stand on it."

I find the only intact brick and, following the voice's instructions, I pull it out and stand atop it. A flicker of a candle from the other side outlines another person, the dark-brown orb of their eye glinting in the dim light.

"Who are you?" I ask.

"You should be quiet."

"He'll come back for me, regardless," I say. "It's only a matter of time."

"You seem to have accepted your fate quicker than the others. That's probably a good thing. No use crying about it, right? He's just going to kill us anyway." Her blunt attitude about her terrible fate makes me pause. She's waiting for death, and it sounds like she wishes it would hurry up.

"How long have you been here?" I ask.

"A few weeks—maybe longer. It's hard to say."

"How did you get here?"

She laughs lightly. "Blowing up the Colossus was a punishable offense. Who would have thought?" Sarcasm colors every word, but it is all tempered with hopelessness.

My foot almost slips off, and I scramble to keep my balance. "You did that? Are you Émile?"

There is a rustle on the other side of the wall. "How do you know my name?"

"I'm with Constance! I'm Sophia. We're here—or I'm here—" My voice catches in my throat and tears well up. I don't even know if Constance has made it to the castle. I don't know if I'll ever get the chance to see her again, but I have to set that aside for now.

"She lives?" Émile asks. "And there is a plan?"

"Yes. But I—I just put my dagger in the king's neck, and he laughed in my face."

She huffs loudly. "That sounds very much like Constance, always stabbing someone." I think I hear her laugh. "But as you saw, it doesn't work with him. He has been poisoned, stabbed, and a few of the girls on this row tried to get close enough to him to slip a rope around his neck. He was quite amused by that attempt. It failed, obviously.

And he made them pay for it. Tell me, have you or Constance been able to find anything else out about him?"

"Yes." I hesitate because I know how it will sound, but I continue anyway. "Do you know that King Manford and Cinderella's Prince Charming are the same person?"

"I've learned the impossible truth from the other girls on this row. Before I was captured, I would have said that it cannot be, but now I have seen too much to discount it." She sighs heavily. "But it doesn't matter. He's killed or captured so many of us that there are barely enough of us left to stage any sort of real resistance."

"How many of them are there?"

"There are seven other girls in the cells next to us, and I hear there are more cells in the bowels of the castle, but none of us are in any shape to fight back. Some of them have been here for months, maybe longer. We don't have enough to eat or drink, and the draining—the draining is too much."

"The draining?" I ask.

"Oh, Sophia." Émile sighs. "You cannot know what it's like. It's like dying. He wraps you up and then you're falling, and if you return, you are—changed."

I press my face against the bricks as I struggle to hear. My heart is beating furiously. "How? Tell me how he does it."

"It's a kind of magic I've never even heard a whisper of.

He siphons the life from your very soul. There is a light, a pull, and whatever he takes from you, he uses to make himself young, to live as long as he so chooses."

My mind runs in circles, and a memory from the ball stands in my mind. The door Liv was taken through stood open for just a moment as the king exited. The old woman with the snow-white hair—wearing Liv's dress. It was her. The king had done that to her. And when I saw him across the crowd, he looked different, happier, his eyes brighter.

I begin to pace the floor. The light from my vision and the pull at my chest, the illustrations in Constance's book of tales, and Cinderella's own words all fit together like a puzzle.

This is how he does it.

This is how he keeps himself young. And just as the thought settles in my mind, another terrible reality makes itself clear. I run back and stand on the brick.

"The ball. Is that its purpose? To bring the young women of Lille here for him to do this?"

"It is a reaping," Émile says. "A way for him to feast on them like the monster he is. And knowing now that he has been doing this since the time of Cinderella, I fear he can go on like this forever." Her voice becomes a whisper. "I've dreamed of finding a way out, but I think that's all it will ever be. A dream. A nightmare, really. He's taken so much from me. I'm changed in the very deepest parts of me."

"When you get out of here, you will have yourself and your freedom, and that will be enough. I promise you."

I think I hear her laugh, but it could have been a sob. "I want to believe you. Really, I do."

I step down and take a deep breath. She's lost all hope. She sounds so much like Erin, like my parents. But I refuse to accept that fate. I need to get out, and I need to find Cinderella's journal.

I go to the door again and peek through the keyhole, listening for a moment. There are no sounds other than the steady drip of water and my own heartbeat. I hold the candle up to the locking mechanism inside the keyhole. It's rusty, and a piece of the keyhole's frame is broken off. I look around the room for something I can use to open the lock. Nothing useful.

I run my hand through my hair, frustrated. My fingers pass over the glass butterflies that still hang there. I yank one down and break off the glass figure, leaving just the metal pin, which looks like it will fit perfectly in the lock. I wonder if my own personal fairy godmother had something to do with crafting these little pins.

I jam the metal rod into the keyhole and try to mimic the motion of a turning key. Flecks of red-orange metal rain down as I probe the lock. I twist the pin as hard as I can, and then *pop!* The lock clicks.

The door groans as it opens just a crack. I expect to be rushed by the guards at any moment, but nothing happens.

I poke my head out and look down the darkened corridor. A patchwork of newer-looking wood planks crisscrosses the hole in the ceiling, but the chilly evening air still gusts through. From somewhere farther off, a melody drifts in, and a sweet smell, like fresh-baked bread, wafts past me. I try the handle on the cell next to mine.

"If you come in here, make sure you kill me. Because if you don't, I'll strangle you with my bare hands!"

"Will you be quiet?" I whisper. "It's just me. From the cell next to you."

I hear her scramble around, and the light under the door flickers.

I put my makeshift key in the lock and try to get it to turn. It clicks gently as I try to find the right angle and then *snap!* The pin breaks off inside the lock.

"Where are the keys?" I ask.

"They're with the guard. You'll never get ahold of them. Just go. Get away from here and never come back."

I see faint lights under each of what must be a half dozen doors down the hall.

"I'll come back for you. I promise," I say. "I'll find the keys or something to break the lock."

Faint sobs fade away as I head toward the end of the hall where I'd found my way out before. I twist the handle. Locked, boarded shut from the outside. The king must have amended his lapse in security.

A monster. Not a fool, I remind myself.

I turn to the opposite end of the hallway. A narrow, spiral staircase is tucked in the far corner. I rush to the foot of the stairs and look up.

The wooden stairway spirals at least two floors into the darkness. The first few feet are passable, and I'm sure this is the way the guards came when they dragged me down here, but beyond that, the staircase is in rough shape. Some of the steps are missing, and cobwebs hang between the slats of the rail. I rush past the sturdy stairs and then ease onto the first tattered step that leads into the darkness. It moans under my weight. I take a deep breath before making my way up cautiously, each step groaning in protest.

The bells toll, marking the half hour.

As I near the top, I narrowly avoid a gaping hole in the structure. When I set my foot on the other side, a sickening crack echoes through the dark. My foot crashes through the wooden stair, and I grab on to the rail to keep myself from plummeting to the floor below.

A shower of debris rains down and clatters to the floor. I scramble to hoist myself up, and when I'm steady, I stand still, listening. Someone must have heard the commotion. I try to calm my racing heart. Just above me, at the top of the staircase, is a door.

I climb the last few steps and lean against it to see if I can hear anyone on the other side.

Silence.

Turning the handle, I push the door in slowly and find myself in a hall much like the one the king had shown me. The walls here are painted a pale blue with white lilies all along the ceiling. Oil lamps light up the space every few feet, set in golden fixtures on the walls. The doorway is built directly into the wall, with no handle on the outside. I gently push it closed and tiptoe down the hall. The floor beneath my feet is a dark oak color and polished to such a shine that I can see myself reflected in its surface.

I pass several rooms before coming to a set of gilded double doors at the end of the hallway. A muffled voice sounds from somewhere behind me. I try the handle on the double doors and they creak open, sending a sprinkling of dust down onto my head. Clearly, no one has been in this room in a very long time. I take a lamp from its holder just outside the door and go inside.

It's a large bedroom, painted the same pale blue as the hallway. The air is stale, and I can taste the dust in it. Windows run along the south-facing side, though they are shuttered, and on the recessed ceiling is a plaster medallion with swirling arms stretching out like the rays of the sun. An enormous gold chandelier hangs from its center, cobwebs dangling between its candle cups like delicate lace. A four-poster bed draped with navy-blue linens sits underneath. It, too, is covered in a blanket of dust.

On the adjacent wall is a vanity with a mirror covered with a black cloth. A portrait of Cinderella hangs above it, but it's much different than the one in the main entryway. Here, she looks straight ahead, no hint of a smile, her mouth pressed into a tight line.

I hold the lamp up. Light cuts through the darkened room, illuminating an open closet filled with beautiful dresses. I walk over and run my hand over the folds of the luxurious fabrics. In the rear of the closet hangs a dress separate from the others: a plain frock frayed around the hem, its long sleeves tattered at the wrists.

Unlike the other dresses, it looks like it's been worn a million times. A picture starts to form in my mind. The dust on every surface, dresses hanging in the closet, the eerie silence.

This room belonged to Cinderella.

35

I back away from the closet as an oppressive sense of sadness washes over me. This is her gilded cage, her pretty
prison.

On the wall next to her bed hangs a small painting no
larger than the cover of a book, showing a man and a
woman standing behind three young girls. They all smile
and the girls hold hands. The tallest of the three has red
hair. This must be Gabrielle. I ache for what was stolen
from them, but now is not the time to mourn the past. Getting to Cinderella's journal is the only thing I can think of
to do. She knew something we don't.

I pull open drawers. I look under her bed and in her
closet but find nothing. Would it still be here after all this
time? Maybe Manford found it and destroyed it long ago.

I move toward the doors of the washroom but feel a tug

at the back of my dress. I spin around to see that my hem is caught on the corner of the little table next to the bed. My dress has pulled it away from the wall, and as I bend to free myself, something catches my eye.

On the back of the table, a small rectangular object sits in a small groove behind the single drawer. I reach down to pick it up, realizing it is a small book. Opening the cover, I see that the words are written by hand in black ink. A journal. My heart ticks up as I read the first page.

The spell has been broken. Every day its effects wane, and I feel something like my old self. The witch lied to me. She said we could end him, but after I drank from her cup, I could think of nothing but Prince Charming. I couldn't harm him, I couldn't speak an ill word against him, and this pleased him so much that he mistook it for genuine affection. But as I return to my senses, I cannot hide how I detest him. I am trying with all my might to keep the ruse up long enough to put a dagger in his chest. I will pay him back for what he has stolen from me.

I skip ahead several pages.

I have learned of something so profane that I can only commit it to paper for now. Speaking it aloud feels like speaking a curse.

With each passing day, he becomes crueler, more indecent. Every time I rebuff him, he acts as if I have struck him; he is wounded anew with each rejection. He cannot stand it.

He's killing me. Slowly, he takes the life from my very soul, and when I am on the edge of death he pulls back, letting me regain my strength only to do it again. He is punishing me, and he is enjoying it.

My skin pricks up as I reread the passage. He drained her, slowly, over time to punish her. My hands tremble as I continue reading.

This is all my fault. With every draw, I am weaker. The sadness in that place, that abyss, it seeps into me with each draining. I do not recognize my own reflection.

I turn the pages as if they are made of glass. I've stumbled upon something sacred. The words of Cinderella herself, in her own hand. In the last pages, the handwriting becomes nothing more than scribbles. I squint against the dark to read the passage.

A channel opened between us, a connection. I could see right into his blackened heart. Something invisible, something unnatural, surrounds the source of the light.

And now I know that there is no hope for me. Or for anyone.

The noise of a door opening in the hall stops me. I tuck the diary away between the shell of my dress and my corset. Someone is walking toward Cinderella's room. A gold candlestick, caked with cobwebs, sits on a table by the door. I pick it up. It's heavy as a brick. Raising it over my head, I listen as the footsteps come closer. Whoever it is pauses just outside the door. I hold my breath.

Right down on his head.

The door creaks open, and in the dim light, I see the guard's eyes. He blinks, confused, as I bring the candlestick down with all the strength I can muster. It impacts his head with a sickening thud, and he falls into a pile, his knees and elbows jutting out in an unnatural way. I quickly hook my arms under his, dragging him into the room and closing the door. Breaths rattle out of him as if his throat is filled with liquid. After rolling him onto his side, I check his pockets for the keys to the cells but find nothing. When he wakes up, he's going to sound the alarm.

I drag him into the closet full of beautiful dresses and close the door. I push the vanity and the small table in front of it and leave the room. Candlestick in hand, I race through the hallway until I come to another staircase.

This one spirals all the way down below the main level of the palace, and as the light from above dims, a gust of cold, fetid air meets me. The sounds of hushed voices drift up, but I can't make out the words. I descend the stairs to find the mouth of a long, dark tunnel.

The dungeon is a narrow hallway with barred cells on both sides. Only one lamp lights up the far end of the dank space. A guard is seated in a chair with an older man standing over him.

"I don't have the money," says the standing man.

"Then we don't have a deal," says the seated man. "Four gold pieces each. No bargains. King's orders."

The old man storms off, stomping up a short flight of stairs at the other end of the hall and slamming the door shut.

A faint whisper from the cell behind me catches my attention. Six or seven people of varying ages huddle together toward the back. A man steps forward, tall and gaunt. I can see his bottom ribs jutting out from under his tattered clothing. His face is covered in a mass of unkempt beard. He stumbles forward and props himself up on the cell bars.

"Sophia?" he asks, his voice thin and weak.

I can't believe it. "Luke?"

He puts out his hand, and I glance down the hall. The darkness gives me some measure of protection as I take his skeletal hand in mine.

"Oh, Sophia," he says, collapsing against the bars.

I kiss the back of his hand as tears sting my eyes. "Luke, what did he do to you? I thought you were dead." I was sure he'd been executed. But it looks like the king has allowed him to languish in the dungeon, waiting for his body to collapse in on itself. He only shakes his head.

"Such is the fate of forfeits," he whispers.

"Just wait," I whisper. "I'm going to get you out of here."

I glance down the hall, debating how to sneak up on the guard. I take the most direct approach and walk quickly past several cells where the prisoners have taken notice of me. As I near the guard, he stands, a look of disbelief plastered on his face.

"Hey, you're not supposed to be down here."

One of the girls in the cell behind him screams at the top of her lungs. As the guard spins around, I bring the candlestick down on his head, and he slumps to his knees, sputtering and groaning.

"Hit him again!" someone yells.

I do, and he falls face-first onto the dirt floor.

"He's got the keys on his belt!" A young girl, perhaps only a year or so older than myself, appears at the front of a cell, frantically waving her hand through the bars.

After tossing the candlestick aside, I unhook the keys dangling from a loop on his belt and go to the cell directly behind where the guard had been sitting.

"Are you all right?" I ask. "You screamed, and I thought—"

"I was only trying to distract the guard," says the girl.

"Which one is it?" I ask. There are a dozen keys, and they all look the same to me.

"It's silver with a square hole at the top," says the girl. She begins to shake uncontrollably. She holds tight to the bars and watches as I fumble with the keys. Her slip dress has come apart at the bottom hem. Her cheeks are smudged with dirt. She wears an unmistakable mask of pain on her face.

I find the key with the square hole and unlock the cell. The girls shuffle out, unsure of what to do next.

"Listen to me," I say. "There is a cotillion going on as we speak, and the king is looking for me. Take these keys and let the others out. There's a man in the last cell who may not be able to walk on his own. He'll need help. Do you know where this door leads?" I gesture to the door where the old man had disappeared.

"To the rear courtyard," says one of the girls.

I hand the keys to her, and she runs to unlock the other cells. My head is spinning. I can't think of a way to get everyone out and still go back for the girls locked away on the upper floor. As the others leave their cells, I look on in revulsion as at least forty girls and a half dozen boys stand before me. Were there so many forfeits in Lille? The young woman from the first cell has looped her arm around Luke, and he leans on her. Most of them are my age or older, but a few girls couldn't be more than eleven or twelve. Is this the fate of the missing girls of Lille?

Suddenly, a thunderous rumble comes from behind the door that leads to the courtyard. I climb the stairs and listen closely before easing it open. Confusion and shouting erupt outside as everyone who has emptied into the rear courtyard rushes away.

"Get out! Everyone out!" I hear a man yell.

"I think the king has ordered everyone to leave," I say. I push the door open wider.

No one moves.

"Go," I say. "Move with the crowd. Don't look back."

"Where are we to go?" asks a young girl. "We can't go home. Some of us don't have a home."

I only know they need to get out of here. Now. "Head up the drive toward the main road. Just keep going, and do not stop."

They rush out, clinging to one another, keeping their heads down. I see the cotillion guests glancing at them and then looking away as they run from the dungeon. This is the one occasion where the people of Lille's indifference to seeing its citizens in such a sad state will work to our benefit. Luke and the young woman who is helping him stop.

"Are you coming with us?" he asks. He can barely

speak, and I cup his face between my hands. I kiss his fore-head before nudging him and the girl toward the door.

"No," I say. "I can't. There is something I have to do."

Luke straightens up, trying his hardest to support his own weight. He puts his arms around me, and I can feel how devastatingly thin he is. If I hold on too tight, I fear I may break him. One of the girls presses the guard's keys into my hand, and I tuck them in my dress, next to Cinder-ella's journal.

I nudge Luke toward the exit, and when he is gone, I turn and race back down the tunnel and up the stairs. A group of guards heads away from me down an adjoining hall, swords drawn, shouting. When they are well out of sight, I cross the landing and descend a short flight of steps that leads to the doors of the main ballroom. I cut across the now-empty expanse of gleaming marble, the king's por-traits in all his guises staring out at me.

I make it halfway through before the doors behind me slam shut. The chandeliers burst to life one by one, casting shadows all around me.

I turn to see the king seated on his throne atop the plat-form, a sickening smile on his face. I run to the outer door and try to force it open, but it won't budge.

"It's no use, Sophia," he calls after me. "Even if you opened it, there are fifty guards on the other side."

Brimming with anger, I lock eyes with him. He

descends the platform. His midnight-black suit melds with the shadows. His eyes glint in the candlelight.

"You killed my friend," I say.

He looks off to the side. "Which one was that now? There have been so many."

I didn't expect him to be sad or sorry for what he's done, but he seems completely lifeless, like a walking shell that only serves as a vessel for his hatred.

"Her name was Liv, and she had a family that loved her. I loved her." I stare him straight in the face and take a few steps toward him. "Your terrible nightmare will end tonight."

"And exactly how are you going to stop me?" It isn't a question I have a solid answer for. I glance at his neck. The place where my dagger had wounded him is a purple color, but the skin has somehow pulled itself back together. He laughs. "I've spent more years in this land than any other living creature. I've molded it, shaped it into everything you see before you. Every man from here to Chione bows to me because I will it to be so."

"Did Cinderella bow to you when she found out what you really are?"

A quiet rage sweeps over him. It's the kind of anger that only comes from hearing a truth he can't accept.

"Even she bowed to me in the end."

Lies.

"You may rule this land," I say, pushing down the swell of terror that threatens to consume me. "But you do not rule me."

"You came here on my orders!" his voice thunders. "You and every other wretched girl in this kingdom, *my* kingdom, will do exactly as I say." He steps closer, his teeth clenched, his black eyes wide and unblinking. "Your father, and his father before him, and all the generations before that have sent their daughters to me in droves so I can have my fill and throw the leftovers to the men who come here like vultures to pick at the broken, rotted pieces of flesh."

"You bring them here to fill the void Cinderella left in your blackened heart," I say defiantly. "Your bitterness, this anger, it only comes from having your heart broken. Was that her crime? That she didn't love you?"

"I deserved her love!" he screams. He is unhinged, his eyes wild. "I took her out of her mundane existence and made her a queen. She should have loved me all her life for it."

"You couldn't control her. You couldn't force her to love you as you loved her." I suddenly understand what's driving him. He has convinced himself that he was entitled to Cinderella's love. He cannot see how his own actions turned her against him.

Manford is only entitled to one thing. The truth. "Did

you know she came here on that night all those years ago to kill you?"

His mouth opens as if he's going to speak, but he doesn't. He clenches his jaw tightly and closes his eyes, drawing a long breath. He sweeps in, reaching his hand behind my back and twirling me around. I struggle to keep my footing as he leads me in a soundless waltz.

"You think you can hurt me with your words? I had hoped you'd be smarter than that. At least make this little game a challenge." He grips my hand. "I will take what I want from you and leave your corpse to rot in a ditch like your pathetic friend, like so many of the wretched girls of Lille." Émile's words flood my mind. He is feeding on the girls of Lille like a monster. I picture him prowling the countryside, leaving a trail of corpses in his wake.

As he leans in, I wrench my arm free, rearing back and striking him with my open palm. He stops but does not let go. I look him in the eye. I know my voice will waver if I don't measure my words, but I want to be clear in what will undoubtedly be the last moments of my short life.

"If you are going to kill me, do it, and spare me your insufferable rantings."

"You can pretend to be brave, but I see right through you. You are racked with fear." He leans in close and breathes me in. "I can smell it on you."

I jerk my body to the side and manage to break his grip.

I stumble back, and he grabs my dress. It splits up the side, and I watch in awe as it mends itself before my eyes. The king lets go. He grins, grabs my arm, and pulls me close, crushing me to him. I claw at his face as he presses his forehead against mine.

He opens his mouth wide and presses his lips over mine. I scream but the sound is muffled. I taste his rancid breath and feel his damp skin, his fingers like knives at my back. Then, everything becomes still. A light hovers between us, a cloud of translucent fog that seems to be coming out of me.

I can't move, can't speak.

I fight to keep my eyes open. A rush of cold ripples across every inch of my skin. I catch a glimpse of my dagger tucked into his belt. I reach for it, but he bats my hand away.

I'm dying. I feel the life being pulled out of me in long, rasping draws. A fire ignites in my chest, burning away any feelings of hope or love or happiness. Something tugs hard at my waist, and suddenly I'm sliding backward across the ballroom floor. I lie still for a moment as my senses flicker on and off. My vision blurs, and a high-pitched ringing fills my ears. I am exhausted, like I haven't slept in days, and a crushing sadness hangs over me. My side aches. I roll over and blink.

A familiar figure stands in the middle of the room.

36

Y ou meddling wench!" the king screams.

My vision clears enough for me to see Constance standing with her dagger drawn and her eyes narrowed, a large book tucked under her arm.

"Stay away from her," Constance says.

Manford's face seems to shift as he glares at Constance, like his skin is too loose over his bones. "Put that dagger away, you stupid girl. It will do you no good here."

Constance glances at me. "Sophia, I—"

The double doors leading into the ballroom groan as they open. My vision is still hazy, but I recognize Amina's squat frame as she enters the room. She's shed her pretend exterior and marches up to the king. A rush of relief washes over me.

"Please," Amina says to him. "Please remember what we discussed before."

I'm still dazed, but even in my haze her words don't make sense. "Before?"

The king looks at me and then back to her. He bursts into a fit of wicked laughter. "You didn't tell her? She couldn't figure it out?"

"Figure what out?" I demand, climbing to my feet. My ribs throb with each heartbeat.

Amina flashes me a tight smile, but her eyes show me nothing but sadness. "I lied to you, Sophia. I had to do it."

The king waltzes over and plants a kiss on the top of Amina's head. "Oh, Mother, you never were a very good liar."

Mother.

No.

It can't be true.

"You—you said he saved you from the pyre," I stammer. "That he came looking for your assistance."

A maniacal grin spreads across Manford's face. "Is that the story you've been telling?" He turns to Amina. "I like that one very much. It's almost the truth."

My gaze returns to the portraits. Yes, they are all Manford, but they are also the boy from the painting hanging by the hearth in Amina's home in White Wood.

"You lying witch," Constance says through gritted teeth.

She opens the book she's clutching and tosses it onto the floor. It's the grimoire. Amina glances up at her.

"Oh, but you, Constance, you had some inkling, didn't you?" Amina grins, and the subtle similarities between her and Manford stare out at me, taunting me. "When?"

Constance grips her dagger. "I knew the little boy in the painting looked familiar, but I couldn't place him. It gnawed at me." Constance trembles as she speaks. "When you left for the cotillion, I looked at the necromancy spell again." She points to the book. The pages containing the necromancy spell lie open.

The conjurer is bound to the raised corpse until death.

"You don't have a good reason for still being alive after all this time," Constance says. "Manford should have killed you if you knew his secret. But now it makes sense. You're bound to him by blood, by love, by magic. He cannot exist without you. I didn't want to believe it. I was blinded by my hatred for him." She shoots a pointed look at Manford.

He cocks his head to the side. "You poor girl. What have I done to make you hate me so?" His tone is mocking, cruel.

"I have plenty of reasons," Constance says angrily. "You have been hunting my family for generations."

Manford is taken aback. He stares at Constance. "Mother, you should have told me we were among such honored guests. You look very much like Gabrielle. Pity."

The horrible realization dawns on me. I turn to Amina. "You brought him back yourself?" I remember the broken seal in her grimoire, Manford's cold skin, his stiffened body. He's a walking corpse. Amina is bound to him and he to her, just like the spell says. Only she has the power to destroy him because she's the one who cast the spell that brought him back from the dead.

Amina claps her hands. "Well done, my dear. Well done. It's true that he saved me from the pyre, but I was only on it because the people in my village found out what I'd done. Necromancy tends to scare the faint of heart."

"You've been working with him the entire time," Constance says.

"I didn't have to do much," Amina says. "You were already planning to come back to Lille. I just gave you a little push." She turns to Manford. "I must admit the things you said to me when you came to visit stung a little."

He puts his hand over his heart. "My temper got the better of me. I'm sorry about that, Mother, truly."

He doesn't sound sorry at all, but he smiles at her like he adores her, and my stomach turns over. All this time, I thought her hesitancy was because she was ashamed, fearful. But it was a lie. Like the Cinderella story. Like the ball. Like everything.

Amina turns to her son. "Your impatience nearly ruined everything. Showing up like that. I told you I'd deliver her to you, but you didn't want to wait."

That night we'd hidden in the root cellar replays in my head. He knew I was close by. The betrayal of it is like a knife twisting in my side.

"There was some truth to what I said," King Manford says.

Amina glances at him, and something like fear washes over her face.

"Your magic has failed me in the past, Mother." The king turns to her. "Your tinctures and tonics didn't hold. She would have loved me had you done a better job of concocting your potions."

"I was sure your wit and charm would win her over without my assistance," Amina says. "It was only meant to be a little push."

A loud screeching sound cuts through the air, and Amina's crow wings into the ballroom from the open side door. It lands on her shoulder.

"I hate that creature," Manford says.

Amina leans toward Manford and draws my dagger from his belt. "Oh stop. He's never done a single thing to you."

They carry on this conversation like Constance and I aren't standing right here.

"You stayed in the woods because you wanted to," Constance says. "Not because you felt bad about what you'd done."

"That's only partially true," Amina says, turning her attention back to Constance. "I do feel a twinge of guilt about Cinderella, but it's nothing that can't be stifled with a full pipe and a stiff drink." She twists the dagger between her fingers. "I told you I was no fairy godmother, that I'd done things you couldn't fathom. You asked me to lay down that burden. But you had no idea what that would mean."

I can't understand. "You knew he was killing people, and that it was how he was extending his own life?"

"Now, Sophia," Manford says, speaking to me as if I were a child. "I have managed to keep some things to myself."

Amina looks down at the floor. "I've never actually seen him do it. I didn't want to know the details. It was better that way. The first time was—when was it?"

"When that beggar woman came to our door in the first months after you'd risen me from the ground," says Manford. "When I realized what I could do, that I could maintain myself indefinitely, well, that was a secret worth keeping even from you, Mother."

"You haven't managed to keep it a secret from everyone," Amina says. "Constance is in possession of a book that has a very interesting illustration in it."

"Is that right?" Manford asks. "We'll have to look into that." He turns to Constance. "Will you give me the book willingly or must I use more . . . persuasive measures?"

"If you take a single step toward me, I will make you regret it," Constance says, her voice unwavering. "Please try it. I'd very much like to kill you."

The king's mouth turns down, and he shakes his head. "A cozy cell might humble you. Make you change your mind."

I think of the girl in the cell next to mine. Did Amina know about her and the others? "Have you spared a thought for anyone else?" I ask, staring at Amina. I cannot believe she has betrayed my trust this way. "Not just the people here in Lille but in the whole of Mersailles, all the lives that have been ruined because of him?" I can't stop the tears from running down my face. "I thought you cared about me. How could you do this?"

The king laughs. "Mother, perhaps your talent for lying is better than I thought. This fool actually thinks you care for her."

Amina draws her mouth into a straight line as she approaches me, her eyes steely. She raises Cinderella's dagger up and gently taps the handle where the pink stone is anchored.

"Just like I saw it," says Amina. "Forgive me." She draws a deep breath and lunges toward me.

I raise my arms in defense, and there is a flurry of footsteps. Amina jerks forward like she's been struck in the back. The look on her face puzzles me. It's pain.

She pushes the handle of Cinderella's knife into my hand and stumbles forward. The crow screeches, beating its wings as it flies up and circles over our heads. A sound, like the roar of a river, shatters the silence. The terrible noise is coming from the king.

The tip of Constance's dagger sticks out of Amina's chest as Constance grips the hilt behind Amina's right shoulder, heaving, her eyes blazing. She has run Amina straight through.

Amina heaves a long, slow sigh as she collapses onto the floor.

"No!" Manford shrieks.

Amina closes her eyes as a luminous cloud engulfs Manford. A sallow light erupts from him. The pulse knocks Constance and me backward with such force it sends us flying in opposite directions. Constance tumbles through a set of double doors on the other side of the room.

Manford, still surrounded by the blinding light, staggers toward me. I scramble through the door closest to me. The bodies of several unconscious palace guards litter the hall like fallen trees. Clutching Cinderella's dagger, gasping for air, my insides twisting around, I stand and run. Glancing behind me, I see Manford picking up his pace.

Careening through the halls, the clatter of swords and guards echoes from somewhere behind me. I find the staircase leading to the dungeon and race down. I can escape to the courtyard and circle back to get Constance.

The cells are empty now, and my heart races as I move to the end of the hallway and open the door.

A monstrous shout erupts from behind me. "Stop!"

I can run. I can go find Constance and get the hell out of here, but that's not what I came to do. If I run now, I'll be running forever. Amina is dead, and I hope that means that the spell she cast on Manford is broken. If there's any chance he'll be vulnerable now, I have to end him.

I close the door and turn to face Manford. He stands in the darkness at the far end of the tunnel. I take a step to the side. He mirrors my movements like a shadow.

"You are resourceful, if nothing else," he says. His voice sounds different. It's rough, and he gurgles in between breaths. "From the looks of things down here, it seems you've cost me quite a bit of money."

"Only tyrants deal in the sale of human beings." My fear has ebbed. Anger comes rushing back.

He takes two steps into the dancing light of the candles. I recoil as he moves closer. I grip Cinderella's dagger so tightly my hand aches. Large swaths of skin have come away from the side of his neck; the white bone shines through a hole in his cheek. I stumble back. His skin, moldering and rotted, falls off in chunks as he lumbers forward.

"They are more of a commodity," he says, his eyes glinting like the creatures that stalk the woods at night. "They fetched top dollar. I don't expect you to understand."

He's a walking corpse with no stolen life holding the shell of his skin and bones together. Staggering as if his legs can't support his weight, he catches himself and smiles as he watches the horror spread across my face, the skin peeling back from his lips.

"Now you cower at the sight of me? Where is that fire I saw in you earlier?" He's taunting me.

"You are a monster. Cinderella knew it. She saw right through you."

"How would you know what Cinderella thought of me?"

"You think you're the only one who can come back from the dead?"

His face changes. Behind the decaying flesh, there is confusion. "Mother." He shakes his head, and another chunk of his neck falls away. "So it seems she was playing both sides. I wonder whose side she was on in the end?"

He closes the gap between us in the blink of an eye, and I scream as he wraps me in a grip that is stronger than it should be. I raise my hand to stab him with the dagger, but he grasps my wrist, folding my arm and the dagger between us. The smell wafting off him hits the back of my throat. Rotted flesh and human waste. I fight to keep myself from gagging as he glowers down at me.

He releases me for a moment to run his hand over the side of my face. I slap it away as hard as I can. A piece of his index finger splinters off like a twig and lands on the floor.

"I didn't say you could touch me," I say.

"The spell is broken," he says. "But make no mistake. I am taking you with me."

He grips my face between his decaying hands, pressing his putrid mouth over mine once again. Pain erupts in my chest, and the light smolders between us. It grows brighter as I close my eyes. This is exactly what I'd seen in my vision. It's coming to pass, and I can't stop it. Is that what it was? Not a warning but a revelation, a glimpse of what would happen no matter what I did? I fall back into a dark, desolate place.

I'm dying. My thoughts ring out as if I'd spoken aloud. Constance's face appears in front of me, and I want to tell her how much she means to me. I see Erin, her face bruised and broken, Amina's lifeless body on the floor of the ballroom, and Luke's skeletal frame. I hear Constance's voice in my head pleading with me to come back to her. I don't want to fall into the void. Suddenly bells begin to toll somewhere in the distance. It is midnight. And then, my own voice echoes in my head again, *I am not ready to die.*

My eyes snap open, and I see the king, his eyes closed into slits, only the bloodshot whites showing. The bells toll, loud and clear. I focus on the translucent tunnel of light between us. This has to be the channel Cinderella spoke of in her journal. It snakes down his open throat and into his chest where a white-hot ball of light sits pulsing, flickering on and off as if it is struggling to stay alight. This is what Amina's spell has been protecting, the source of his power.

He squeezes me tighter, desperately trying to feed the light in his chest, but it's futile. He'll die, but I will too if I can't find a way to stop him. I grip Cinderella's dagger, feeling the outline of the stone in the handle. The crystal suddenly grows bright, and I'm awash in a pale pink haze that surrounds only me, severing the tunnel of light between us. I step back, still clutching the dagger, as the king falls to his knees.

The clock begins its final toll, and the enchanted dress Amina had provided melts away in a wash of silver and starlight. The soft slippers disappear from my feet, my hair hangs around my face, and I am left in the tunic and trousers Constance had given me. I am left just as I am, and after all this time, I know it is enough.

I gather myself as Manford sputters, swiping at me, and lift my arm to bring Cinderella's dagger, my dagger, straight down into his chest, right where I imagine the light is sitting. I lean on it with all my weight and look directly into his wild, searching eyes.

"For Liv," I say. "For Lille. For Cinderella."

Bright, hot, and crimson like a heatless flame, the light in his chest erupts out of his mouth and engulfs the king's entire head as he rears back, his hands clutching wildly at the air. A sound escapes his throat, the cries of a dying animal. What is left of his skin begins to shrivel and crack like burned paper. The crimson cloud dims, and the king's body shrinks down until it resembles a human-shaped cocoon of white ash.

I feel like I'm floating, like my head is no longer sitting properly on my shoulders. I steady myself and take the torch from its holder on the wall. I plunge it into the pile of dust that had once been the king of Mersailles.

The flames render the ash weightless, and it floats on the air as the fire spreads to the wooden chair the guard had been sitting in. The flames climb up until they engulf the wooden beams running across the ceiling. The embers from the burning structure find the piles of straw in the cells and set them alight. I run up the short flight of stairs and out into the rear courtyard, panting, my vision still blurred, my heart still racing.

The girls in the other cells, the ones on the upper floor.

A rush of panic washes over me. I drag my heavy limbs

through the now-abandoned courtyard to the side of the castle where the cells are hidden. The flames from the fire paint the darkened sky orange. It's burning quickly and spreading fast.

They will burn to death if I don't get them out.

I run to the little door I'd escaped from during the ball. My head begins to clear, and I remember I had the keys in the folds of my dress before the enchantment wore off. I frantically search my pockets and find them safely tucked away. I pull them out and fumble with the lock. None of the dozens of keys seem to fit.

Constance, where are you?

My hands are unsteady, and the sky grows brighter with each wasted second. I pause for a moment and then back up enough to get a running start. I have to knock the damn thing down.

I rush forward, shoving my shoulder into the wooden door. It breaks from the frame, and I kick it the rest of the way in. Inside the passageway, I can smell smoke, though the flames have not yet reached the hall. I bang on each of the cell doors.

"Hello! Just hang on! I'm going to get you out!"

Coughs and pleas for help ring out as a thick black haze penetrates the confines of the hallway. I'm running out of time. *They* are running out of time. I go to the cell next to the one I'd been held in and try each key until finally one fits, and the lock pops open. I push the door in to find a woman standing in the far corner. Her long brown hair hangs around her face, two streaks of white at her temples. She comes forward, sputtering as the smoke fills the cell. I put my arm around her waist, and we hobble out into the hallway.

"Where is the king?" she asks, searching the hall frantically.

"He's dead," I say. Even in the haze of smoke, I can see the astonishment in her eyes.

"You've done it?" she asks, tears filling her eyes. "You've done it!"

"You need to get out of here." I still need to unlock the other doors, and smoke is starting to stream into the hallway. I guide her to the door, and she falls onto the snow-covered ground. I take a swallow of fresh air and duck back inside to open the other doors.

Excitement begins to mount. The king is dead, I can free his prisoners, and maybe things can be different in Lille. One by one, the girls emerge, and I rush them outside. My head swims as I approach the last door. I can no longer see the lock in my hands, so thick is the smoke. I fit the key in by feeling where the opening is, and as the last girl stumbles out, the smoke overtakes me.

I fall to the floor of the servants' passage; a thick cloud of black smoke lies over me like a blanket. My lungs burn, and my eyes water. I can't move, so I close my eyes. All I can think of is Constance. I see her face in the darkness as I give in to the falling, sinking feeling. Manford is dead. The people will be free, but there will be no escape for me.

37

G et up."

I'm floating. Drifting away. There isn't any pain. I'm letting go.

"Sophia!"

I know that voice, but it's so far away, and I can't answer.

"Sophia! You open your eyes right now!"

I try, but I can't. Then I realize they are already open, and I'm staring up at the blazing orange sky.

"Breathe," says the voice. "Please, Sophia . . . please."

Clean, crisp air fills my chest, but it only makes the pain worse. I gasp, taking in breath after breath. Someone is there. Her hair melds with the sky, and her hands clutch at my face.

Constance.

"That's it, Sophia."

I roll onto my side and suck in the cold air, my throat raw from the smoke. Constance leans in next to me as I cough until my ribs ache. I reach up and put my arm over her shoulder. We are far from the castle, which is ablaze on nearly every floor.

"How did I get out here?" I ask, still disoriented.

"I saw the girls coming out of the castle, and I went in to help. You were on the floor, just like the vision I had, and I thought—" Her voice catches, and she pulls me closer to her.

"You saved me," I say. She has. And in more ways than I can count.

Thick black smoke billows out the windows. A crowd gathers. Girls from the cotillion stand in shock as more and more people arrive in carriages and on horseback. Everyone rushes around, unsure of what to do.

"Where's the king?" someone shouts.

Constance helps me to my feet, and I scan the crowd. Even now, as the palace burns, some of the suitors hold tight to their newly won prizes. One young woman struggles in her partner's grip as he looks around, wild-eyed. The king may be a pile of ash, but his ideas are still alive and well. I steady myself before marching through the parted crowd. I stand in front of the man and turn to the girl.

"Is this what you want?" I ask her. She stares at me, afraid.

"What do you think you're doing, wretch?" the man yells.

"The king is dead!" I shout back, putting my face very close to his. A hush falls over the crowd, and the man gawks at me as if I've struck him. Constance does a double take. This is news to her, too. "He is dead, and his disgusting laws and rules will die with him. This ends now."

Everyone stares at me in confusion. The parents of many of the girls descend on the scene and find their daughters in the crowd. The flames crackle and snap behind me.

Much more than beams and timber are burning to the ground.

Determination swells inside me. I watch as the young woman in front of me pulls her arm from the man's grip, scowling at him. He leans over her, and several of the other girls rush to stand in front of her. A murmur of voices ripples through the crowd.

"Cinderella's story is a lie," I say. "It was used to manipulate you. To make you feel as if your voice shouldn't be heard. The king lied to us." I pull out the journal and hold it up. "The words written here are in Cinderella's own hand. It's all right here."

Constance stares at the little book. A man walks toward me, gritting his teeth and spewing obscenities. Before I can confront him, Constance steps between us. She pulls out her dagger and shoves it against his chest.

"If you dare touch her, I will end you. Is that in any

way unclear?" Constance's tone leaves no room for discussion. A young woman pushes through the crowd, sword in hand, and stands at Constance's side. Constance seems shocked.

"Émile?" she asks.

It's the young woman from the cell. They share wide smiles, and Émile glances back at me. "Leave it to Constance to find the girl who could bring all this to an end."

The man backs away and disappears into the mass of bodies gathered in front of the castle. There is a shift in the crowd. Many of them have never seen a woman defend herself. This is how it will be from now on.

"Everything Sophia said is true," Constance says. "My family is descended from Gabrielle, Cinderella's sister, and she was not the monster the king made her out to be. None of them were. You've been lied to. But you have a chance to change things. Right here. Right now."

I see fathers with tears in their eyes. "You can keep your girls from harm," I say. "And more important, they can be allowed to keep themselves from harm. These girls don't want to be here tonight. Look at your children, your friends, your wives, and your daughters. Don't do what is right because they hold those titles. Do what is right because they are people. Make a choice to change things."

The entirety of Lille has gathered in the front drive of the palace. A few people nod and embrace each other, but even more have looks of disbelief, of confusion. They need more convincing.

"I know this is hard to understand," I say. "Many of us have never known anything other than Manford's way."

"How do we know he's dead?" a woman yells, fear distorting every syllable.

"I put him in the ground myself," I say. "You don't have to fear him anymore."

Constance stares at me as tears well up in her eyes. A murmur runs through the crowd. A group of people have broken off and are talking among themselves. Forty deep, at least a half dozen palace guards and many suitors from the ball among their ranks, they shove their way toward me.

"We're going to have a problem here," I say to Constance, who follows my gaze.

"Are we?" she asks as she holds up her dagger.

Émile takes a wide stance. Even though her frame is skeletal and her face bears the look of someone who has seen unspeakable horrors, she is ready to fight.

Shouting erupts as this faction of angry men push their way through the crowd. The man at the lead is the same man I'd seen haggling with the guard in the dungeon. He's found a sword and apparently has made himself the leader of this mob.

"Who is the king's lawful successor?" the man asks.

"He has no heirs," I say. I stare at the man unflinchingly.

"And if you think we are going to allow another monster to sit on that throne, you're mistaken."

"Why should we listen to you?" The man clasps his hands together around the sword's grip. "You're just a girl."

Constance steps in and disarms the man so quickly that I don't know exactly how she's done it. All I see is her flaming red hair and then the man lying on his back in the dirt, clutching his chest, a trickle of blood dripping down his lip. I pick up his sword and stick it in the ground.

The crowd pushes in, surrounding the mob who at the very first opportunity are trying to put us right back where we'd been before. I didn't kill the king and almost lose my life in the process for them to do this. The people of Lille—women, men, the children from the dungeon, the girls from the ball, the families who've come looking for them—stand at the ready, glaring down at the man.

"We want a say in what happens next," the man on the ground says as he scrambles to his feet.

"You've sat idly by while the people of Mersailles suffered and died, and now you want a say in what happens to us?" I'm shocked at his arrogance. "You're not in a position to make demands. I watched you try to buy a young girl in the dungeon."

Whispers and groans ring out. Some people in this crowd have no idea what the king did behind the walls of the castle. All they have are rumors and hearsay. The man glares at me with contempt.

"Leave," I say to him. "Leave. Or stay. You have choices now, but I suggest you make the right ones. Your actions will have consequences from now on."

The man scrambles back, tripping over himself as he flees. Some of the others follow him. Some stay. An uneasy calm settles over the crowd. I turn to Constance and sigh.

"They'll be back," I say.

"I know," Constance says. "But we will be prepared." She nods at Émile, who tilts her head and gazes up at the sky. I wonder how long it's been since these prisoners have seen the stars.

As I look out over the gathering, two familiar faces emerge. My parents. My mother's knees buckle when she spots me, but my father catches her, and they push through the crowd toward me. My father seems to have aged ten years, and my mother looks as if she hasn't slept in days. I search my father's face for the anger I'd last seen when I left home, but find only sadness.

"I thought you were dead." His voice breaks as tears roll down his face.

I've never seen him so broken. I don't know what to say or how to feel. I look at my mother, who is unable to speak.

"I had to put a stop to this," I say.

My father stares up at the palace. "You did this?"

I nod. I wait to see if he'll chastise me, but instead he holds out his hands. I hesitate, then slip my hands into his.

All I've ever wanted is to be seen by them, to be precious to them. I don't know if what has been broken between us can be fixed, but this feels like a good start. I hug my father, and over his shoulder, I see Luke in the embrace of his parents and his sister. Constance comes to stand at my side, and I gently pull away from my parents to take her hand. They look at each other and then at me. My mother smiles. Something I haven't seen her do in a very long time.

"Your family would be proud," I say to Constance. I hand her Cinderella's journal.

"Your grandmother would be proud," Constance says.

Tears come again, but she wipes them away with the tips of her fingers, kissing my hand and pulling me close.

"I couldn't have done this without you," I say. "I don't know how I can ever repay you."

She leans in and kisses me, but it's no longer a sorrowful goodbye. It's full of hope and tenderness. This is what all our planning has come to. She and I at the edge of an uncertain future, but one that is bright for the first time.

38

THE TRUE STORY OF CINDERELLA
People's Approved Text

. . .

*Recorded this First Day of the Growing Season
by Sophia Grimmins*

Once upon a time there were three young women:
Gabrielle, Isla, and Cinderella. The sisters loved each
other dearly, but in a land ruled by a ruthless king who was
cursed by dark magic, love was not enough to save them.
The sisters were brave, and each of them did what they
could to stand against the king, but forces outside their
control made that an impossible feat.

Cinderella's father had been the favorite to rule Mersailles before Prince Charming came to power. He should

have taken his place on the throne, but fate had other plans.

King Manford, in his many guises, ruled Mersailles for two hundred horrid years, until a time came when the people of Mersailles stood up for themselves and broke the curse. It was then that a new ruler emerged.

Constance.

As the only kin to Cinderella, the rightful heir to the throne, Constance presided over Mersailles as head of a council made up of six individuals, handpicked by her. They care only for the safety and well-being of Mersailles's people.

Constance and the council immediately abolished every single law Manford had set forth and put in place new rules that allow all the people of Mersailles access to the same privileges once only afforded to men.

The transition was fast, and of course, some rebelled. The council considered making changes slowly over time, but ultimately decided that the equal treatment of Mersailles's citizens was far more important than some people's inability to handle those changes.

The faction of angry townspeople who'd confronted us the night of the cotillion came back and burned down several houses in an attempt to seize power. Émile, a member of the resistance before she'd been captured by Manford, led the effort to push them back. With a well-armed battalion at her side, she drove most of them out past our borders into the Forbidden Lands. The others, including the prominent Baron Marcellus Moreau and his sons, Édouard and Morris, were rounded up and sent to a tribunal for their abuses. No amount of money or power would allow the mistreatment of Mersailles's people to go unchallenged ever again. Constance made sure of that.

We record here the true history of Cinderella and her family, who fought hard to ensure that the people of Mersailles could live their lives in the way that brought them the most happiness. They began a movement, a resistance that persists to this day in the hearts and minds of all who seek justice and equality. King Manford tried very hard to deny the people these things. But we will not be denied. We will not be silenced.

Let Cinderella's truth stand as a testament to her persistence and her bravery even in the face of oppression. Understand that what King Manford, in all his incarnations, feared the most was the will of the people he so desperately wanted to control.

Do not be silent.

Raise your voice.

Be a light in the dark.

ACKNOWLEDGMENTS

When I sat down to draft *Cinderella* I started with a few questions: What effect do the fairy tales we are told as children have on us? What happens to our view of the world when the characters in these stories don't look like us or love like us? When do we get to be the heroes of our own stories? From there, over countless cups of coffee, over innumerable late nights and early mornings, through tears and self-doubt, *Cinderella Is Dead* took shape. It really has become, with the help of so many others, the book of my heart.

To my amazing agent, Jamie Vankirk—all I can say is thank you, a thousand times thank you. When we started this journey, I wasn't sure there was a place for this story. You told me, unequivocally, that not only was there a place for it, but that my story was important and worth sharing.

I couldn't have done this without your support, your hard work, your tenacious spirit, your kind heart. Thank you for being *Cinderella*'s champion and for helping pick me up when I'm down.

To my wonderful team at Bloomsbury—Mary Kate Castellani, Erica Barmash, Anna Bernard, Lily Yengle— thank you for all your hard work. I don't take any of this for granted, I'm so incredibly thankful to everyone at Bloomsbury for this opportunity. Mary Kate, you have made this entire experience a dream come true. Thank you for your insight, your unfailing encouragement, and for taking a chance on me and on *Cinderella*. You have made this story what it is and I am forever grateful.

To my family—my amazing partner, Mike, thank you for supporting me. You never doubted me, even when I doubted myself. I love you with my whole heart. To my babies—Amya, Nylah, Elijah, and Lyla—I see you in the worlds and characters I create, it's why I love them so. You are, and will always be, my greatest inspiration. To my brother, Spencer, thank you for always being there for me, for encouraging me, and for listening to me go on and on about this book. I love you! To my dad, Errol Brown—I miss you every second of every day. You taught me to be proud of who I am and where I come from, and that if I have a dream, I should go for it no matter how impossible it might seem. I went for it, Dad. I hope you're proud of me.

To my BFF Sherrida—your friendship over the years has never wavered. No matter the distance, you're always in my heart. I love you, boo! Thanks for always being there.

To the booksellers who got to read early copies of *Cinderella*—I want yall to know that I printed out the wonderful things you said and put them up on my wall. On days when writing is hard, when I feel like I should just throw in the towel and move to a cabin in the woods, your kind words encourage me and make me want to keep pushin'. Your support is invaluable. Thank you.

And finally, to anyone and everyone who picks up *Cinderella Is Dead*, I want you to know how much it means to me that you would give your time to this story. I wrote it for you, for us. Be a light in the dark.